SQL SURVIVOR

SOL SURVIVOR

The Qaldreth Warriors #1

Vic's dream was to expand the solar farm her mother left her. Instead, she must survive as an arena gladiator for Carne Corp. to pay off her father's gambling debts. Now her dream is ultimate freedom which is granted to the arena champion. At last, the future she planned for is within her grasp, but when Carne conspires against her and augments her against her will, she flees into outer space, hoping to disappear. A chance encounter with an unknown alien species awakens her sexuality. Plans go awry, and there is much she must defeat before she can truly be free.

Meorri aac Drafe is on a mission to find who assassinated the Ivoyan Ot he was tasked to protect. As a Qaldreth warrior, his tribe's honor rests on finding the killer. Forming an unheard-of union with a servant Ivoy, the other witness to the crime, they locate the killer's homeworld. There, Drafe encounters a female like no other.

To regain his honor, he will need to ask for her aid, go against his protective instincts, and endanger her.

Hunted by Carne, Vic must trust her heart, life, and newfound freedom to a Qaldreth warrior she cannot resist.

ALSO BY SEVANNAH STORM

The Blood of Legends Series

The Huntress

The Healer

The Gifting Series

Soul Forged

Fate Forged

Sun Forged

War Forged

Star Forged

Shadow Forged

Earth Forged

Lust Forged

Standalones

Xiaxan Fox

Ire of Silver

The Shikari

Seven Cursed Sisters

Plump Playwright Series

Plump Jane

Seducing Amelia

Loving Finley

Keeping Tessa

Kissing Navy

COMING SOON

Inkoded

Fire Forged

The Crucible of the Eternal

GLOSSARY OR PRONUNCIATIONS

Places or Planets

Aguura – agg-oo-rah

Ivoy – eye-voy

Ki'irinzi – key-rinze-zee

Nadaar – nay-daar

Qaldreth – kal-dreath

Creatures

Garak – gah-ruck

Hudu – hoodoo

Itaya – itt-tigh-yah - yellow creatures – attach to the outside of ships and feed off sol.

Kurrula — coo-roo-lah - winged creatures (the meat is eaten raw)

Vasquva – vass-coo-vah

Terminology

Audinna — or-dee-nah - a variegated-yellow mushroom that grew inches above bubbling lava.

Carne – car-nay – Carne Corporation

Cucooya – coo-coo-yah - a bulbous tree, a mixture between cactus and baobab. Has beautiful white flowers.

Darasaho – darr-uss-ah-hoe – brother

Girda– gur-dah – a stone used to sharpen blades.

Gevatia – geh-var-tee-ah - beloved

Jakar – jah-kar - priest

Koq - cock

Mhi' vatia – mee-var-tee-ah - my love

Uhann – oo-han - The Rite of Uhann

Vatia Sahaar – var-tee-ah sah-haar - love mates

Venai – venn-igh - stones that glow.

Military

Rankings

Udap – oo-dapp - Commander

Arrak – ah-ruck - Protector

Sava – sar-vah - Security

Karu – kah-roo - Trainee/cadet

Maed – mah-eed - Med-tech

Taed – tah-eed - Tech

Ot – ott - General

Zi – zee - Traveler

Lo – low - Teacher

Uz – ooz – Servant

Names

Qaldreth

[tribal name] + [first name] + [rank]

Bavu – bah-voo

Caah - car

Cainus – cay-niss

Drafe – dray-fe

Gusin – goo-sin

Igar – eye-gar

Juunn - june

Kael - kale

Kish - kish

Larya - lah-ree-yah

Nenn – nen

Saha – sah-hah

Srim – s-rim

Tiyl - tail

Umda -oom-dah

Ulvus -ull-viss

Vaen – vah-en

Ivoyan

[last name] + [first name] + [rank]

Luharp Vadril – loo-harp vah-drill

Fumart Dau – foo-mart dow

Vizen Aehort – vizz-enn ay-ort

Human

Ande – andie

Dieter – dee-ter

Leah – lee-ah

Nikko – nick-oh

Themba – tem-bah

Religion

Qaldreth

Kreta – kree-tah - evil (she)

Osnir – oz-sneer - good (he)

Tribes

Awayar – ah-vigh-yar - live in or around water – coloring is: white hair (Like a polar bears)/gray skin/white eyes

Borven – bore-ven - live in and around canyons – coloring is: brown hair/gray skin/gold eyes

Giniiri – gin-ee-ree - live around volcanoes – coloring is: red-orange hair/gray skin/red eyes

Jeerlud – jeer-lood - live in the jungle – coloring is: brown eyes/gray skin/green eyes

Meorri – me-orr-ree - live in the desert – coloring is: black hair/gray skin/amber eyes

Riermus – rear-miss - live in the mountains – coloring is: gold hair/gray skin/black eyes

Zuphayr – zoo-fah-yer - live high in the clouds (snow/mountains) – coloring is: white hair/gray skin/dark blue eyes.

Contents

CHAPTER ONE

ON ALL SIDES OF Vic's solar farm sprawled the littered remnants of the Pacific Ocean. With a flick of a finger, the binogs fell into place, bringing the shimmering horizon closer. A flutter exploded in her chest. Every dawn that sliver of silver stole her breath. Soon, this wonder of nature would disappear. What ocean remained shrank by a meter every year as they desalinated it for consumption. Strictly guarded, the only way to see it up close was by drone, that is, if the military didn't shoot it down. She'd tried, just to see a large pool of water. South lay Old Ren's solar farm, but Vic's was the biggest in Deadweed by far. If she headed west toward the 'shore,' she'd hit the old North American continent.

A chilly breeze teased the curls at her neck. She pushed the binogs up to rest on her forehead. Her eyes stung from the cold. The temperature dipped before sunrise. The Great Water Shortage had triggered a shift in technology and space travel. Without oceans and lakes, the weather had warmed, and now going into the sun without cover was suicide.

Protected forests produced and recycled oxygen, and there were rumors of idiot scientists attempting to reclaim deserts by planting thousands of trees. She didn't place too much stock in that being successful, especially with water at a minimum. Unless they imported it...

She raised her gaze to the night sky, wondering what worlds lay in wait for colonization. Not that she'd ever leave Earth. She couldn't afford it, and no space conquering conglomerate would sponsor her when fixing farm equipment was all she could do.

The sunrise would be in a few minutes. The butterfly plates would unfold, beginning the sol harvesting. Pa was due home any second, drunker than a farm-hopper.

He'd named the farm after her ma, Millie, when he'd bought it for her. It had over a thousand plates that Vic maintained, along with other equipment. If she didn't ensure peak performance, she received a walloping. That didn't faze her, since Pa beat her either way, depending on his mood. She had learned to lean back enough for the punch to sting but never to bruise. To avoid it entirely, meant a furious man swinging wild punches. If she allowed one glancing blow, he felt vindicated.

She rose onto her tiptoes and winced when her aching thigh muscles twanged. A few years ago, she'd downloaded an instructional vid on ancient fighting techniques. Not that she had mastered the stances yet, and without a sparring partner, she wasn't sure she'd survive in a fight. Still, every night after Pa left, she'd run through the vids. She gritted her teeth, bouncing on her feet. Hours wasted trying to learn to protect herself. Quick reflexes meant fewer injuries when Pa was in one of his combative moods.

As the heat notched higher with the rising sun, she fitted the parts she'd dug out of the store. More would arrive in a few days. Her ma hadn't raised a fool, so when Pa gave Vic signing rights to the farm's accounts, she'd split their funds. The demand for sol-power was high thanks to evolving inventions which meant earning more tokens. Of course, she had to keep the profits separate, not wanting Pa to know how flush they were. He would piss it away on booze and sorrow.

Tugging the binogs over her left eye, she scanned the horizon sliced with powerlines running from the farms. No dust cloud marked Pa's impending arrival. She grimaced, dread and excitement warring within her stomach, churning until it was one twisted ball of pain. She would have to fetch him. Visiting Deadweed's only bar, Leviathan, meant curious gazes scanning the curves she had developed. Leaving Pa there was out of the question, no matter how tempted she was. The owner, Cleg, would charge to deliver Pa home.

With a twist, she latched the door on Plate-47. She tossed the all-tool into a bag, slung it across her shoulder, then climbed onto her skid-cycle. Black panels covered every clunky inch of it for maximum sol absorption, but it was one of the original designs able to withstand the harsher elements on the dry beds. She wrapped strips of cloth around her arms where the heat-res suit had torn. Buying a new one or clothes wasn't an argument she wanted to suffer through. Soon, though, she'd have to endure. At seventeen, she was outgrowing everything.

As she sped home, she cast a glance east. For Pa, dusk meant distilled-seaweed liquor, or sweed, and Cleg was happy to provide. By dawn, she'd find Pa sprawled across his bunk, stinking worse than a bloated corpse.

She hovered her cycle and darted down into the rock-hewn rooms buried under the seabed. As she stepped into the shadowed confines, she removed her helm and hung up the bag, grateful for the warmer temperatures of her home. Decades ago, it had been an underwater observation base, small in size with a small kitchen, a bunk room, and a glass-walled common room that now looked out onto fossil-rich sand. In a storeroom, she slept on a pile of rags amid crates, tools, and spare parts. The compact room granted her privacy with the lock she'd fitted on the inside.

The scent of baked sand stung her nose, but the stench of old sweed and vomit watered her eyes. There wasn't a free counter anywhere in the kitchen. She'd need to clean after she fetched Pa, obligated to do so in her ma's stead. Besides, he would wallop her if she didn't.

Flicking open the cooling drawer, she pulled out a cyan-dyed hydro-gel and squeezed the thick sweetness onto her tongue before swapping her binogs for sunvisors. The short trip to Deadweed meant stinging sand particles finding every orifice of her body. Shrugging on a jacket to serve as additional protection, she activated the magnetic fasteners, tapped on the helm, and bounded up the makeshift stairs to her skid-cycle. The sun's rays painted the dunes a glorious orange-gold. The heat hit her hard. The shock of it snatched her breath. Throwing a leg over the cycle, she flipped her visor down and wiggled her gloved hands under the handle guards.

She sped forward, skidding across the surface of the pale dunes, once hundreds of meters underwater, or so the old folks claimed. On boring nights, she'd slip inside the bar, find a dark corner, and listen to the whispered stories of a world covered in water. The Global Warming War had been over water resources, yet as she understood it, no clear winner had risen out of the chaos. Those who could afford it had moved into domed cities or off-world. Those who remained harvested sol as a power source, fueling newer inventions in medical technology, weapons, and any way solar could replace water—like a sol-bath.

She snorted, skidding over a chasm too deep and dark to be of any importance except as shelter from the sun. Bath? She stood naked on a circular plate in front of a panel, and as it rotated her, solar rays scanned her body to eradicate bacteria, sweat molecules, and other detritus. Med-rays neutralized her waste by-products still inside her. She'd never seen a 'bath' in her life. To be honest, the idea of sitting in a tub filled with water was a shameful waste of resources.

The morning sun scorched the crown of her padded head, but it was tolerable. Later, when she returned home with Pa, she'd activate the cooling system in her heat-res suit. She didn't want to use her secret stash of tokens on medical care so avoiding sunburn was preferable. Through a shimmering dome, white half-buried egg-shaped buildings marked the town of Deadweed. Sol vehicles of various ages circled the Leviathan, and folks scurried between the buildings, purchasing goods from the mercantile store, or visiting Aunt Mei's for a decent rehydrated meal.

Vic deactivated her skid-cycle and attached it to the rear of Pa's skid-car, assuming she would have to drive it home. Yanking the helm off, she tossed it into the back, along with her jacket. She squared her shoulders and strolled into the bar.

Sweed lay thick in the air, a musky stench merged with it and the aroma of refried rehydrates. Some sport or arena played on the hologram fixed above the bar, and most patrons had their eyes rolled upward as they watched it.

"My tokens are on Angel. She's as lethal as she's beautiful," someone said from the back of the bar.

Vic grunted. Angel was a Ring champion, and why she still participated after she had won her freedom, Vic couldn't understand. She sought the woman's dark face, her cybernetic eyes glowing blue as she fired sol bolts from her forearm. Vic grimaced, wondering what they'd removed from her bone structure and muscle mass to cater for the sol canisters.

Scanning the bar, she saw no sign of Pa's blond hair. She dodged robo-servs as they carried jars of deep-green sweed en route to Cleg behind the counter. When she slid onto a seat, she smothered a sigh as it conformed to her backside, offering the maximum of comfort. These were a recent addition to the Leviathan. Cleg must be doing well.

"Seen Pa?" She wagged a dismissive forefinger when he offered her a hydro-gel. At the prices he charged, she'd rather die of thirst.

"Yep, dang near broke my new music box." Cleg nudged his head at the panel in the wall. Not that it was playing, what with the arena on the holo.

"It looks fine, so where is he?" She met Cleg's dark gaze, refusing to look away until he answered her.

"He's in the back. Started trouble with a few noobs."

"Did you call Jolson?" She leaped off the seat. "Call him, Cleg, or I'll break your music box so badly a city-tech can't repair it."

"You wouldn't." Fear coated Cleg's voice, but he pinned his right palm to his cheek to call the sheriff.

She couldn't wait, jogging around the tables, through the swinging door at the back, and out into filtered sunlight. Heat warmed her skin, but thanks to the dome, it didn't burn her.

Pa sprawled on his stomach. A man pressed his foot to the nape of Pa's neck, forcing his face into the sand. Two men stood to the side, laughing and slapping each other on the back. Pa's arms flailed, digging furrows in the sand as he struggled for air.

"What the fuck do you think you're doing?" Vic rushed forward, drawing Man Two and Three's attention.

They snickered at her distress, but Two stepped in to hinder her. She took him down with a knee to the groin, dropping him to the sand as Three lunged for her. A punch to his throat left him gasping and falling to his knees. They weren't laughing anymore. One removed his foot from Pa's head. Pa spluttered and coughed up sand while One circled him, his gaze flicking between his two men and Vic.

"Not so little are you, girl?" A scar marred one side of his face, but his eyes were soulless. No joy or eagerness were in their depths. As soon as he was clear of Pa's legs, he grabbed for her, his fingers brushing her upper arms as she lurched back. He swung a fist, and she ducked, coming up with a groin punch, a downward cut to his jaw, then an elbow to the back of his neck.

Two wrapped her in a tight embrace, pinning her arms to her body. She slid her hips to the side and threw her elbow back, hard enough to wind him or crack a rib. He grunted, bending over. She brought the same elbow up to strike him in the jaw. Three still gasped for air, now on all fours, barking like a robo-dog. He peered at her. His expression promised her a painful death, but he didn't look away from her, keeping his gaze fixed as if she was a pissed-off snake. He grappled for his gun. Oh, no, that wouldn't do. She kicked it out of his hand, shattering his wrist. He howled, crumpling to the sand.

She hurried to Pa's side, hesitating to offer him aid. He wouldn't tolerate her touching him and hadn't hugged her since Ma died. Part of her hated him, the lines etched in his skin, his sad brown eyes like hers, the way his fist formed when he was about to swing at her. Fire burned in her chest, consuming her emotions as if they were tinder. She should leave him, should have let them kill him and eradicate him from her life.

Ma's pale face flickered before Vic. She fought off tears of helplessness, forcing her to succumb to the promise she had made on Ma's deathbed—take care of Pa.

"What have you done?" He gripped Vic's shoulder, digging his fingers into her muscles, his face chaffed red from the sand. She hoped it was that and not fury mottling his cheeks. With the agony of his grip summoning a cry from her, she saw a beating in her future. "These men belong to the Ring, Vic." He darted his gaze at the fallen men, concern spiking his voice.

Ice drenched her innards, not from possible retribution, but that her Pa had gambled when he had promised Ma he wouldn't. "You lost tokens?" Vic yanked out of his arms as anger dismissed her cowardice, along with her survival instincts. "Why the hell didn't Cleg mention that?"

"Look at this, Victoria Harper." Sheriff Trev Jolson strode across the sand, his careful steps not disturbing it nor dusting his polished boots. He barreled toward her, his movements stiff and threatening. Yet when he gripped her, his touch was gentle. A dark curl fell across his brow, escaping his wide-brimmed hat, and he stared into her eyes, his as blue as hydro-gel.

"Sorry, Jolson. I thought I was saving Pa's life." Vic rubbed her shoulder where Pa had bruised her.

The sheriff scowled at her lack of respect, but she couldn't show him any, not since she had known him from childhood. "You saved his life but lost yours, Vic," he said, gesturing to the cameras mounted above the bar's door.

"I'll pay Pa's debts. That should appease them." She shrugged. "Let's go home."

Pa grunted and headed for the bar, but a hand on her elbow stilled her. She raised her gaze to meet Jolson's again.

"Don't let him hurt you, Vic. You deserve better." He brushed an escaped tendril off her cheek, tucking it behind her ear. "I'll do what I can to protect you and warn you if the Ring heads your way."

"Thanks, Trev," she said, sparing him a small smile.

A bigger one would encourage him, and he had pestered her since she turned fifteen. She didn't want to be someone's wife or a kept woman, not when she wanted to own Millie's and expand it. Miles and miles of wasteland surrounded them, promising untold riches if she could increase the harvested capacity of sol. There were better, more efficient butterfly panels and battery stores. She would have replaced theirs one by one if she had a say.

Sliding into the skid-car, she wrapped her fingers around the control level to unlock and power it up until it hovered off the ground. With a forceful tap, she activated the sun shield. She reversed, then shot forward, aware of her father's steady gaze on her. Her knuckles burned where her skin had split and bled with purple bruises forming.

"Next time, mind your damn business." He curled his fingers into fists.

She snuck a glare at him. "Next time, I'll let them kill you. Do this world a favor."

He leaped for her. She spun the skid-car, thrusting him against the side. He roared warnings, promises of beatings, but after the eleventh spin, his skin mottled green, and his sweed-colored vomit splattered the inside of the shield. She straightened the car and headed for home once more.

"I made a promise to Ma." She pinched her lips from the enormity of her decision. "But I'm done with you. Come tomorrow, you'll have to pay for a hopper, Pa, 'cos I ain't your daughter no more."

He laughed and wiped the spittle off his mouth with the back of his hand. "You won't survive a day on your own, and don't think you can crawl back here."

A tense silence fell between them. She clenched her jaw, fighting the need to spew her disappointment, anger, hatred, everything she wished she could say to him. A deep well of sorrow tore through her. Cold and hot pain crushed her chest, hindering her ability to breathe. She wished she had let him die.

Chapter Two

VIC ROSE EARLY, UNABLE to find rest for fear that Pa might chain her to a crate. She needn't have worried. He snored where he sprawled on his bunk. She crept through the rooms, snagging items like a digi-pic of her ma, the electronic deed to the farm she'd left to Vic, a handful of hydro-gel sticks, and a few hidden tokens. She could use the split account to start a new life. The sun was on the cusp of rising, painting the horizon in a palette of deep browns and yellows. She drew in the cold air, gazed once more at the butterfly panels she'd so lovingly repaired, then flicked the visor down.

With a small bag of possessions tied to the back of her skid-cycle, she headed for Deadweed, skimming through on her way to New Westlands. She parked outside Leviathan, planning to cut off Pa's sweed supply. All Cleg needed to know was that Pa was penniless. With a gaze at Jolson's office, she strode into the bar's cool interior.

She almost jerked to a stop. The Ring lay in waiting, sipping on purified sweed—the expensive kind. By Ring, she meant one man: Erv Lawson. He stepped off the seat in graceful silence. His cybernetics from his eyes, shoulders, arms, and right thigh didn't hinder him when the additional weight should have.

"My timing is perfect." His voice rumbled in the unnatural quiet of the bar. No one spoke, as crowded as it was for that time of day.

She scowled, accepting that she was the entertainment and would have to face the man alone.

Preferring to take care of business before leaving, she ignored him. If he wanted her, he'd have to make his intentions clear. "Cleg, Pa's without tokens." She held his gaze as best she could with him slicing glances at a looming Lawson. "Cleg," she barked, snapping his attention to her.

"Gotcha, Vic." His strangled voice had her sighing. For someone running the only bar in Deadweed, he sure was a coward.

She faced the room, slipping past the great bulk of a gladiator in his prime. Lawson tried to grab her, but she was adept at dodging fists, searching fingers, and robo-servs. She left Leviathan and marched to her skid-cycle, determined to face the next phase in her life with a little courage.

Lawson trailed her, his gait irritated or perhaps his jerky movements were natural for him. After his previous graceful display, she doubted it. "Victoria Harper, you best be coming with me, gal."

"How much does Pa owe the Ring?" She fiddled with the visor, on the verge of flipping it into place. The sun warmed one side of Deadweed's shielding dome. Farg it, she'd wanted to reach New Westland before the sun baked the dunes. "I'll settle his debts one last time, then I'm no longer responsible."

"David Harper has paid all ten-thousand tokens owed in exchange for...you."

"What?" Shaking her head, she tried to rid herself of disbelief. She must have misheard Erv or misunderstood. Her mind whirled at the implication that Pa had bartered her like bottles of poorly-distilled sweed.

"Your father sold you, little gal." Erv flicked something at her. Whatever it was, it landed on her neck, biting into her skin.

She screamed, clapping a palm over the flat device and half-expecting blood to smear her skin. The full realization settled on her. She couldn't move. In fact, she stood there like a scarecrow with a hand plastered to her neck.

Grateful her eyes could move despite shadows hiding Erv's face, she peered at him. He gripped her jacket and tossed her over his shoulder as if she weighed nothing. Folks trickled out of the buildings to watch the spectacle, and amid them, stood Jolson. His lips tugged downward. He said and did nothing except curl his fingers in his silly belt. She landed and bounced once on the back seat of Erv's sleek skid-car. Unable to brace herself, her shoulder and jutting elbow stung from the abuse. A grunt lodged in her throat. She fought to twitch a finger.

"Quit squirming," Erv snapped, the back of his head in her line of vision.

Farg him. As soon as this device was off her, she'd show him what she could do. Images flooded her mind from her latest instructional vid. One of those moves had to take the ox down.

As the skid-car flew across the sands toward the domed city, the purring engines didn't drown his words. "Feisty, but that won't last long, gal. Glaring at me won't harm me. You'll soon find out, violence is the only answer." He raised his hand and clicked a button. A fresh wave of fiery agony spasmed her limbs, granting her blessed darkness.

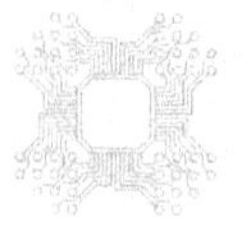

GRUNTS, THWACKS, AND MOANS drew Vic from sleep. As she crawled to wakefulness, her body pinged news of stiff, aching muscles when she'd done nothing more than repair sol panels and learn fighting techniques. This pain went bone deep. She frowned then flicked her eyes open when something nudged her boot.

Gasping, she sat up, blinking at the kids brawling or dueling while someone zigzagged within a rolling barrel, dodging pendulums and arrows. Farg. Her stomach lurched, coiling and writhing from what her pa had done.

"Good, you're awake. Mr. Carne will see you now."

Scrambling to her feet, she glowered at Erv. "I said I'd settle Da's debts. Ten thousand tokens is nothing to sneeze at."

Erv faced her. A smirk contorted his lips but crinkled his eyes with good humor. "Entertaining too. I'm beginning to like you." He raised his hand and waved a button. "Feel like another jolt?"

She slapped her neck, finding the thing still attached. No amount of scratching gained her enough traction to remove the device. "This is barbaric and...and illegal."

He blinked at her, threw back his head, and guffawed, his massive shoulders shaking. "Yes, I *do* like you." Waving his hand, he gestured for her to follow.

Huffing, she did, striding after him like a cybernetic lapdog.

"You showed remarkable skill." He paused while two teenage boys grappled on a mat. A snap echoed when a bone broke, but the injured boy made no sound. Despite his arm hanging limp by his side, he tackled the other boy, punching him in the gut.

She gaped.

"We don't take someone your age, but we're not starting from scratch with you." Erv faced her. "Where did you learn to fight like that?"

Meeting his gaze, she tried not to recall the day she was assaulted. Just a kid at nine, and without the protection of her drunken pa, she'd had to defend herself, to kick and scratch. After that, any spare moment she had, she went through old vids she had found on the intra. Some of those techniques had injured her—pulling muscles, scrapping toes, or bruising shoulders. She'd persevered when the alternative was worse.

"Here and there." She shrugged without lowering her gaze. He needed to earn her respect, and despite him being the infamous Ring trainer, so far, she wasn't impressed.

"Well, we'll see after your interview. Mr. Carne will decide where you go, gal."

"The name's Vic."

His lack of response was dismissive, as if her name didn't matter. She trudged after him when they left the massive room behind, its many red doors intriguing, but a curiosity she could live with not satisfying. The long passage was wide enough to fit a skid-car, and the metallic flooring was matte, scuffed, and in need of a good clean. In the high ceiling were skylights fitted with grills. She could work one loose and escape if she could find a ladder. The walls were as smooth as the floor with no toe holds. She would need cybernetic limbs to leap that high.

There had to be an exit somewhere.

Erv wrapping his fingers around her elbow shook her out of her daze. She curled her arm free.

His chuckle grated, as did him holding up his hands as if in surrender. "We're here. Now show him respect, or you will be knocked out again."

She nodded. Making an enemy of the most powerful man in New Westlands wasn't wise. All she wanted was her freedom, so controlling her anger was in her best interest.

Erv preceded her, holding the door open with misplaced gallantry. The office was extensive, all in dark fabrics, and...she gasped, real wood. Farg, even the walls were lined with wood paneling and bookshelves holding actual paperbacks. After the Great Water Shortage most plant life died unless protected by domes. So paper was rare and super expensive.

Downlighters illuminated the room, but they weren't needed with the floor-to-ceiling wall of glass overlooking the arena. Heavy leather chairs were in front of his desk that squatted like a beast, dominating the vast space. Behind it sat a man too gentle-looking to be the purveyor of blood, pain, indentured servitude, and violent death. White hair cascaded over a wrinkled brow, and hazel eyes warmed when Erv nudged her deeper into evil's lair.

"Ah, Victoria Harper," Sebastian Carne boomed, his voice too bombastic for her pinging temple. He gestured to a chair.

She spread her legs and clasped her hands behind her back. "I'd prefer to stand if you don't mind."

With a shove on her shoulder, Erv had her sitting. She glared at him but bit her tongue.

"Fire." Sebastian slapped the desk. "Now that's what we've been missing." He rose from his swivel chair and faced the arena. His white hair was trimmed an inch from his crisp collar. "Our contesters are boring. The crowd wants someone they can get behind, cheer, or mourn the loss of." He gestured to Erv.

"Seventeen years old, deceased mother, and a drunken father," Erv rattled off like she wasn't sitting there.

"So, no hope of a good future." Sebastian sliced a glance at her. "Are you still a virgin, gal?"

She gritted her teeth, fighting the wave of heat pouring over her face. "The name's Vic." Erv digging his fingers into her shoulder lanced pain through her. She jerked out of his reach, casting him another glare. "Yes, I'm still a virgin, not that it's any of your business." Fargen hell, she'd worked hard to keep something of herself private and hers alone.

"Impressive." Sebastian turned his back on the arena and splayed his fingers on the desk as he leaned over it. She snorted. Like she cared what he thought. "As I see it, you have two things you value: home and your virginity. The former is denied you, but your virginity is a prize many will want."

"I am not your whore." She clipped each word, twitching away from Erv in case he wanted to abuse her again. "No, home isn't valued."

Sebastian arched a white fluffy eyebrow. "Then your freedom?"

She bit her lip, trying to keep her face impassive. *Fargen hell.*

"Only after ten years, *if* you survive, can you fight for it. Work your way up the ranks and during a deca-match, you can challenge for your freedom."

"Ten years?" She gripped her knees. "No, fighting for you makes no sense, not when I have the tokens."

"Look around you, gal. Why would I need your tokens?" Sebastian sank into his chair, balancing his elbows on its arms while he steepled his fingers. "Test her, determine her rank, and throw her into the arena."

"As you command, Mr. Carne." Erv gripped her upper arm and hoisted her to her feet.

Hell fargen no. She tossed a glance at Carne and grimaced. Nothing she said would save her. She had to escape though, but how? Slumping with her ass almost touching the floor, she forced Erv to drag her.

When he huffed and bent to grab her other arm, she elbowed him in the ribs, spun into his embrace, and kneed him in the groin. Without pausing to ensure he crumpled mid-groan, she bolted, sprinting out of the office. The first two red doors were locked so she ignored the doors and headed for the practice grounds. When she burst through the door with Erv's thundering steps behind her, she swept her gaze across, searching for exits. The contenders paused in mid-kicks, punches, or lunges to gape at her.

Too many doors lined the walls, so she aimed for the double gates on the opposite side. Erv was closing in, and a few kids were eager to assist him, like crabs in a bucket. She didn't hesitate, taking down those too close. With her hands at her side, she roared like a wounded lioness. When they hesitated, she weaved through them, hoping to dodge their futile attacks.

Her frantic breaths tore from her throat when she slammed into the gates. They didn't budge. With a shuddering breath, she faced Erv, a sense of helplessness engulfing her . He had halted a few meters away, gripping his side as he too fought for air. Worse, he wore a satisfied grin on his ruddy face.

"Fire. Fargen hell, gal, you may have skill but you lack strategy." He straightened and gestured behind him. "How many enemies have you just made?"

"Like I care. I want out, now." She'd intended to sound commanding, but instead, her voice cracked as the seriousness of her situation settled upon her. Her thoughts pinged. Her mind reeled, unable to accept the lack of options closing in on her. A buzzing in her ears drove a blast of agony to her temple. She winced but didn't dare shift her gaze or appear the slightest bit weak.

"There is no escape." Erv drew the small black box from his pocket and waved it. "Had you made it through the doors, you would have been stunned."

Tears threatened to spill, but she shook her head, denying them freedom when she had none. She curled her fingers into fists, digging her nails into her palms as she raised her hands in front of her face. Others had gathered behind Erv, some bleeding or limping, a few running an eager gaze over her body. She smothered a shiver, letting it tingle her knees.

"Gladiators, meet Vic. Ande," Erv swung out his arm, "train her."

She growled, holding each person's gaze with blatant challenge.

A young man stepped forward, his skin dark, his hair and eyes black. "Come." He held out a hand, offering her refuge.

She hesitated, not sure she could trust him. Scanning the crowd, she waited, tense, like a cobra ready to strike. Erv flicked his hand, and they dispersed. Inhaling sharply, she lowered her fists but didn't relax her stance.

"Come." Ande waited, letting her decide even though she didn't have any options left.

Taking a step, she slipped her hand in his and allowed him to tug her behind him. He led her through a weathered door and along a narrow passage that opened into a long room.

"This is the canteen." The stench of burned food filled the air. He pointed to another door as they strolled between the metal trestle tables. "The ablutions. Don't ever shower alone." He held her gaze until she nodded. They stepped through double doors into a room lined with bunk beds. No windows meant no escape. "You can sleep next to me."

She stiffened, curling her fingers into fists. "Farg, no."

"You're pretty but not my type if you get my meaning." He focused on a blond man sprawled on a bunker. "Stick with me, Vic, and you might survive this."

Clasping her hands behind her back, she opted for a casual air, as if she hadn't been about to pummel him. "How long have you been here?" She tested the bunker he bumped with his booted foot.

"Four years." He flexed his arm, showing a bulging bicep. "I get my freedom in six years if I don't lose a challenge or die during the deca-match."

She winced, running a fingertip over her bleeding and bruised knuckles. The pain was negligible compared to the panic squeezing her ribs. Aware he studied her, she drew in slow, silent, and deep breaths.

He tapped his gray vest. "We need to find you a uniform." Dark gray pants clung to muscled thighs, hiding nothing from her admiring gaze. Also in gray, a sleeveless and padded vest molded to his chest. "Come."

Throwing her legs off the side, she pushed off the bunker and hurried after him to an open door. Inside were shelves lined with folded garments. He grabbed items and tossed them at her before pointing at thick black boots.

While she peeled off her oil-stained worker breeches and dirty tank, she kept her gaze on his back. He faced the metallic wall, the gesture of privacy appreciated. As she crisscrossed the straps of the vest around her waist, he tapped a red button on the wall. A panel glided aside to reveal a window.

Her breath lodged in her throat. A tear slipped past her defenses, and a deafening roar consumed her mind.

"There is no escape." He dipped his head.

Through the portal were endless parsecs of space with the curve of Earth in the left corner.

"Farg." She gasped and pressed a splayed hand on the cold glass.

"Yup, welcome to the *Conqueror*, Carne's out-in-space training academy."

Chapter Three

DRAFE SQUEEZED FIVE DROPLETS of water onto his tongue. The sweet liquid nourished and cooled as it slid down his throat. His pouch sloshed with the heavenly goodness, but drinking more than the allowance was taboo. Still, he was tempted, hefting the bladder in his hand while trailing a thumb over his father's star burned into the leather. Sighing, he set it aside. Any water he returned with would add to tomorrow's rations. Not that he could recall having quenched his thirst. He, like all Meorri, survived on Osnir-blessed five drops at a time to hold back thirst.

On a pale-yellow stone ledge, he rested. Enjoying the cool shade of a cucooya tree—its thick, bulbous roots offering him a backrest—he stared across the Aguura salt plains. In the distance, hazy mountains rose, dark and mysterious. The Riermus tribe reigned over the Ki'ir-inzi Mountains stretching as far as the eye can see. He had never hunted far enough across the plains to meet a Riermus. There was talk their skin was the color of pale-yellow rock, mottled green and brown.

He sprawled with two dead garaks beside him. The length of his forearm, they would provide food for a few days, and their thick fur would please Larya, his sister. It was nearing midday. Qaldreth's two suns tortured the soil, burned the air, and siphoned what water trickled to the surface. He slumped, resting against the spongy bark. Having set out before daybreak, exhaustion drained him. Every big prey he'd targeted had slipped through his fingers.

His symbiotes flooded him with memories of his past fathers' hunts, hoping Drafe would learn from their skill and mistakes. A poor substitute for a lost parent. When he had a son, he would share the symbiotes as his father had done with him. So did the knowledge and condemnation of his ancestors survive.

"My thanks," he grumbled.

None of the symbiotes' guidance helped him. They slithered under the surface of his skin, rippling like a vasquva under the desert sands. Now that would be a worthy kill. The massive worm would feed his village for a year. Holy Osnir, even a baby vasquva would be worth the effort.

He shifted his legs, bare beneath the leather loincloth, his koq tucked into its pocket. His feet and chest were bare too. To hunt clothed was cowardly. To his right lay his father's sword. The shimmering Borven blade caught the suns' light. The hilt had strips of leather, hinting at past kills. It wasn't a Cainus-made sword, but it had survived generations. He had his spear beside that, the Borven head sharp enough to kill. No vasquva leather wrapped around the butt, only garak. One day soon, he would add a worthy kill to his symbiotes' memories.

The pebbles beneath his hand trembled and hopped. He rested his gaze on the plains before him. His symbiotes whispered of vasquva, but he dismissed it. The worms didn't travel the plains, preferring the Nadaar dunes west of him.

The whiskers bursting through the hard-packed soil proved him wrong.

A cold shiver shot down his back as he gaped. Scrambling to his feet, he scooped up the sword, and bolted, sprinting across the sand with tiny puffs of dust under his feet. As a Meorri, moving without disturbing his surroundings was taught from a young age. Many a danger lay beneath the salt and sand. He pumped his arms, chasing the swerving, slithering worm as it crossed the plains. Salt crystals exploded, stinging his skin. He shook his head to dislodge the white powder off his eyelashes. If he could just reach its neck. Sweat beaded his forehead, drenching the plume of hair curling from his temple down his spine, now sticking to his skin. His breathing labored, but he pushed on.

Such a kill would bring great honor and secure a good mating for Larya. As primary male, he had to care for her.

The amber beads in the guard of his sword dug into his hand. He tightened his grip and leaped onto one of the vasquva's many tails. The slimy yellow skin burned where it touched him. He scrambled up its length, dodging the other tails as they whipped over his head. It tried to dislodge him with flicks and jerks. He held on. Hand over hand, despite the burn of his skin flaking off, he climbed. His symbiotes hurried to heal him, whispering curses in an unknown, ancient language. The tone was the same.

On the vasquva's back, he wrapped one of its long hairs around his arm and tugged, pulling himself from strand to strand until he neared the creature's head. He needed an eye, its weak point. The

Ki'irinzi Mountains drew closer, variegated greens changing the hazy grays into a riot of color. Foq. He twisted, spying the cucooya tree he'd but moments ago rested under. It was no bigger than his thumbnail. The hot wind baked by the suns whipped at his hair, dusting his skin with salt. He grabbed a strand of hair and yanked to the right, needing the vasquva to turn around. A laugh erupted at his silliness, but it didn't smother the sadness claiming his soul. If he didn't abandon the hunt, it would take him days to reach home.

The annual challenge was tomorrow.

Even if he plunged his sword into the vasquva's eye, all this meat would rot before he could gather the village. He grunted, released the strand of hair, rolled down the vasquva's back, and leaped off its ass, hitting the ground with a grunt. With a final backward glance, he sprinted toward the cucooya tree, evading the vasquva's nine tails.

A rumble behind him spun him on his heel. A whisker broke the surface of the plains too close for comfort. Gathering his dwindling energy, swallowing past the thick mucus clinging to his tongue, he ran, the sword still gripped in his hand.

At his heels, the sand cracked as the vasquva hunted him, its whiskers caressing his hair. He shivered while his symbiotes screamed instructions he had to ignore. Only the rock outcropping mattered. If he could just reach the tree surrounded by solid rock, the vasquva would abandon the hunt. His feet burned from the hot sand and his heels itched at the constant vibrations. Glances behind him revealed the creature's persistence. He was close. Just a little more...

The ground beneath his back foot fell away. Roaring a battle cry and with the power of his legs, he launched himself, hand outstretched. Fear chilled his bones, so dark, whispering he would fail, he wouldn't make it, his sister would fall to slave status. For a moment, he succumbed to Kreta's seductive words. The goddess of death awaited him.

His fingertips caught the edge. He scrambled to hold on, to pull himself up and over, scraping the skin off his shoulders. A thunderous wail pierced the air and trembled the rock beneath him, but he lay there, on his back, his ragged breaths jarring his chest. Sweat trickled down his scalp, past his ears to the ground beneath him.

He threw out a hand to where he'd left his water pouch.

Nothing. Sitting up with a groan, he stared at the cucooya's thick roots. Where the foq was his water pouch? His spear? The two garaks?

To steal one's water was beyond dishonorable and was punishable with the loss of a hand. No one would dare. The tenacious vasquva circled him, wailing and sending out its whiskers to taste the air. South of him lay the caves. Home, half a day's walk.

Here he sat, waterless.

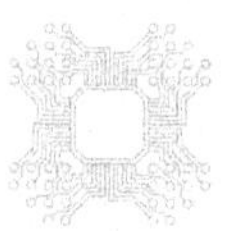

HOURS PASSED WITH HIM unable to head home. The setting suns took the light while the vasquva ranted as it circled the rock. The cooling temperatures racked shivers across Drafe's exposed skin. It lasted a moment before his symbiotes warmed him. With his tongue swollen, he watched the moons cross the sky, the stars bright, beckoning. One was the Ivoyan world where he longed to train as a Qaldreth warrior.

He huffed. Not if he stayed on this rock.

To witness the challenge, Ivoyan aldermen would descend from their sky crafts and choose the next trainee. From when he was a boy, he had longed to join those who left the hot sands of Meorri. Leaping to his feet, he gripped his father's sword and carved a niche in the cucooya's root, asking for nothing more but five droplets. It conceded, and he gathered the sticky liquid on his fingertips. One could not survive for long on the tree's salty sap, but it should sustain him until he reached home.

The wind whipped his hair, tickling his back as he stared south, peering into the thick darkness. Used to the suns' light, his eyes didn't handle night well. Drawing in a deep breath, he squared his shoulders, rocked on his toes, and bolted, sprinting across the sands with the wail of the vasquva trailing him.

He was a fool to have tried to kill it alone.

Lessons came after he needed them.

His arms and legs burned, but he persevered, zigzagging from rock to shade, often resting on boulders when he could. As the moon crossed the sky, the vasquva persisted, hunting him. Its whiskers dipped and danced as it sought his scent. A mournful cry followed.

In the distance, the white bobbing globes of the venai stones served as guiding lights. He was close to home.

Two tails flicked across the boulder, and he ducked, hissing as they brushed across his scalp. One caught him across the midriff, throwing him off the boulder. He rolled and burst into a run, weaving as he sprinted for his life. Another wail pierced the air, its whiskers brushing across his shoulders. Too close. It dived underground, spraying him with salt and sand.

Two guards rushed to meet him, their spears ready.

Umda hurried closer. "Young Drafe, what have you done now?"

Drafe stumbled to a halt, fighting for breath, to keep standing, to speak. Before he could answer, the vasquva keened, bursting out of the sands, its whiskers tasting the air.

"Holy Kreta." Umda spun his spear, roared, and charged.

Exhaustion trembled Drafe's limbs, but he raised his sword, throwing himself after the older male. The other guard, Tiyl, joined in the battle cry. Following the path he had taken earlier, Drafe clung to the vasquva's tail. Umda vaulted past him, so Drafe scrambled up the creature's back as well. At its thrashing head, Umda raised his spear and nodded at Tiyl, who stabbed the flesh of the worm's ass.

As it bucked and shrieked, Umda yelled, "Now," and plunged his spear into the vasquva's ear. It squealed, its whiskers splaying out, its thrashes more violent.

Drafe clung to a strand of hair, spread his legs wide, and buried his blade into the vasquva's black eye.

Its wail was deafening. With its yellow blood drenching him, he struggled to hold onto his father's sword. At his desperate cry, his symbiotes reacted, adding texture to his fingers. Able to tighten his hold, he yanked and slid the blade free. The vasquva arched its back on a forlorn squeal and slumped, crashing to the sand in a great plume of dust. Drafe tumbled off, slipping on its blood-slicked skin to land on his back with a grunt.

Umda and Tiyl leaped off the creature to stand beside him. As pain lanced across Drafe's body, he bit his lip, careful not to make a noise as he dragged himself to his feet.

"Well, this was fortuitous." Umda's grin was bright in the moonlight. "Osnir has blessed you, young Drafe."

Drafe accepted the thump on his shoulder, despite it almost bringing him to his knees. He doubted the god of light had anything to do with this.

Cries rose from the direction of the village, and more venai lights bobbed.

"Go, we will tend to this." Tiyl gestured to the mass of vasquva to be carved and shared.

"My thanks." Drafe splayed his hand on his chest, then swayed as he turned for home.

Umda halted him with a hand on his forearm. "Where is your water pouch?"

Drafe closed his eyes against the loss. To replace it required the bladder of a hudu. Regardless of the effort, his father had burned the star into the leather. Where his father had touched, that was now lost to Drafe.

"Taken."

Umda jerked back, raising a wide-eyed yellow gaze. "Your oath?"

Drafe nodded. "Along with my day's hunt and a spear."

"This does not bode well, young Drafe." Umda ground his teeth. "Leave this to me. Go, seek your rest, for the rite of Uhann is tomorrow."

Drafe stumbled to where Larya waited. A frown marred her delicate brow, and her mass of braids quivered as she hurried to him.

"What happened?" Her soft voice soothed him despite his dwindling energy. His symbiotes had no more to give until he ate something and tasted the sweetness of water.

"I endangered the village by bringing a vasquva to our borders."
He accepted whatever fate the elders chose for him. "I am sorry,
Larya."

She said no more, slipped her arm around him, and led him
home. Taking the carved steps into the caves trembled his thighs,
and bending his knees was beyond him. Placing his hand on the
smooth cave walls gave him strength, but when she guided him onto
his bed, he groaned.

"Here." She held up a stone bowl of water.

With trembling fingers, he tipped it to his lips, careful to sip and
take no more.

"Drink, my brother. I saved from yesterday."

He hesitated, but she forced his hand, tilting the bowl with a
finger. The coolness soothed his grated throat, and he groaned,
savoring each drop. It wasn't enough, but it would do.

"Hungry?"

He shook his head.

She placed a flat stone beside him with strips of garak across it.
"Your symbiotes need it, Drafe."

Taking a sliver, he chewed slowly. His strength had all but left
him, and he slumped against the wall. She moved around their small
home, gathering a bowl and a cloth. He trailed her with his gaze. The
decadent splash of water followed as she poured it into the bowl.

"What are you doing?" His voice was hoarse.

"Washing you." She soaked the cloth and rung it out, but when
she tried to touch him with it, he jerked away.

"We do not waste water, Larya." He glared at her, prepared to
argue with her.

"You stink of vasquva blood." She met his glare, her yellow gaze clashing with his. "I will walk to the pools in the morning. For the injured, they will allow an extra ration."

"When?" He flinched when she ran the wet cloth across his arm. White spots marred where the vasquva's skin had burned his. "The challenge is at daybreak. I dare not keep the Ivoyan waiting while you fetch more water."

"Ulvus will be challenging you."

Drafe's breath hitched. That massive son of a Kreta whore had been a pain in his ass since childhood, worse so when Larya reached womanhood. "Holy Osnir, Larya, you cannot mate him."

"I know." She stilled, dipping her chin to hide her delicate face. Her tiny body would be no match against Ulvus's brutishness.

"If I let him win, the Ivoyan will choose him." It went against Drafe's very soul to do that, but he had to. One more year would not be too long to wait until the next rite of Uhann. He could train on his own, learn to hunt better, and take the time to find Larya a worthy mate.

She sniffed, raising her shimmering gaze to meet his. "As challenge victor, he will demand I go to his family and await his return."

Drafe winced. If Ulvus didn't survive Ivoy, Larya would never bear children. "The Ivoyan have to choose me then."

She leaped to her feet to refill the stone platter. Not that Drafe could recall eating it all.

"When I go, I leave you unguarded, Larya. Who will you mate?" Darkness hit his chest like a boulder dropping into the unknown caverns beneath the village. He couldn't abandon his sister without knowing her future was secure.

"Kael has asked."

Drafe sat up and groaned, slumping again. "He has? You like him?"

"He is a strong male and a good hunter."

Kael was honorable too, but not favored because of the jagged scar across his face. Drafe pursed his lips. "He will cherish you. Have him come see me, Larya. I want this settled before the challenge. Once the Ivoy arrive, your fate is sealed."

A sweet smile graced her dark lips, as black as his own. She gathered her leather skirts and ran, leaving him alone with his thoughts.

Kael? Drafe was blindsided by the male's interest. Although, he could not fault him, for Larya was a typical Meorri woman with her black moonstone skin, her golden eyes, and the thick braids down her back. She had the gentlest nature and the biggest heart, willing to sacrifice much for another.

Kael was a massive male, scarred from childhood, ostracized because of it, despite having lost his family in the incident. The symbiotes were quiet on the details, except to say, Kael needed Larya's softness.

Drafe ate the meat, sucking the juices off his fingertips before dragging himself off the bed. While she was away, he used the bowl of water to clean himself. Its brown depths swirled with yellow blood when he was done. Slipping on a fresh tunic over pants, he settled onto his bed again.

Heat generated from a stack of venai stones warmed the rooms. Stories were told of tribes burning trees for fuel. He didn't believe them.

"Meorri aac Drafe," Kael greeted from the doorway.

"Meorri aac Kael." Drafe gestured to him to enter. "Larya tells me—"

"She speaks the truth." Kael stood before Drafe, his stance wide, his hands at his sides—a male with nothing to hide.

Drafe studied him. Kael was a big male, his presence filling the small room. When he sliced a glance at Larya hovering at the door, his face softened, and warmth glowed in his yellow eyes.

That was what Drafe had been waiting for. "On the love Osnir once bore Kreta, do you swear to honor Meorri aac Larya, to care for her and cherish her?"

Kael's chest puffed out, and in the steady light from the venai stones, his scar twitched. "As the suns bathe the sands, I do."

Larya gasped and ventured deeper into the room, her eyes wide, her smile more so.

"Larya, sister of mine, do you accept Kael's offer of protection, to bear his children, to care for him?"

She clasped her trembling fingers in front of her. "As the moon births the night, I do."

Drafe laughed, holding out his palms to accept Larya and Kael's hands. He guided hers to Kael's and released them. "It is done. Congratulations, Kael, brother of mine."

Kael roared and scooped a laughing Larya into his arms. Nuzzling her neck, he carried her out.

A deafening silence settled in the home he had shared with his sister and father. The night winds battered the walls but didn't intrude on his thoughts. Mating Larya before the challenge was frowned upon, but Drafe didn't care what the elders said. For tomorrow, he would die, or Osnir willing, fly the stars.

CHAPTER FOUR

DRAFE RAN HIS GIRDA stone along the shimmering blade of his father's sword—a slow hiss, a flick of his wrist, and repeat. The suns had yet to crest the Ki'irinzi Mountains to the east, bringing with it the unbearable heat. This day, he would make his ancestors proud.

His symbiotes hummed with anticipation, thrilled at the impending match. He was ready, having practiced with his father's sword since he could wield its ungainly weight. His nose twitched as Larya stirred in a fresh batch of tulsig. Bitterness saturated the air. He paused and drew in a long inhale, filling his chest to maximum. The sunbaked soil merged with his sweat, the sweetness of water, and the salt cakes she was frying in garak lard.

Her shadow fell across his outstretched legs. He flicked his gaze to hers while he sharpened the sword. His muscles knew the back-and-forth glide without endangering his fingers on the razor-sharp blade.

"Morning, Drafe." She lifted her face to a stray breeze. "It is a good day for dying."

"Morning. You have your mate to see to." Although, he was grateful for the meal she prepared. If this was farewell, it would be the last meal she ever made him.

She met his gaze, her yellow eyes so like his. "Come, break your fast." Pushing off the rock wall, she dusted her pant legs and entered their home.

The smooth pale rock had been carved with water in a time long gone. The little rooms now served the Meorri. Their home was on the outskirts of their village and received the brunt of the heat. Mating Kael hadn't improved her status by much, but the male adored her, and that was all Drafe needed to bless their union.

He pulled himself to his feet with a grunt. Yesterday's adventure had taxed him, and his muscles were stiff. While he slept, his symbiotes had healed his burns and grazes and eased some of the pain.

"Morning, Drafe." Kael appeared at the door, carrying a rack of drying meat. The sprinkle of salt crystals showed the meat had been spiced. "The elders wish to see you."

Drafe grimaced, then bit into a hot salt cake, relishing the savory flavor.

"I will deliver this to our home, *gevatia*." Kael winked and was gone.

"My heart? Endearments already?" Drafe couldn't resist teasing her, especially when her cheeks paled to gray.

She shoved two cakes into his hand, held out his sword, and gestured to the door. "Best see what they want. I will clean up and follow."

He trudged to the village well where they held court. Many were gathered, obscuring the older Meorri seated on smoothed stone blocks. As Drafe neared, the crowd parted. Smiles, frowns, and a few glowers greeted him.

"Elders." He bowed his head as soon as he stepped into the small clearing. This was it, his punishment announced, all symbiotes recording this moment to be remembered for an eternity.

"Young Drafe, primary male, we have much to discuss." Elder Bavu rose on wobbly knees to stand in the center. "You mated Larya without seeking our permission."

Kael growled, shouldering his way to stand beside Drafe.

Bavu's cheeks paled, but he cleared his throat to continue. "This can be forgiven in the light of recent events. For an absent primary male cannot serve his family."

Foq, they were going to exile him. Drafe snuck a glance at Kael. He had done well to mate his sister so quickly.

"Bringing a vasquva to our borders is beyond foolish. Helping the guards to kill it and in doing so supplying this village with food for a year, impressive."

Drafe frowned. Wait, what was the old male saying?

Bavu continued, "The Ivoyan aldermen are en route for this year's rite of Uhann. Are you prepared to challenge this day?"

Drafe jerked back and bumped into Kael, who nudged him forward. "I am, Elder Bavu."

"So am I." Ulvus thrust his way into the clearing. "This is garak shit, Elder Bavu. Had I lured a vasquva, you would have skinned my ass." He folded his massive arms across his chest.

"You would have run and hidden behind your mother's skirts," someone called from the crowd.

"Who said that? Face me." Ulvus spun, his face darkening as his eyes paled.

"Challenges happen in the circle, Ulvus. Confirm you wish to challenge Drafe for Qaldreth training." Elder Bavu stared him down, his gaze unflinching.

"By Kreta, yes. I will show this son of a—"

"Ulvus has declared challenge. Do you accept, Drafe?" Elder Bavu met Drafe's gaze, but laughter twinkled in his eyes. All knew, he had no patience for Ulvus or anyone in his family.

Drafe grinned. "I do."

"Let the rite of Uhann proceed." At Elder Bavu's announcement, the crowd cheered.

As one, they shoved past Drafe. Just south of the village, stone pillars had been settled into the dunes in a circle. Over the centuries, as the sands shifted, more stones were added. How deep they went, no one knew, not even the symbiotes.

When Kael drew Larya against his side, Drafe faced them. He smiled, cupped her cheek, and slapped Kael on the shoulder. "May Osnir bless your mating."

"May Kreta whisper your name in fear." Kael gripped Drafe's shoulder.

"Make him suffer, Drafe," Larya whispered, her paling eyes belied the strength in her words. She feared for his life.

Drafe grunted and strode through the water-carved tunnels to the circle. Many gathered, eager for entertainment. The symbiotes robbed them of storytellers when everyone knew the history of the Meorri from the first symbiotic relationship. Merchants who traveled between tribes brought fresh stories. Meorri discarded most of their tales as nonsensical. A sky village, tribes with too much water, food in abundance, slithering or flying predators? He huffed. Absurd.

Ulvus waited in the center of the circle, spinning his Cainus sword. Drafe's family could never afford such a blade, but one day, he would bless his son with the finest. Perhaps, if Osnir smiled upon him, hi3s mate wouldn't be a Meorri but from a land blessed with much.

"Only you would escape judgment," Ulvus hissed when Drafe entered the circle.

Raising his sword, Drafe spread his feet, preparing for Ulvus's usual charging like an enraged hudu. Drafe smirked. Ulvus was the size of one and as awkward on his feet.

A silver object darted across the sky, close enough to stir up spiraling eddies and plumes of sand. Drafe squinted, his symbiotes hurrying to shield his eyes. Through thin film, all watched the craft descend. Like a single drop of water, it glimmered in iridescent silvers and grays. Its door slid open, and two Ivoy stepped out. Their orange bodies glowed in the morning suns' light, and their dark blue garments flapped in the breeze. They descended, marring the sand with their footsteps. Tall, with long limbs and bulbous heads, they moved with efficiency on four-toed feet. Masks hid the top half of their faces. Visible were two holes for a nose and a small mouth drawn into a grim line.

They paused on the outside of the circle, alongside a smiling Bavu. He chatted away, bobbing his head whenever the Ivoy spoke. Drafe strained to listen above the shifting sands, despite it being futile. Only Bavu spoke Ivoyan. An Ivoy stepped closer and gestured with his four fingers for the match to commence.

With a roar, Ulvus charged.

Drafe stepped to the side without looking at him. Settling his gaze on his challenger, he waited and watched. Ulvus pushed his foot deep into the sand, preparing to lunge. Drafe sighed, wishing this was done, that he was en route to Ivoy, the heat of the suns no longer baking his head, shoulders, and his future optimistic. He could serve as a warrior or spend endless years mining the salt plains. His stomach churned as a weight settled on his chest.

Ulvus grunted and swung his sword.

Drafe leaned back, the whisper of a breeze trailing the blade's path.

Another strike, another dodge.

Sidestep, duck, back step, and repeat.

For every attack Ulvus made, Drafe evaded.

"Stand still, you son of a Kreta whore." Ulvus panted, his great shoulders jerking. He whipped his sword from side-to-side. Sweat glistened on his skin, and his yellow eyes paled.

Just a little more. Drafe smirked. "Why? Not everything in life is handed to you, Ulvus. This time your mother cannot help you."

Ulvus growled and lunged again. Instead of stumbling past Drafe, he switched tactics mid-charge and caught Drafe in the stomach with an elbow. He grunted and raised his sword in time to catch Ulvus's downward swing. The force of the colliding blades rippled down his arms. He pinched his lips to smother a moan. It would do no good to reveal a weakness.

Swing, swing, backward leap, duck, roll, and block. Exhaustion tugged on his limbs, but Drafe refused to concede, to allow Ulvus a victory of any kind. At the edge of the circle, he fought for air, his lungs burning, crisscrossed wounds bled clear blood while sweat dripped off his chin. Ulvus stood on the opposite side, worse than Drafe.

A horn blew, marking the end of the first half. Drafe strode across to Kael and Larya. He handed Kael his sword and accepted the offered water pouch. After squeezing five droplets on his tongue, he faced the circle for the last battle.

As if a phantom finger ran down his spine, he shivered. Ulvus drank deeply from Drafe's stolen water pouch. On the edge of the leather was his father's star. Fury rattled his bones, and he ground his teeth, almost biting his tongue to remain silent. He had to win the challenge first before accusations flew.

"Is that Father's—?"

Drafe gave Larya a slight nod. Her cheeks paled, and she twitched, her hands forming fists. Kael wrapped an arm around her shoulders and hugged her against his side.

Without his sword, Drafe strode into the circle and waited. Closing his eyes, he fought for calm and willed his anger to subside, for now. He trembled with restrained energy, and the urge to kill the male gripped him. Kreta whispered her seduction, how best to take his life, how Drafe would be doing the Meorri a great service if he killed Ulvus. To do so would make him an exile.

Drafe rolled his shoulders, his arms burning from meeting Ulvus's strikes. His symbiotes scrambled to heal his cuts and fuel his attacks. He was so tired. What he longed to do was sleep for days. His cool home called to him, his bed a few strides away.

He clenched his jaw and raised his hands. All Ulvus had to do was sit on Drafe to end the challenge. He had to ensure that didn't happen. Which meant more dodging, strategic kicks, and punches to the knees, thighs, eyes, ears. The first two were doable, the last two required a longer arm-reach than Drafe had.

As soon as Ulvus assumed position, Drafe struck with a kick to the knee. He leaped back and orbited while Ulvus howled and hopped on one leg.

"Holy Kreta, Drafe," he whined and rested the toes of his injured leg on the sand.

Drafe bounced, weaved, ducked, constantly moving between feints. Ulvus struggled to focus on Drafe, his gaze darting a second or two after Drafe moved. He pecked at the lumbering hudu, jabbed, kicked at newly healed wounds, at sore points, at weaknesses. With one arm-swing, Ulvus caught Drafe across the chest and sent him flying. He landed on his back with a grunt, sliding across the sand and stopping too close to the circle's edge. Moving out of it with any part of his body forfeited the challenge.

The ground trembled when Ulvus charged. Drafe's symbiotes whispered a warning, and he rolled several times to the side. When he leaped to his feet, he was in time to catch a kick to his stomach. Again he hit the sand and skimmed backward. He struggled to rise. Something squeezed his throat with his ability to breathe taken from him. A shadow fell across him. Ulvus prepared to throw his weight on Drafe, who raised his knees at the last minute. Ulvus's eyes bulged as his chest met Drafe's knees. The stale stench of salt cakes on his breath bathed Drafe's face, and he grimaced. Howling, Ulvus fell to the sand and curled on his side. Drafe rolled again and scrambled to his feet, swaying where he stood.

He brought his heel down on Ulvus's jaw, but the male caught his foot and dragged him off his feet. As pain throbbed in his shoulder and the sharp bolt of fire shot up his leg, Ulvus landed on top of him, pinning him to the ground. Drafe sank into the sand, hindering his ability to fight, to escape. Failure loomed while his symbiotes screamed suggestions.

His gaze fell to the side, to where Larya bit a clenched fist while Kael spoke to an animated Umda. No expression crossed the exposed part of the Ivoys's faces. Bavu frowned, no doubt unhappy with Ulvus winning.

Drafe slumped, dropped his hands, and pretended to pass out. In times like this, he would play the weakling. Ulvus chuckled and jerked back, a slave to his nature.

Drafe struck, punching the male in the face. Clear blood drenched him at the snap of a bone. Ulvus howled, pulling away to wipe his chin. His eyes paled to white, and before Drafe could thrust the male off him, Ulvus punched him. His body registered the excruciating burn of agony as his head snapped to the side. By the fourth blow across his jaw and cheek, the pain merged into one.

"Enough."

The blue sky filled Drafe's fading vision when someone dragged Ulvus off him. Drafe's symbiotes muttered, cursed, but hurried to heal him. Yesterday and today had tested them, and for that, he was sorry. One eye began to close when Bavu leaned over him.

"Young Drafe, do you require a healer?"

Drafe winced. To summon a healer proved his unworthiness. "Is it *that* bad?" His words were mumbled with his lips smashed against his teeth. The salty tang of his blood coated his tongue. He chuckled, then moaned when his ribs constricted.

"I have seen worse." Bavu grinned and offered a hand.

"I lost. That is worse enough for me," Drafe mumbled.

"Against Ulvus you could never have won, Drafe."

Hoisted to his feet, he smothered a groan and focused on standing still. His world tilted. Trickling blood from his ear dripped onto his shoulder.

"This day is not set." Bavu patted Drafe on the shoulder. "The Ivoy will choose, and there is the small matter of your stolen water pouch."

Drafe whipped his head up and gaped, despite his vision spinning. "How did you—?"

"Umda is our finest peacekeeper, Drafe. Did you doubt he would look into this?" Bavu shook his head. "The theft of a water pouch is not to be taken lightly."

Ulvus stood to the side, laughing despite his bloody nose. Hanging from his belt was the evidence of his crime, but the foolish male was too arrogant for his own good.

Bavu strode toward the Ivoy instead of confronting Ulvus. A discussion ensued with Bavu pointing and gesticulating before he pulled his lips into a grim line. Marching to the center of the circle, he waved his hand, summoning Ulvus to his side.

"The Ivoy have chosen, but before I announce the next Qaldreth trainee or Karu, I would like to discuss Ulvus's punishment."

His mother gasped, her cheeks darkening.

Ulvus blustered, as if he was innocent of whatever crime Bavu would mention.

"Whose water pouch is that, Ulvus?" Umda called from beside Tiyl, both having thrust the butts of their spears into the sand.

"Mine?"

Drafe laughed. "You are not sure?"

Ulvus glared at him. "Of course I am sure. It is mine."

"It bears your father's symbol?" Bavu arched a brow.

Ulvus's cheeks paled. "Um...yes?"

"So, if I were to examine it, a tall cucooya tree would be burned into the leather?" Bavu folded his arms across his chest, twisting his face in disbelief.

Ulvus trembled. He opened and closed his mouth, choking on his words.

"Whose symbol is it?" Bavu raised his arms above his head. "Elders and primary males, gather around and share your wisdom."

Males strode into the circle, studied the water pouch still hanging from Ulvus's belt, with most raising startled glances to Drafe.

Ulvus stilled. "But—?"

"You wish to defend your actions, young Ulvus?" Umda asked.

Ulvus rocked from side-to-side. "Drafe gave it to me."

Laughter rippled across the males, for such an event would never occur. A water pouch was as sacred as the symbiotes, passed on from father to son for generations.

"Young Drafe, what say you?" Umda stood firm, gripping his spear's shaft close to him.

Drafe hesitated. To reveal Ulvus as a thief would cost the male a hand. He could not lie either. With a grimace, he forced the truth past his lips. "It was taken while I rode the vasquva's back toward the Ki'irinzi Mountains."

Gasps rippled across the males with Ulvus's mother wailing in the background. Females held her back. To enter the ring without invitation was suicide.

"Ulvus, you have been judged." Bavu swept a hand over his shoulder, stating the matter settled. "Umda, he is yours to deal with."

"No." Ulvus shoved males aside. "I found them unattended."

"Them?" Bavu widened his eyes. "You stole more than a pouch? No more lies, Ulvus, or does the loss of more limbs not matter to you?"

"It was but a water pouch, a spear, and two dead garak," Ulvus muttered, lowering his chin.

"Did you present them to Drafe or Larya when you returned from the hunt?" Bavu pursed his lips when Ulvus said no more. "Very well, failure to accept punishment means banishment for you and your family. Is this acceptable?"

"No." Ulvus settled his gaze on his mother, raised his head, and trailed Umda.

The village waited. Silence reigned except for the hiss of shifting sands and the howls of the winds as they raced through the tunnels. An agonizing cry pierced the air. As one, the village gasped. The deed was done. The punishment was carried out.

Umda returned, ushering a gray-tinged Ulvus into the circle. He gripped his forearm, with a bloodied cloth wrapped around his wrist. Sweat dewed his temple and saturated his black hair. His eyes were a rich gold and his lips drawn into a narrow line.

Umda held up Drafe's water pouch. He accepted it with his hand on his chest in thanks.

"The Ivoy have chosen." Bavu gestured to Ulvus. "They will take you as you are."

Drafe tried not to show his disappointment. This was as expected. He would try again next year. Squeezing his eyes shut for a moment, he envisioned a future in silence. Without Larya, no one would care for him, ensure he ate, or force him to converse.

An Ivoy sliced through the crowds, parting them. He raised a four-fingered hand. When Bavu bowed his head, so did the tribes.

"Ivoyans do not care that you are missing a limb for this is repairable." His voice was smooth, cool, like trickling water in a deep well. "Your size is what is valuable. But," his lip curled in derision, "a thief is not tolerated. Continue this dishonorable behavior, and your service will be terminated. You have been warned, Meorri aac Ulvus."

The Ivoy turned, not waiting for a response from Ulvus, and rested his gaze on Drafe. "Meorri aac Drafe, the Ivoy will accept your service." The crowd gasped, but he sliced a glance, silencing them. "Your determination, strength of will, and use of strategy makes you a worthy selection. Elder Bavu informs me that you also killed a vasquva, yet here you stand, able to participate in a challenge despite your recent injuries. Commendable. Do you accept?"

Violent emotions bubbled in Drafe's chest. He struggled to hold back his joy or a wide triumphant smile. "I do."

"You have a few minutes to bid your loved ones farewell." The Ivoy strode past his companion and climbed into the craft.

"May I?" Drafe gestured to where Larya bounced on her toes, her smile bright against her dark face.

Bavu pressed a hand to his chest. "You may, Drafe."

Drafe ran, dodging the males eager to grip his arm. He paused beside Umda and rested his hand on his shoulder. Nothing needed to be said. As soon as Drafe neared Larya, Kael reached across the circle's edge and yanked Drafe over it.

No tears trickled down Larya's cheeks. To do so was to waste precious liquid, but she gripped his hands. "So happy for you, Drafe."

"Take care of my sword and Father's water pouch. I will return." He handed the pouch to her and cupped her cheek one last time. With a nod at Kael, he strode to the craft and climbed into the dark depths, the smell metallic and foreign. A strange coolness swept across his skin as he waited, unsure what was expected of him.

"Sit," an Ivoy said, gesturing to a wall-mounted ledge.

Drafe obeyed. Straps shot across his legs and around his waist, holding him to the structure. He could move and wasn't uncomfortable. An Ivoy sat on the opposite ledge, strapped in place, so nothing Drafe needed to be alarmed by.

Ulvus staggered into the craft, and the last standing Ivoy ushered him to a ledge. The male was in agony, his shoulders curled in, his cheeks still gray and glimmering in the craft's pale lighting. The door closed, sealing them inside. As soon as the Ivoy assumed a ledge, the craft lifted. Images of Meorri flitted across one wall, the Ki'irinzi Mountains in the distance until blue skies darkened into a star-studded black.

"Drink," an Ivoy commanded, holding out a cylindrical container. "As much as you want, Meorri, for water is abundant on Ivoy."

Drafe twitched but accepted the gift. The sweet scent of water tickled his nose, and he tipped the bowl to his lips. Ice cold droplets fell onto his tongue. He paused after five.

"As much as you want," the Ivoy repeated.

Drafe did so, drinking his full, feeling like a child with too much garak meat on his birthing day. As he leaned back, cradling the container to his chest, his stomach cramped. For the first time in his life, he'd quenched his thirst.

CHAPTER FIVE

VIC HADN'T BEEN ABLE to sleep, thrust into a world not of her choosing. She tried to think of ways to escape but ended in the same spot, here, in a bunker beneath Ande, on a spaceship orbiting Earth.

Trapped.

Running a fingertip over the neck device, she winced at the raw skin where she had tried to scratch it free.

Snores peppered the barracks. A dim glow illuminated the path to the ablutions. Her cheeks warmed, and she ran her hands along her thighs. Before light's out, men and women had disrobed, standing in the sol rays without shame. Ande had stared at her, his lips curling, as if her clothing was hideous. Sure, it was stained and brown, but then working on machinery would ruin her best clothes. Though, nothing she owned could compare to the soft pants he'd given her.

She rolled her lip to swallow a whimper. Her things were gone, lost forever, along with her cycle. She had nothing and no one. Gathering the thin blanket around her, she crushed her shirt's hem in her fist. Fire ebbed and flowed, climbing up her chest to squeeze her throat.

She blinked back the tears brimming on her eyelashes. *Farg, I hate my pa.*

Sucking in slow breaths, she struggled to clear her vision. This was her life...for now. Her ma hadn't raised a fool. Vic was a hard worker. She would knuckle down and earn her freedom.

A low drone began, building in volume until it vibrated the beds. She flung the blanket aside and her legs off the bed as the other captives did. The boy with the busted arm sported a cast.

Relief was swift to slump her shoulders. At least, medical treatment wasn't denied to them.

Ande rolled off his top bunk and glowered. So, not a morning person?

"Get dressed." He gathered her folded garments and shoved them at her. "Canteen is a free-for-all. If you want the most palatable food, you get there first." He stomped off after yanking on similar clothing to yesterday's. Watching him disappear into the ablutions, she hurried to snap her boots on, not wanting to lose her one ally, as grumpy as he was.

"Mm, you're too old for this. Where've you been?" With her hands on her hips, a dark-skinned, black-haired girl smiled at Vic.

"Working my sol farm." Vic rose, forcing the girl back.

"Name's Fiona."

Vic stared at the outstretched hand. *'Nice to meet you'* seemed trite. "Vic," she muttered and took the offered hand for a quick shake. "Got to get food." She darted around Fiona for the canteen. Used to odorless, cubed pastes, the unusual aromas were intriguing. She hoped it was edible and would assuage the ravenous monster in her belly.

A wall of muscle halted her progress. Blond, tall, and solid, the blue-eyed boy side-stepped when she did. She'd dealt with his kind before, thinking his God-given attributes entitled him to 'special' treatment. A knee to the groin would be a treat. She smirked and dipped her head to hide it. Aggravating him wouldn't help her.

"Name's Devlin, princess. Ready for some serious action?" He rolled his hips, his meaning clear, despite his gaze resting on Ande. Why he bothered with her, she couldn't say.

"Devlin working his magic." Someone laughed.

His eyes narrowed before he settled his focus on her, at last.

"I'm used to real men." Lies, but he didn't need to know that. She patted his chest and slipped past him, throwing an arched brow at Erv leaning against the canteen's metallic wall.

"Sleep well?" The older man pushed off the wall to approach her.

She glared at him. Like he cared. "Perfectly fine." She grinned to show him her teeth, all of them.

He grunted and gestured to her to follow. Her stomach cramped. She cast a longing glance at the trestle tables and the colorful food items she wouldn't get to sample. Sighing, she trailed Erv, hesitating when he pointed at Ande. "To me."

Ande grabbed round objects and shoved one in his mouth as he clambered over a bench to reach them. He pressed the softness into her hand when he fell into step beside her. She sniffed the sweetness and bit into the warm gooey substance. Moaning, she shoved the thing in her mouth, barely able to chew. That wasn't necessary when it melted on her tongue.

Licking her fingers, she asked, "what was that?"

"Sugar bun."

She slowed to a crawl while she gaped at him. "Real sugar?"

He smirked. "Of course not." He wrapped his fingers around her wrist and tugged her to catch up. Erv hadn't waited, but when he reached the massive obstacle course set to the side of the training room, he stopped.

"Farg," Ande whispered. "Good luck, Vic."

Cold drenched her spine. A white metallic drum, its diameter about ten feet, spun but switched direction without reason. Rectangular cutouts made running through the drum more difficult. Dark red splotches on the gleaming metal suggested blood stains. She clenched her jaw, praying the red was paint and not...well, the real thing. Before the drum, massive arms with spiked balls swung across a narrow bridge. The starting platform was wide enough to stand on but nothing more. To reach it, she would have to climb a ladder. The end platform on the other side of the drum held a flag—the target. She settled a wide-eyed gaze on Erv, who waved that wretched device that triggered the thing in her neck.

"Didn't peg you for a coward." He nudged his head at the death-defying contraption.

"Nor am I stupid." She folded her arms, challenging him.

"It's too soon, Erv." Ande slid glances between the drum and Erv.

"If she grabs the flag, Ande, it will determine what training she receives. Mr. Carne wants her in the arena tomorrow. I must know who to pit her against."

"*Her* is standing right here," Vic snapped.

"*Her* should be climbing the fargen ladder." Erv threw out his arm in a wide sweep.

"Try, at least, Vic." Ande patted her shoulder as if to say 'it's been nice knowing you, kid.'

She inched toward the ladder, then gripped the rungs, enjoying the solid feel of them beneath her hands. Clambering up, she balanced on the small platform and eyed the static flag. She wasn't scared of heights. Some of the solar plates she'd worked on were high off the ground. Placing her feet with care, she faced the swaying pendulums between her and the drum. There was a timing to it. Thwack, pause, pause, thwack, thwack, pause, thwack could read as left, go, go, right, left, go, left. Easy, except for the arrows whizzing across the bridge.

This was insanity at its finest.

Raising her foot, she waited. The unstable bridge was comparable to the platforms she balanced on when she did repairs. On Earth, the wind was at its worst behavior. Here, not a breeze stirred. She could do this.

The red flag beckoned.

"Left, go, go, right, left, go, left," and she bolted.

Dodging left, she underestimated the moving floor and slipped. She caught her toes on the edge of the bridge and teetered, throwing out her arms to catch her balance. A faint whistle preceded an arrow. She ducked, mimicked the action of the first metallic arm and leaped forward. On the padded floor below was a tumbling dart, as long as her forearm but as thin as her pinky finger. If that had hit her, it would have killed her.

"Fargen hell," she growled.

Taking a step brought her close to the second pendulum, as more whistles warned her to duck. As soon as the arm swung past, she lunged across. She cried out when a spike scratched her thigh, but she couldn't pause to check. Ignoring the blazing agony trembling her leg, she rolled across the bridge, a dart flicking out one of her curls while the third pendulum thrummed past her ass.

The returning swing of the fourth metallic arm descended. She had a left, go, and a left to do before she reached the drum. Why the hell was she doing this? A glance down caught Ande's pensive face and Erv's nod, his arms folded across his chest. Instead of inching across, she lunged for the pendulum, catching its arm with her left hand. Its momentum dragged her off the bridge and flicked her up, her legs flying outward.

Ande whooped.

As she rode the pendulum, she grinned but didn't dare focus on him. Three more to go, but from this angle, she swung from arm to arm and land firmly on the narrow section of the bridge between the seventh pendulum and the drum.

This close to the drum, she spread her legs to handle the shuddering bridge. Before her tumbled the final challenge. The flag twitched, taunting her. Seven feet of gaps and spinning metal separated her from the end platform. Taking a moment to catch her breath, she waited until a gapless path aligned before exploding into action. When her foot hit the moving metal, she lost her balance and had to leap over a gaping hole rolling toward her. She slammed into the side, wincing when her shoulder took the brunt of it.

Panting for air, she splayed her fingers on the metal and watched the impending hole draw nearer.

There was no going back. *Farg it.* She jumped onto the side of the drum, sprinted high along the top, as far as the centrifugal force would allow her, and landed on the platform. The seconds it took for her fingers to brush the flag's course fabric sent her plummeting through a trapdoor. A tear reached her ears despite the whistles and thwacks continuing.

"No," she cried out, having not once considered the end platform unsafe. She landed on a padded mat, the wind knocked from her lungs. They could make the exit gentler, but she doubted they'd soften the blow of failure.

"What does this mean?" Ande asked Erv.

"No one gets the flag on their first try." Erv's words preceded him, then he rounded the corner and strode to where she lay under the massive rotating drums. It wasn't just one but many, tumbling in opposite directions and often changing without warning. "You did well, gal."

"Vic." She huffed and rolled onto her side to meet his gaze. Her thigh burned, but she didn't look away, just pressed a hand to the wound. Wet stickiness warmed her palm.

"You came close." Ande crouched beside her and gestured to the elbow she leaned on. She twisted to find a piece of the flag.

"A part of a flag isn't a win, but it's fargen close." Erv grinned. "Vic for Victorious?" He offered her his back when he strolled off. "Mm, I like that. Needs something, though." Pausing when he was halfway across the practice mats, he called without glancing over his shoulder, "Have the medics attend to the scratch."

"Holy farg, did she get the flag?" Fiona rose onto her toes to see better. Crowded around her were the other captives.

"A piece. It doesn't count." Devlin scowled. "Time to spar. Show's over." He stomped as he headed for the weights.

Ande helped Vic to her feet. "Can you walk?"

She tested her weight on her leg and nodded. With a last glance, she met Devlin's gaze across the room. "What the farg is his problem?"

"You were close to beating him."

Vic spun to gape at Ande. "He got the flag?"

"At his second attempt." Ande paused by another door, no different than the others. "If you train hard, you might be his equal, Vic. Good thing Carne doesn't mix genders. Devlin's a vindictive bastard if he doesn't win, in the arena or here." Ande rubbed his shoulder as if he nursed an old wound.

"Right, so don't get caught in a dark room with him."

"It's best to avoid his radar completely." Ande settled his gaze on Devlin. "Although, I suspect it's too late for you."

CHAPTER SIX

The Qaldreth Command Council

Planet of Ivoy

DRAFE SAT ON THE outskirts of the training ring, running a cloth along the sword's blade. The repetitive motion gave him focus and brought him a sense of peace. He raised his gaze to the dome above, its opaque glass revealing the lilac sky misty from a morning deluge. Another thing he'd had to get used to. Water so precious on Qaldreth fell from the Ivoyan sky so much that he longed for sunlight. Never would he have thought he'd find himself in such a blessed situation. If he could send home water, he would. No Ivoyan ships traveled to Qaldreth unless to attend the rite of Uhann, and besides, what would an abundance of water teach the Meorri but to waste? No, it was best he enjoy this time and allow his symbiotes to share his experiences when he stepped foot on Meorri soil.

Thwack.

He lowered his gaze to a male from the mountain tribe. Like a comet, his golden hair trailed every strike he made. He swung a staff, hitting the target with such force, the pole bowed.

"Riermus aac Vaen, where is your sparring partner?" Fumart Dau Lo asked, his hands clasped behind his back. He strolled the grounds, checking each event or exercise.

"At the med-tech, Dau Lo." Vaen dipped his head in a show of respect.

"I see." The Ivoyan teacher pursed his dark-orange lips. "Find another. One cannot test one's strength *and* agility alone."

Newer to the training arena, Drafe had yet to spar with all karu. Setting the sword to the side, he folded the cloth and placed it on top of the gleaming blade.

"I am available," he said and pushed off the bench, picking a staff out of a nearby barrel en route.

Vaen scowled, made more menacing with his black eyes. "Your training has just commenced. You have not yet earned—"

"Consider it practice then." Drafe smiled. "After all, I am willing to be humiliated at your hands."

"You waste my time, Meorri." He swept the staff wide, smacking the padded target without glancing at it.

Drafe bristled but maintained a calm exterior. Vaen could not irritate more than Ulvus. "I did not think a Riermus would fear a Meorri. I am certain my symbiotes will be delighted to tell of this moment."

"Fear?" Vaen glowered then tapped the mark on the mat beside his.

Drafe stepped into place and ducked when Vaen spun, sweeping the staff at Drafe's head. The weapon slammed into the target with a reverberating thud. Drafe responded with the same. The exercise required a duck and whack but in unison. Both had to be aware of their partner's movements while using the correct stances when swinging the staff—weight on the front leg, swivel on the ball of the foot, with the full force of the body to power the strike.

Dau Lo watched then strolled off. Time slowed with the repetitive motion, though Drafe's limbs marked the effort. Sweat coated his skin, but he wiped his palms on his pants during ducks. His connection with the staff began at the grip. Weakening would jeopardize his control of the weapon. Lose that, and he would wound himself or worse, Vaen.

At last, the male stepped aside, breaking the hypnotic routine. Drafe stiffened his shoulders, not wanting to slump no matter how much relief coursed through him. His symbiotes hurried to heal and energize, starting with his trembling knees and throbbing arms.

"Mm, better than I expected." Vaen layered his forearm over Drafe's in a show of respect.

"From a static target?" A male laughed.

Drafe gritted his teeth and glared at Ulvus who scratched his regrown hand—a startling orange against his obsidian skin. True to their word, the Ivoy had 'healed' him. His new hand was a mirrored replication of the other down to the fingerprints. What was amazing was that the symbiotes had adapted, matching the skin tones when they formed armor.

"Ah, Ulvus Karu, why not demonstrate the skill?" Dau Lo strolled through the gathering trainees, clasping his long arms behind his back.

Vaen's scowl darkened. He gripped and released the staff in agitation.

When Ulvus shifted to the side, his new hand twitching, Drafe smothered a smirk. "Please, show me how it is done, Ulvus."

"Against you?" His eyebrows arched in a hopeful expression.

"Against me," Vaen snapped, tapping the spot as he'd done with Drafe.

Ulvus scowled. "I challenged Drafe."

"That you have done and won. What would another battle accomplish?" Vaen smacked the spot, this time bowing the staff.

Ulvus jerked back.

Drafe palmed his staff and handed it to the male. "Do not fear. Vaen will not hit you unless you are unable to match his rhythm."

"I fear nothing, Meorri aac Drafe," Ulvus spat, snatching the offered staff. He stepped onto the mark and raised the long weapon as if he swung a stick.

"The Qaldreth has an issue with this male."

All turned to the source of the intrusion. Authority resonated in the Ivoyan's voice. As it should. Before them stood the highest-ranked Ivoyan, Luharp Vadril Ot. A white tunic, embossed with golden thread, draped over the towering Ot. His narrowed gaze assessed the situation while his expression remained neutral.

The focus shifted to Ulvus whose cheeks had taken on a pale gray hue. "I... I do, Great Ot."

"Why? Do you blame him for the loss of your appendage? Are you not satisfied with our craftmanship? What will your resentment gain you?"

Ulvus flinched at each question, the staff in his hand slipping until the butt hit the padded mat.

Vadril Ot gestured to Drafe. "Accept his challenge, and whoever does well, I shall consider for my next protector."

Gasps rippled through the crowd.

Drafe pursed his lips. To be given such an opportunity, he had to try. No matter how much exhaustion still weakened his limbs. With a nod to Vaen, Drafe took up position when the male stepped aside and handed him the staff.

"Remember, Ulvus Karu, it is not the chance to inflict pain that is measured but the ability to work as a team, awareness of one's surroundings, and the use of one's might against the target." Dau Lo dipped his head to whisper to the superior Ivoyan.

"Begin," Vadril Ot commanded after meeting Dau Lo's gaze.

Drafe gripped the staff as Vaen had demonstrated—one hand a short distance from the butt, the other below the middle. Ulvus clasped it with both hands at the butt. Drafe thudded the staff against the target, narrowly missing Ulvus's head when he ducked. Drafe knelt, not checking if Ulvus would swing. No thwack followed. Drafe didn't hesitate and leaped to his feet, the staff ready.

Pain exploded across his upper arm. He sucked in a sharp breath, reigned in his fury, and slid back from the mark. His symbiotes vibrated, demanding he retaliate. Once was an accident. Despite the fire spreading down his arm, he arched a brow at Ulvus. "Shall we begin again?"

"Of course," Ulvus grinned and raised the staff to ear-height.

Drafe forced his legs to move, to step into place. Without hesitation, he ducked, wincing when Ulvus hit the target. Drafe jumped up and swung, the force of his anger traveling along the staff to the padded target. He dropped to a knee and waited.

No connection sounded. He glanced up, catching Ulvus's smirk. When the staff hit Drafe's ear, he swallowed a cry of surprise and sheer agony as if his head would explode. Sharp needles ricocheted from the side of his head to behind his eye, making it water. He cupped his ear, grimacing at the stickiness of his blood wetting his palm.

"Enough," Dau Lo roared, snatching the staff from Ulvus.

"Oh, my apologies, Dau Lo." Ulvus bowed. "I did not mean—"

"I am not blind, Ulvus Karu," Vadril Ot said, his calm tone slicing through the chaos.

A red-orange-haired male from the Giniiri tribe leaned over Drafe, running his arm over the injury. The glowing name across his vest said 'Borven aac Nenn.' The burning ceased, along with the persistent humming. Given time, Drafe's symbiotes would have healed him. Vaen took up a protective stance between Ulvus and Drafe.

Scowling, he staggered to his feet, gripped Vaen by the upper arm, and nudged him aside. "Ulvus Karu, my apologies. I did not demonstrate the process." He took the staff from a stiff Vaen. "Shall we try again?"

"This is illogical," Vadril Ot stated.

"In Ulvus's defense, the process was not demonstrated, Vadril Ot." Drafe dipped his head to show respect. "I had hours to observe Vaen."

Dau Lo frowned and whispered to Vadril Ot. The superior stiffened and gestured to security.

Borven aac Igar drew near, his gold eyes narrowed, almost lost against his dark orange skin so like the canyons he called home. "Great Ot?"

"Send the recording to the Senate and the Qaldreth Command Council." Silence settled while Vadril Ot stared at Drafe. "Escort Ulvus Karu to the vault to await sentencing."

Ulvus trembled and fell to his knees. "Please, Great Ot—"

"Dau Lo warned you, Ulvus. Yet you allowed your lust for vengeance to govern your behavior." Vadril Ot flicked a dismissive hand, elegance in his long fingers. "Drafe Karu, walk with me."

Drafe stiffened, shoved the staff at Vaen, and trailed the Ot. He said nothing, waiting for the Ivoyan to reveal his thoughts.

Once they had left the training grounds and were alone on a sun-lit pathway toward the Senate—a hovering building on the horizon, Vadril Ot drew to a halt.

"Tell me, Qaldreth, why did you allow that male to harm you?"

"It costs me nothing to bow like a cucooya tree in a gale. I will not break if I maintain humility. Against a male stronger than me, I cannot stand firm. It would be my death."

"So you allow him to believe he is the victor." Vadril Ot chuckled. "A flawed strategy. Ulvus Karu knows what you are doing, Drafe Karu, which is why he will repeatedly challenge you. I suggest you find another approach."

Drafe slumped for a second before straightening. "You are wise to suggest this, Great Ot."

"I *do* like you. You remained calm, gave him the benefit of the doubt when you knew his actions were deliberate, and still, you offered him a way out of his consequences." Vadril Ot grasped Drafe's cheeks, cupping him from jaw to hairline. Tilting his head, the Ivoyan studied Drafe's face before releasing him. "Once you have completed your training, I will request your service as arrak."

Drafe stared after the Ot, too stunned to form words. His symbiotes bounced as they'd done the first time he'd quenched his thirst. A slow smile blossomed into a grin.

Osnir had seen fit to bless him again.

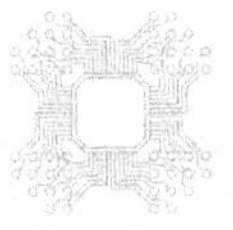

A decade later.
The Senate
Planet of Ivoy

DRAFE STIFFENED, SLIDING HIS hand onto his pulsar holstered to his back. He held his breath, his gaze tracing the Ivoyan running out of the Senate. Boxes teetered in his long-limbed arms, his extended fingers splaying out to stabilize the shifting mass. Drafe drew in a deep breath, the tension between his shoulders easing. The Ivoyan was an Uz, a servant, as categorized at birth and by the blue uniform molding his orange form.

Drafe raised his focus to the deep lilac and yellow skies, watching ships zip across. As pleasant as the sight was, he should have been inside the Senate, guarding Vadril Ot. His language implant behind his left ear had malfunctioned. Now, he waited for a med-tech to assess the device and repair it.

Pacing, his long strides covered the distance on the floating platform. He neared the edge, activated the air-barriers with his proximity, then spun on his heel, striding across to the other side. Unmasking and masking his armored obsidian skin on his fingers, he sighed. His symbiotes thrummed their displeasure, but at least, it was something different to do.

The number of scurrying servants had dwindled. Fewer demands from the attending Ots indicated the intensity of the debate. They met once a lunar cycle to discuss expansion, inventions, discoveries, and economics. This was an unscheduled gathering. A new species had been discovered. He had caught a brief sighting of the body sprawled on a table in the middle of the auditorium. Hating the delay, he grunted. Xenology was a hobby of his. He needed to be inside, to see for himself what this species was.

Lifting his bared hand—the lilac sunlight didn't taint the obsidian tone of his skin, he pressed the device in his neck. "How much longer, Nenn?" He flicked his gaze upward again, searching for the med-tech, a maed. Despite belonging to separate tribes, Drafe had grown to respect the incoming male. This cycle, he would kill him for the delay.

"Why? You have a female awaiting your return?" Nenn chuckled, the sound reverberating through Drafe's mind. The nodule had a distance limitation but was effective during guard duty and short excursions. A response meant the male was close.

Drafe snorted. "A female on Ivoy? Sure."

"Ivoyans are androgynous so finding a compatible female *is* possible," Nenn said with a huff that only his shoulders conveyed when he landed on the platform and deactivated his powered boots. The huff wasn't emotive enough for the nodule to communicate.

A grunt would have, though, which Drafe used again. "I am attempting to banter with you. Try it before you reject the skill."

"Would this be from your xenology studies I've heard rumors of?" Nenn's derision silenced Drafe.

No one understood his fascination with the lesser species that inhabited the universe. Their biology, cultures, and mannerisms intrigued him. The Ivoyans and Qaldreth were once as primitive, but to suggest such a time existed was blasphemous.

Nenn strode toward him with insufficient enthusiasm for Drafe's liking. He spun, tilting his head for easier access to his ear. His bald head, similar in shape to the new species, aided access. Qaldreth shaved their heads but allowed a strip to grow from the brow to the base of his spine. He kept most of it hidden under his dark gray, armored body-suit, and since his fur was the exact shade of his suit, it blended in.

Nenn paused beside him, raising his arm to scan Drafe's ear. "Is your Ot inside?" he asked, soft beeps marking his progress.

Agony pierced Drafe's skull, and he gritted his teeth against it. He didn't answer for a while, focusing on controlling his breathing while his symbiotes fought to heal the cause of the pain. They couldn't, but they would at least repair the area around the implant.

"Diagnosis?"

"Replacement," Nenn said, lowering his arm.

"Here?" Drafe didn't smother his hopeful tone. The quicker he received the new nodule, the quicker he could return to Vadril Ot's side.

"No, you'll have to come with me."

"Curse it, Nenn. I cannot leave, not with my Ot unguarded." Drafe sliced an irritated glance at the male. A blend of orange and red fell from his brow to his nape before disappearing into his red suit. The male tsked, tilted Drafe's head, and cold metal clipped into place...a temp-device.

"See me when you can," Nenn said. "I'll have the implant waiting at med-tech."

"My thanks." Spinning to enter the Senate, Drafe approached the hovering Uz to test his temp-device. "Greetings," he said.

The servant's head shot up, his brow furrowing in confusion with fear lingering in his black eyes. A Qaldreth warrior never spoke to an Uz unless they had been implicated in a crime.

"Be at ease. I need to test my language translator." Drafe brushed his armor-coated fingers over his ear.

The uz flicked his gaze there. His narrow shoulders sagged with relief, and his fear faded. Drafe grimaced; if only the male would babble, then this test would be over sooner.

Clenching his jaw against the continued silence, he asked, "How fare's the gathering?"

The uz twitched. "Meorri Arrak, this discovery has the Ots eagerly chatting above each other."

Drafe pinched his lips to smother a smile, understanding the Ots' enthusiasm. "Good." He wrapped his fingers around the ornate handle of the large metal door, unraveling his armor for the scanner to read his genetic markers. The door unlocked with a soft click.

Intense heat engulfed his face and body. A force blasted him back, shoving him across the platform. He bounced off the air-balustrade to sprawl face-down across the floor. His symbiotes bombarded him with reports, bruises, and instructions. His vision spun, so he took a second to draw in a calming breath. He raised a stunned gaze to the Senate. Debris rained down in numbed silence. The uz leaned over him, peering into his eyes with his wide black orbs. His fear was too strong, drowning Drafe's other senses.

In a discordant roar, his hearing returned, slamming into his skull. He cried out, slapping a hand over the temp-device; wet and warm blood staining his armored fingers. An explosion? He scrambled to his feet, shoving the uz aside to stagger down the causeway. A void filled his soul, where the warm glow of the connection to his Ot had once resided. No, no, he refused to believe it.

The platform grumbled, shuddered, then tilted, sending him flying once more. He activated his boots, hoping to make it inside the crumbling Senate to find his Ot alive. To lose one on duty brought shame upon his tribe. The causeway creaked, then splintered off, sending the flame-engulfed Senate falling to the planet below seconds before the section he stood on dropped, as well.

A scream behind him jerked him around. The uz gripped the air-balustrade, then he grabbed nothing as the safety mechanisms failed. Scrambling for a handhold, he toppled over the side. Drafe shot forward, the thrust of his boots driving him after the uz. Touching his neck, he bellowed instructions and warnings to anyone close enough to pick up his signal. He tucked in his arms, streamlining his body, and aimed for the panicking uz.

Something or someone had killed the reigning Ots, their Uz servants, and many Qaldreth. Drafe gritted his teeth, fighting the shock stinging his eyes. Wrapping his arms around the Uz, he halted his fall, trusting his powered boots to carry their combined weight.

"Do you know who did this?" he asked the gaping Ivoyan. "Did you see who planted the explosive?"

The uz shook his head.

Salvage ships swarmed the plummeting carnage; their safety protocols would halt the platform's impact and minimize further damage. Drafe landed on the extended platform of a sec-ship and lowered the Ivoyan. He stumbled away from Drafe to vomit over the air-balustrade. A pounding in Drafe's skull reminded him that he had sustained an injury. Regardless, he faced the males jogging toward him.

"What happened, Drafe?" Vaen demanded, his black gaze on the chaos around them.

"Hell if I know." Drafe ran a hand over his face. "I was outside waiting for Nenn to insert a temp-device, and when I unlocked the door, everything exploded."

"Yet you saved an Uz instead of your Ot," Vaen said, a scowl twisting his features. That didn't bother Drafe when that was Vaen's usual disposition.

"I take no insult, Vaen." Drafe sighed, his shoulders drooping at his failure. It might have been better for him to have died in the burning wreckage.

"I will defend you to your commander." Vaen faced him and gripped Drafe's upper arm. "If they have their way, you'll return to Qaldreth in disgrace."

"I am a Qaldreth warrior of the tribe Moerri. I face my judgment without fear." Drafe's symbiotes bounced in agitation, but he ignored them, allowing Vaen to lead him away.

He would argue his case, perhaps the council would listen and send someone to investigate this new species. They had to be behind this catastrophic event or know someone who was.

CHAPTER SEVEN

The Qaldreth Command Council
Planet of Ivoy

DRAFE'S ARMOR UNMASKED FROM the waist up, baring his obsidian skin. At his most vulnerable, he stepped onto the platform. He raised his gaze to the dais upon which sat seven Qaldreth commanders, the strength of the tribes combined. All warriors in attendance were bare-chested, for to remain masked was an act of deceit. An exposed Qaldreth had nothing to hide.

Beams of light bathed them in artificial sunlight. The warmth of their suns upon their faces was craved by all. The yellow glow struck a chord, a yearning for home Drafe's symbiotes echoed. He tamped them down, willing them to calm.

They would have Qaldreth sunlight soon enough.

He winced. As a protector, an arrak, he had brought honor to the tribe. Across so many parsecs, the symbiotes could not communicate, but once he stepped foot on the salt plains, all would know of his failure...for generations to come.

"Meorri aac Drafe Arrak, you have been brought before the council in the direst of circumstances." Meorri aac Kish Udap paused, rolling his lips inward as if what he had to do was distasteful.

Drafe didn't doubt that. Exiling a warrior from the commander's tribe wasn't a pleasant task. He said nothing, though, for it was disrespectful to interrupt an Udap.

"By the grace of Ivoy and Osnir, you were welcomed as a karu, to train under those who *earned* their place as protectors." Kish Udap settled his gaze on Ulvus, and his lip curled further.

Drafe restrained the urge to nod. Despite Ulvus winning the challenge, he had only made the rank of sava, that of security or a foot soldier. Drafe had surpassed him, having earned the honor to protect, to share his symbiotes with an Ot—the highest rank an Ivoyan could be born to. Luharp Vadril Ot was from the most influential family on Ivoy.

Drafe had let him die. Along with the other twenty-three prime Ots in attendance and their Qaldreth warriors. Had his language implant not malfunctioned, he would have died alongside them. An honorable death he'd been denied. He'd responded by saving the witness, a lowly servant, an uz.

The planet of Ivoy was in chaos, losing its leadership in one strike. The second rank of Zi had to be summoned from their travels and studies. Some came from far-off galaxies Drafe had yet to learn about. This upheaval had toppled the Ivoy hierarchy, with the next generation of Ots still in training.

Many fingers pointed at the Qaldreth warriors, charged with the protection of the Ivoyan leaders and failed to do so. It would take decades to restore the tribes' combined honor on Ivoy and centuries for the Meorri tribe.

Yes, it would have been better had he died with his Ot.

"Worse, instead of rushing to save *the* Luharp Vadril Ot or any high-ranking Ot, you rescued Vizen Aehort Uz...a servant." Grumbles rippled through the council and the witnesses behind him. "What say you, Drafe Arrak?"

Drafe opened his mouth to speak.

"Borven aac Nenn Maed claims your language implant failed, explaining your presence outside the Senate." Borven aac Eran Udap gestured to Nenn to step forward.

Drafe tilted his head to acknowledge the male.

"It is defective, Great Council." Nenn's hair tucked in, his shoulders stiff, but he held his chin high. "I offered a temp-device until his could be replaced."

"Happenstance led you to abandon your Ot?" Zuphayr aac Srim Udap tapped his chin, his white hair bobbing. His blue eyes were striking, as were all the Qaldreths from the sky tribe of Zuphayr.

Drafe waited, scanning the council to ensure none would speak. He didn't need to add disrespect to his charges. "I rescued the only witness, Great Council, and yes, my implant did malfunction, causing Luharp Vadril Ot to suffer alongside me. Unable to bear the shared pain, he instructed me to seek medical attention." Drafe sucked in a deep breath. "I ensured he was well-guarded, tasking Meorri aac Saha Karu to protect him. Under the circumstances, twenty-two arraks, twenty-three karu, and a dozen sava were sufficient protection against a corpse."

The council nodded.

"You are wise to mention the protectors, the trainees, and the additional security, Drafe Arrak. Had I been in your situation, I would have acted the same." Kish Udap's words stiffened Drafe's spine. Agreeing with him made his symbiotes ripple to the surface of his skin, threatening to form his armor to shield him.

"This was an attack none of us foresaw." Srim Udap scanned the crowd. "An illogical strategy is required. You will share your symbiotes with the uz, Drafe Arrak."

Gasps rippled across the room. Kish Udap slapped the stone desk, and silence prevailed.

Drafe reeled. To share his symbiotes with an Ivoy was the prerequisite to becoming a protector. The higher the Ivoy's rank, the more honorable. An uz would bring no honor to his tribe. Drafe would have to guard the uz until the Ivoyan's death, natural or otherwise.

"The acting Ivoyan leadership has demanded justice be served. You and your uz will travel the galaxy and hunt down the culprits."

Exiled but not to Qaldreth. Under their vigilance, he could not react. Dishonor, enslavement, and banishment were his punishments. He fought for calm, running an imaginary hand over his symbiotes to soothe them. There was honor to be found on a revenge quest.

"All findings will be reported to me," Kish Udap continued.

Drafe straightened. "As you command, Kish Udap."

"You leave as soon as the symbiote transfer is complete, your implant replaced, and a ship fueled." Eran Udap gestured to the hall. "Choose your crew. Additional security will be provided."

"Do not take this mission as leniency on our part," Kish Udap sliced glances at his council members. "Fail this, and dishonor and exile won't be the worst of your punishment."

Drafe frowned. This wasn't exile? Dishonor? What could be worse than sharing his symbiotes with a servant? "I thank you for this opportunity, Great Council." Offering his back to the Q.C.C., he scanned the room. "One from each tribe would suffice." Picking faces he knew were Ot-less, he listed them. "Riermus aac Vaen, Zuphayr aac Gusin, Jeerlud aac Juunn, Borven aac Igar, Giniiri aac Nenn, and Awayar aac Caah."

Each male jogged to the dais, scowls marring their features. Drafe may have doomed them to a lonely death or exile, but *when* this quest succeeded, they too would receive the honor.

"So noted," Srim Udap announced, banging his fist on the desk. The Q.C.C. followed, stating the end of the council.

"You are a lucky male," Vaen growled. "Not that I thank you for dragging me along."

"Same." Juunn scanned the dissipating crowds. His green eyes flashed, and his brown hair rose and fell, revealing his displeasure.

"Is this punishment for making you wait for the temp-device?" Nenn rocked on his heels, a smile teasing his lips.

Drafe chuckled. "You were there, Nenn. I assumed you'd want to see justice done."

"As Osnir is my witness, Drafe, the killers will pay. To stand aside, let you go off on this mission alone, my children's children will forever curse my name." Nenn grasped Drafe's forearm.

"You believe we can find them?" Vaen arched a golden brow, bright against his brown skin.

"I do." Drafe raised his chin, showing his determination.

"Yet again, you escape justice." Ulvus nudged the others aside to glare at Drafe. "You should not have been accepted as a karu then awarded an Ot. Now, this." He growled. "Kreta curse you, Drafe."

"Ah, Meorri aac Ulvus Sava, it is good I see you wishing Osnir's blessings upon this journey." Kish Udap, striding through, parted the males gathered. "For you too shall be tasked to assist Drafe Arrak."

Ulvus's cheeks paled, but he offered a nod to Kish Udap as if pleased to be included.

Drafe gritted his teeth when Kish Udap sauntered across the hall and out the building. Lilac sunlight bathed the platform outside, bringing little warmth.

Vaen's golden eyes faded to brown when he glared at Ulvus. "Foq, I'd prefer to bring all the untrained karu than that idiot." His tone dipped, his words meant only for Drafe's ears.

"Same." Drafe chuckled. "A vasquva would be a more helpful addition."

Vaen snorted, then slapped Drafe on the shoulder. "Have Nenn see to your implant. I'll ensure the ship is prepped." He paused, tossing a glance over his shoulder. "May Osnir bless your symbiote transfer with the uz, Drafe. Let us pray the servant survives it."

Drafe stilled. Killing another Ivoyan would not be well received. They...*he* needed the uz. The male had to remember something about the events leading up to the explosion. Once Drafe left the hall, he summoned his armor, relishing the excited buzz from his symbiotes. Trailing Nenn along the wide, ostentatious passages of the Q.C.C., he ignored the lilac sunlight creeping through the stained windows. Gold inlaid the stone walls in intricate patterns—a blurring of the seven tribes' art and history, with images of a giant vasquva, the kind whispered across generations.

He strolled into a med-tech ward to where Nenn gestured to a chair. Drafe lowered himself, obedient for now. Tilting his head, he stared at the instructional signage on the floor-to-wall metal cabinets, not understanding the symbols and not caring to learn. Nenn sprayed something cold across Drafe's neck, numbing his skin.

The red-orange-haired male paused to grin at him. "I am excited. To see other stars and species. There is much I can learn." He leaned closer, dabbed Drafe's neck, and stepped back, holding a circular temp-device in his palm. "Whore."

Drafe growled and leaped to his feet.

Nenn threw out a hand. "My apologies, Drafe. That is the only word I know in Ivoy."

Drafe relaxed his stance. "Then the new nodule works."

"Good. I assume the uz is awaiting your presence in the transfer chamber?" Nenn arched a brow.

"I assume the same. Until we depart." Drafe strode out, cupping his neck where the temp-device had been inserted.

Now it was smooth skin if a little numb. His symbiotes remained silent, as if they resented what they had to do. This was for Meorri, Qaldreth, and Ivoy. His symbiotes had to comply. Taking the steps into the bowels of the building, he ignored the flickering venai stones casting ripples on the walls. The artwork was still present, carved into the stone but without the gold inlay. He burst into the small chamber and slid onto an S-shaped solid stone table alongside the uz sprawled on his own. The stiff male widened his eyes when he glanced at Drafe.

Compelled to speak, Drafe met his black gaze, hoping to convey a sense of peace. "Have no fear."

The uz nodded.

"I have explained the process to Vizen Aehort Uz, the opportunity this affords him." The Jakar's black markings on his temple stated his role in the priesthood. He pointed at the table with a graceful flick of a finger, the dark gray of his cloak draping his form. "Please extend your arm."

Between the two tables was a bridge upon which Drafe laid his arm, his gaze fixed on the ceiling studded with venai stones meant to replicate a Qaldreth sky. A glance confirmed the uz had draped his arm parallel to Drafe's.

A hum started in his core. The sensation was one he had forgotten. The Jakar raised his arms high and droned a low song. Light caught the blade a second before he brought it down, slicing across Drafe and the Uz's forearms. The pain was negligible. His blood pooled in the small basin at the center of the bridge. The Ivoy's blood flowed blue. Drafe was taught, if his symbiotes accepted the Ivoy, they would travel along the blue rivulet and enter through the narrow wound. Due to his clear blood not being as visible, he had to contend with watching the Ivoy's blood roll toward him.

When it entered him, he gritted his teeth, fighting the burn. He hadn't forgotten about that.

The pain thickened and intensified. His mind roared in agony. Curling his fingers into fists, he forced himself to relax. Fighting the intrusion would make it worse.

The uz whimpered but did not twitch a finger.

Unlike Vadril Ot who had screamed like a pregnant hudu.

The Jakar wrapped a strip of garak leather around their wrists, binding them together. He hummed words, lyrical, nonsensical, as the pain ebbed and flowed and time passed on silent feet.

"It is done." The Jakar's words snapped Drafe out of his daze.

He swung his legs over the side, the leather strap and thin wound gone.

The uz did the same while stroking his arm. "I feel...different yet the same."

"Our thoughts and memories will begin to align." Drafe forced a smile as exhaustion sapped the last of his strength. "Until one of us dies, Aehort Uz."

The orange male jerked, stared at Drafe, then nodded. "As you say, Drafe Arrak."

Chapter Eight

VIC SPIT OUT BLOOD, staring at it for a second when it pooled on the sand. Her body's alarms blared warnings she had to ignore—cracked or broken ribs and a gash in her shoulder plastering her red faux-leather vest to her skin. A dull ache replaced the piercing agony, merging with the burn in her ribs. Numbness spread outward, and she would soon lose the use of her arm.

Blowing escaped tendrils of her hair out of her face, she scanned the arena. High metallic walls kept the fans from the gladiators standing in the center of a sand-filled floor. Above the twelve rows were massive screens interspersed with banners flapping as if a breeze swept through. Like a barrel vault, a transparent dome capped the arena. Lighting and fireworks canons were mounted to the support beams with the expanse of space beyond.

The cacophonous roar of the crowds faded away as she slowed her breathing and listened to the steady thump of her heart. This was her final match. Win this, and she earned her freedom. It was Fiona's last match too. Losing meant waiting another year for the next deathmatch. Vic wasn't prepared to give Carne Corp and the Ring another hour of her life, let alone a year.

Fiona, known to the world as Fortuna, waited, a confident grin splitting her cheeks while she incited the crowd, arms raised high. Braided ebony hair swirled when she moved her head, in stark contrast to her green suit and dark skin. As Vic staggered to her feet, she analyzed her opponent's posture. She slanted a little to the side, nursing her cybernetic right arm and a spark flickered, proving Vic had caused a malfunction when she'd stomped on it with her spiked boot. She had to get that arm off her. If Fortuna activated it, mini heat-seeking missiles could be on Vic's ass in an instant. She was too exhausted to let that happen with her blood draining and her breathing restricted by her injuries. Bolting forward, she zig-zagged to confuse Fortuna's cybernetic eyes. They were state-of-the-art but slow to focus on erratic movements.

Vic vaulted into the air, swooping in with a tight fist. Fortuna dodged to the side at the last moment, taking the brunt of Vic's downward punch on the chin. It doubled her over, but Vic didn't hesitate, swinging a backward hammer fist, catching Fortuna on a cheekbone, spinning her.

Fighting for air, Vic threw out a side kick, catching Fortuna on her sternum. She flew backward, sprawling with a groan. A cloud of dust rose around her. Mics in their outfits caught each breath, groan, cry, or spoken word. It registered their heart rate and injuries, with a projected duration remaining of the match. The crowds lived for this, and Vic hated them for it. Not once did she look at them; no smile or encouragement, yet they adored her.

"Victorious," they chanted when she strode toward Fortuna, who'd managed to push herself onto her elbows.

"Don't bother bargaining, Fortuna. You know the stakes." Vic's words shushed the crowds for a moment before they roared, the arena thundering with their combined cries and stamping. She gripped the low collar of her shirt as if to adjust it, pushing her breasts up for added emphasis when, in fact, she covered the mic. Catcalls and whistles from the crowd showed their appreciation for Vic's minor display of her assets. She ignored them. "I'm tired and done. Wait one more damn year, Fiona."

She shook her head.

Vic drew in a shallow breath, spun on her heels, and round-house-kicked her opponent in the face. The force threw Fortuna to the side like a rag doll. She caught herself on her palms, spitting blood and groaning. Lights flickered on her right arm. She was powering it up. Vic leaped across and grabbed the woman by the wrist. Wrenching a cybernetic limb off took skill, but Vic would try it anyway. She might damage it enough to cost Fortuna the advantage. Placing her boot on the shoulder, Vic pinned her to the ground, holding her arm up. The crowd roared their bloodthirsty eagerness, having anticipated this. Fiona balked, kicked, wriggled but to no avail.

"Sorry, Fortuna," Vic said before twisting her body side-to-side and wrenching the limb off. It grated and screeched as metal disconnected, pseudo-skin tore, and neuro-wires pulled taut, then snapped.

Fortuna cried out, her skin turning ashen. She scrambled back, tossing up dust with her scraping boots. "Farg, Vic, why'd you do that?"

"Concede, Fortuna." Vic studied the cybernetic arm in her hand. Numbness had spread to her bicep so she tossed the cybernetic limb to her other hand. Despite the disconnection, Fortuna *had* armed the missiles. Raising her gaze, Vic jerked back at finding Fortuna had crawled farther away than expected and was powering up her left arm. Vic eyed the squares glowing through the pseudo-skin on the limb and sprinted toward Fortuna, holding the arm in front of her like a gun. She pressed the buttons, firing the missiles without thought.

Fortuna screamed, throwing out holographic shields to disarm or detonate the missiles before they reached her. One slipped through. Her holos shielded Vic from the blast. There where she had sprawled was a charred, limp Fortuna. The crowd fell silent, their gazes pinned to the stats board flickering Fortuna's life signs. The green blip of her heartbeat slowed. The crowd waited. All Vic cared about was that Fortuna lived, barely. The arena trembled, straining to contain the stamping of a hundred-thousand feet.

Vic approached her and placed the limb on Fortuna's chest. "You were a formidable opponent, Fiona," she said, uncaring that the crowd eavesdropped. She'd never see the woman again, and the months of recuperation that lay ahead had Vic pitying her.

A blue holo sphere appeared on the sand. Vic staggered onto it. A cylinder formed, cocooning her in bright light as it assessed the extent of her injuries and captured her for posterity. They would market merchandise and avatars from her deathmatch. Lifelike replicas of this moment would bring in a sizable profit. It was one of the reasons Carne offered freedom to their veteran gladiators.

"Ladies and gentlemen, Carne Corp and the Ring are proud to announce Victorious as the arena champion. This was the deca-match that determined Victoria Harper's freedom and end of service. We wish her well."

Black ribbons shot into the arena, tossed by the crowds as tribute and in farewell. Joy, relief, and fear of the unknown, of a life of her own, warred with her distrust of Carne. They'd hounded her this last year to allow them to alter her, amp her muscles, strengthen her bones, purify her blood, and add ammunition implants. She'd declined every offer, and according to International Arena law, they couldn't force her. One word from her, and they'd lose their license.

Ande bounced on the side, whooping and hollering, his bright smile shining through the chaos. Beside him wearing a ferocious glower was Devlin. His gaze wasn't on Vic but on her best friend. She stiffened, wishing she could capture the asshat's expression. A deep yearning twisted his lips. Ande refused to take Devlin as a real threat, dismissing the man as beneath his care. Next to Ande's great bulk, Devlin appeared smaller despite his broad shoulders and mop of tussled blond hair.

When a new unit of seven A.I.-sec-bots marched in on heavy feet, Vic expected the worst. Circling the arena floor, they leveled their glimmering black weapons on her. Despite their threatening presence, she marveled at the sleek design, how they matched the bots' metallic frames even as her heart rate spiked. The bell rang, ending the match. The bots raised their weapons, firing above her. A shower of red fireworks—to match her suit and hair—filled the dome, clouding the streaming ribbons.

Her shoulders slumped. It was over. Raising her good arm in the air to acknowledge her victory, she did something she never did. She grinned.

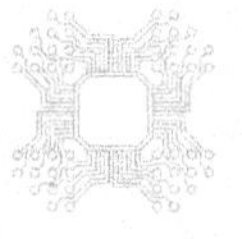

Two days later
The city of New Westlands

"Morning, sleepyhead." Ande sat on the edge of Vic's bed. "I'm off to Carne."

"Hate that," Vic mumbled and rolled over. She huffed her hair out of her face to focus on Ande.

As gorgeous as he was, they didn't have that kind of a relationship. Best friends and house mates summed it up.

"Try not to get into any trouble," he said, then chuckled when she glared at him.

He kissed her temple. She waved him off then listened to him heading out the door of the apartment they shared. Still belonging to Carne, he had to attend training sessions and medical appointments. She had nothing on her agenda. Despite all the time she'd had to think about her future, the possibilities had seemed surreal. Now, she was free, and she had no idea what to do with her time. Credits weren't a problem, but learning a hobby or working at a menial job held no appeal.

While sucking on a hydro-gel, she jumped into leggings, a sports bra, and sneakers and headed out the door. Beyond the apartment block was Endis Gardens with massive sol trees that filtered the dome's sunlight to the real fauna and flora beneath them. She crossed the busy intersection, paying attention to non-autodrive vehicles. Manually driven cars were more unpredictable. While warming up, she drew in long breaths. The air tasted sweeter. She smiled, settling her gaze on children playing nearby. Mothers chatted, their gazes vigilant.

Vic broke into a run, keeping to the dedicated paths. She relished the energy powering her limbs, more alive in every inch of her well-toned body. At the Ring, exercise was done indoors until the nineth year. Gladiators were considered trustworthy in their 'final' year, under the assumption they wouldn't jeopardize their chance at freedom. Ande had been living on Earth for the last two years. After he lost his deca-match.

She darted between the sol trees. The shifting shadows from their manmade branches reminded her of Millie's, of home. Despite Pa selling her to the Ring, Vic still had fond memories of her time alone, working the butterfly plates in the pre-dawn light.

The warmth of the sun burned her upturned cheeks, but she didn't mind when a breeze cooled her flushed face. She found a café and ordered a cup of Ganymede coffee. Time passed while she surveyed the folks going about their business. Ten years in a cocoon had meant a culture adjustment was needed. Fashion hadn't been a factor pre-Carne, so what people wore didn't surprise her. Technology had progressed, of that she didn't doubt. She'd love to learn how better to harvest sol, perhaps roll out those changes on Millie's. The farm was hers, of course. She'd planned to sell it and throw Pa out into the sand. Now, she was having doubts.

She needed something to do with her time. Paying for the coffee with the swipe of her wrist, she turned for home, planning on joining Ande for dinner, then perhaps a sparring session before bedtime.

While waiting to cross the intersection, an odd whirring caught her attention. As if in slow motion, an autodrive swerved off its programmed route, something unheard of. She blinked at it, then swept her gaze to what lay in its path. A little girl swung her legs where she sat on the bus stop's bench.

Ice drenched Vic, shooting shivers to the tips of her fingers.

Without hesitation, she bolted across the street, dodging vehicles, courier drones, and pedestrians. Had she been augmented, stopping the autodrive with a rocket might have worked. She managed to pick up the child, but twisting to leap aside only half-worked. The little girl tumbled free when the autodrive clipped Vic.

The pain was indescribable but also unreal. Her mind struggled to latch onto what was happening. Her left arm, torn from her body, flew to the side, landing with a squelch on the heated walkway. At the same time, something smacked her hip, spinning her. She hit the walkway and bounced, coming to a standstill on her right side. Dazed, she lay there, unable to understand what her body was telling her. Pain beyond anything she'd ever experienced. Fire, and in strange places, like her throat, as if she couldn't breathe. People crowded her. The traffic stopped. A man knelt before her, yelling in a garbled voice.

As if time had caught up, everything slammed into her—the agony, screams, and unbearable noise. She whimpered, and when the man touched her, she fainted.

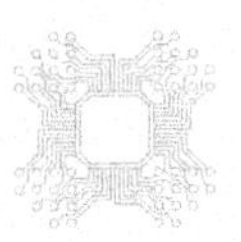

A DEAFENING ROAR AWOKE her. Nausea and dulled pain came next followed by the sensation that something was…odd.

She blinked unfocused eyes at the muted white walls and sea-green lights. Her mind blurred, phasing memories on the back of her eyelids like flicking through archaic prints of photographs. Similar to the one she used to keep in her locker at the Ring—a faded full-color glossy of her ma Erv had returned to Vic after her first victory.

"How do you feel?"

Recognizing that sibilant voice, she whipped her head and smothered a shudder born of revulsion. Why was a Carne representative in her room? How long had he been watching her? His gray suit was impeccable, his ebony hair coiffed to perfection against the backdrop of his olive skin and plastic-white smile. She closed her eyes, willing his presence to be a nightmare.

"What do you want?" She clipped the words, not wanting to waste her breath on the obsequious man.

"So ungrateful after what Carne did for you."

Heat burned along her nerve endings, churning nausea in the pit of her stomach. She didn't want to look, couldn't bring herself to. Lying still, she focused on her legs first. They were heavy, as if weighted by the blankets, but she could wriggle her toes. Lifting her arms, she studied them, testing their mobility by touching each finger to her thumbs.

"A new liver?" She grimaced at her hopeful tone, then shook her head. Her internal organs were healthy, not like Pa's, who'd no doubt drunk himself into a stupor with the tokens the Ring had given him. She cupped her breasts and sighed. Their familiar shape calmed the palpitation of her heart.

"Do you remember what happened, Ms. Harper?"

"Of course I do," she said, throwing him an irritated look, but his expression didn't change—self-assured and oozing patience.

Images flashed in her mind along with morphed sounds as if in slow motion. The out-of-control autodrive aiming for that little girl. Vic saving the child but watching her arm fly past her.

Losing a limb makes no sound. The senses merge until Vic *smelled* the fiery agony and *felt* the stench of burned skin. Her mind switched off reality, and the subconscious kicked into survival mode but didn't make the right connections.

She sat up. A cry escaped her lips. Her body was hers, no one else's, and for farg's sake, not Carne's. She shoved her left arm in front of her, studying the skin, the shape, the tension and release of her muscles. There was no pain now, but a burning wrenching lingered on the edges of her subconscious. *What did they do to me?* Visions of her dismembered arm snapped across her mind. The memory was incongruent with what she could see—her left arm intact and still attached to her body. *No, no, anything but augmentation.* Sweeping over her was that same helplessness from the day Carne imprisoned her. Her vow to never experience that again had driven her to work hard, to survive.

"What the fuck did you do? It was a no then and a no now." She flicked the blankets off, uncaring that she exposed her bare legs to his avid gaze.

"We did what we could to save you," he said, his voice calm with a hint of eagerness. He watched her with bated breath as if expecting a moment of revelation.

"*You* had the autodrive hacked. They *never* malfunction. That girl could've died." She shoved her finger in his face; his wince hit her with a spike of dopamine. "You did what you did for your stakeholders, and advertising the champion as having your cybernetics is good for business." She clambered off the bed but grabbed the railing to ward off dizziness. It was the last sign of weakness she would afford him. "Yet you violated international autodrive-protocol and clipped me. For what? A stronger, faster me when you no longer *own* me?"

She strode toward him, clenching and unfurling her left fist. Her mind reeled at what shouldn't have been there—her fingers. He scrambled back, a bright smile warring with the fear darkening his eyes. Snatching the chair he hid behind, she tossed it across the room, testing her new strength and the dexterity of her fingers. Then, with righteousness filling every pore and empowering her decisions and actions, she gripped his jaw to lift him off the floor.

That infernal grin still splayed across his face so she punched him, pain burning across her right knuckles. That was good; it meant they hadn't converted all her limbs while they were at it. His blood dribbled from his deformed nose, splashing over her splayed hand. Outside the hospital, the setting sun cast shadows on the bustling city of New Westlands far below. No one could survive a fall from this height. He was no exception. Spinning, she dragged him through the window, shattering it. She dangled him over the edge. A jagged piece of glass pierced her new limb, but she didn't feel it. He squealed and grasped her forearm, smearing her blood across the torn synthetic skin and the mechanics beneath.

"I was the Ring's champion, but that wasn't enough for you. I'd *earned* my freedom. What gave you the right to do this?" She shook him, his legs flying out like a puppet's. He screamed, his smile, for once, absent.

"The Ring is down as next of kin," he said. With the fear contorting his face and her grip crushing his larynx, she could forgive him for strangling his words.

Cool wind whipped her hair around her. The fading sunlight dropped the temperatures and brought relief to the baked soil for an hour before chilling it. The urge to return home twanged through her, and as her room filled with the hospital's security guards, she studied the representative, the last obstacle to her freedom. "I no longer belong to Carne. Repeat it."

He whimpered so she jolted him again, shaking her head at the guards not to come closer. Their mouths moved in slow motion, demanding she pull him inside. She laughed since she had the upper hand. They couldn't take her down without losing him.

"Say it," she roared.

"You are free of the Ring and any obligations to Carne. All ownership of Victoria Harper is hereby relinquished," he said, his eyes pleading with her not to kill him.

"Thank you," she said and released him.

CHAPTER NINE

ANDE SUCKED HYDRO-GEL INTO his mouth, his gaze fixed on the holo as his fingers controlled his avatar's movements. Some sort of racing car whizzed around a corner, killing a pedestrian. "Where the fuck have you been, Vic?"

"How long have I been gone?" She disappeared into her room, throwing her carry-all onto the bed. The memory foam dented to accommodate it.

"Six days, but the Ring said they were videoing you or some such bullshit," he said, leaning against the doorframe, stuttering the door as it attempted to close. "You look good though, no bruising, no hindered movements. I expected worse after Fortuna's defeat. Gotta love Carne's medical teams." His black curls flopped over his umber brow, snagging her gaze which traveled over his bulging arms straining his F-suit.

"Did you just come from sparring?" Vic flicked her fingers at his fight-suit made of a steel-thread-polymer mesh. It fit him like a glove, curling over his tight ass like a lover's caress. She sighed, cursing the fates that made her best friend gay.

"The question is, where did you come from? Is that a hygiene wrap?"

"Carne thought I needed improvements," she said, tossing in her oldest clothing. Where she was heading, evening and sparring garments wouldn't be of use.

"Shit." Ande's curls bounced when he jerked forward to grab her shoulders. "What did they do?"

He ran his fingers over her bare skin, summoning shivers. She wasn't used to caresses of any sort. Yanked, punched, shoved, or flipped was the extent of her physical contact. Able to feel his touch meant her nervous system had accepted the cybernetics. It took a few days, so they said. It explained why she'd yanked out the shard of glass without writhing in agony. Nanos had swarmed the wound, repairing the severed mechanics and lacerated pseudo-skin.

"They caused an accident that tore off my left arm and leg." She separated the magnets and shucked off her hygiene wrap, letting it pool on the floor. Uncaring that she stood there in the nude, she twisted her left arm, showing Ande all the angles.

He whistled, tracing a thin scar that ran over her shoulder, around her breast, and across her ribs. "That's a beaut, sweetheart." A similar scar curved over her hip, denting her ass cheek. She watched him in the mirror trace the line with a steady fingertip. "They did this in days? Holy shit, Vic, they must have thrown their best at you."

"It's the final straw, Ande. I said no to cybernetic enhancements. I was proud of my all-natural ability to defeat my opponents." She dipped, scooped up the medical wrap, and tossed it on the bed. "I made the representative relinquish ownership, but despite the witnesses, I doubt Carne will consider this legally valid."

"Farg no. You are...were their biggest draw." Ande flopped onto the bed. "They care nothing for human lives, Vic. Those witnesses will be dead by tomorrow."

She stilled, sucked in a sharp breath, then slumped. "I know."

He was right. Carne wouldn't see this as done. They'd rise to the challenge, hunt her down by all means necessary. She had to leave...Earth. Kicking Pa off the farm and running it herself was no longer an option. A lump formed in her throat, matching the heavy weight squeezing her heart in a vice.

With a yank and tug, she wore her old worker breeches, the oil stains having taken up residence. It was a little tight over her backside, but she'd been a decade younger when she'd last worn them. Next were her trusty old boots. Thankfully, Ande hadn't incinerated them when she'd swapped them for new ones so many years ago. She pulled on a plain white tank, which shimmered as it shrank to conform to her body. Sex sells, and accentuating her curves meant she was a whore-extraordinaire, selling more Ring tickets. It wasn't unusual for the P.R. department to fake relationships between fellow fighters. Too many times she had to drape herself across a gladiator's body, but the contact was fleeting and brought no comfort to her lonely soul.

"Now what? If you skip out before the ceremony, you're under the Ring's thumb anyway?"

"Farg them, not when their 'word' means nothing." She zipped shut the heat-res suit, the final layer protective against the sun's rays. With flicks of her fingers, she wrapped the aged strips around her wrists and forearms to cover the tears in the suit. Farg, she should have invested in a new suit, rather than deal with this. "I'm heading home, selling the farm, and taking to the stars. You in, or are you going to waste more time on them? No offense, babe, but winning your next deca-match isn't guaranteed."

She tried not to hold her breath, to place too much importance on Ande coming with her. He stood to lose so much more with time left in his contract. After losing his deca-match, he had two more years to become a champion before they renewed his contract for another decade. Yet... Ignoring the fluttering in her chest, she nibbled on her bottom lip. She *needed* him to share this adventure with her. Doing this alone was too daunting to contemplate.

"What's the destination?" He folded his arms across his sculpted chest. Scars marred his forearms, some from lucky opponents, some from cybernetics. He had to accept the enhancements after his first near-death match.

"I'll take anything off-world." With a biometric thumbprint, she activated the magnetic fastenings sealing the bag. She faced the mirror, her fingers flying over the controls as it scanned her face and hair, removing the artificial coloring. Her auburn hair faded to fawn, and her eyes once more their lackluster mud-brown. Around them, crow's feet had formed. She forced a smile, staring at the single dimple on her left cheek as if it was new. She didn't recognize her older self.

"Fine, want to wait for me, or should I meet you at Lunar Base?"

Tears stung her eyes, but she didn't shed them, having not cried since her father betrayed her. She was so grateful to Ande that she wasn't facing this path on her own. Not making eye contact in the mirror, she kept her head down, just needing a moment to gain control of her silly emotions.

"I'll send you a location marker when I get there," she said, squeezing his arm before striding out of her apartment, not looking back.

Having moved up the rungs, feeling any attachment to materialistic things meant giving her trainers leverage. Even attachments to fellow fighters cost her. Ande was big and downright menacing. Their friendship had stood against manipulations and rumors.

She latched her bag to her sol-cycle and swung her leg over the seat as the Ring's security pulled in front of the building. From the shadows, she watched them scurry through the glass doors as their autodrives' hovered.

Not sparing Ande a thought when he could handle a small security band, she tapped her helmet on and steered her sol-cycle toward the old harbor. A tunnel separated the safe and unsafe zones. She climbed out, gasping when the sun hit her. The heat was intense, but no worse than she remembered. She just wasn't used to it anymore. Still, she relished the burn, as if it greeted her after her long absence.

Outside the dome's protection, the sun beat down, killing anyone foolish enough not to wear protection. Abandoned and rusted tankers cast sharp shadows, cooling the sand. The homeless occupied the cruise liner leaning to the side and many cabins from yachts, fishing boats, or tugboats protruded from the shifting sands. She drove down a dune and skimmed the dry-bed's surface in the direction of Deadweed. No roads scarred the seabed since the winds shifted them daily, obscuring any definitive paths.

She opened the throttle. It had been a decade since she last saw her home. Ten long years since the day Erv had collected her. She had a score to settle with the folks of Deadweed, with Jolson, with Pa. If she saw them, she would consider her next venture blessed. She would make fargen sure that both men would see her fist coming.

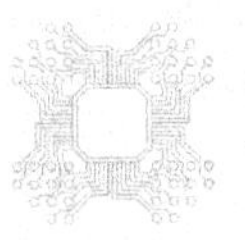

Year: 2219

Deadweed

VIC STEPPED INSIDE LEVIATHAN, and the stench of old sweed hit her. It tweaked her nose even as nostalgia snatched her breath. The customers turned as one, watching her stride to the bar behind which stood Cleg, older but none the smarter.

"Vic?" He arched a bushy eyebrow, sneaking glances between her and the holo announcing her death. *So, that's how they want to play it?* She snorted. The images showed her spinning full circle amid ticker tape stats and past kills. She had to admit that the last decade had treated her well. The holo of her was from the deathmatch.

"You haven't seen me, Cleg." Vic faced the room. "None of you have. I'm popping in to visit Ren, then I'm gone."

"What do you want with my pa?" Junior rose, his lank body as shriveled as she remembered.

She smiled, delighted for something to have gone her way. Nudging her head toward the door, she asked him in a genteel manner to meet her outside. He hesitated, and she didn't blame him. Anyone with a little intelligence would expect death at her skilled hands, yet he scurried out the door just as Jolson burst in. The sight of him ripped a fresh hole through her. Sharp pain pierced and throbbed, cinching her chest with renewed anger.

"Cursed hell, Vic. When they said you'd arrived, I couldn't believe it." He strode forward as if to hug her, but she dodged his sweeping arms and kneed him in the groin. With an animalistic howl, he crumpled to the floor.

"I'm in a good mood on account of Junior, so I won't maim you for betraying me, Trev. For a man who claimed to care for me as his future whore, you stood by and let the Ring take me." In a dramatic show of power, she curled and unfurled her left hand then gripped Trev by the jaw, lifting his coiled body, his feet dangling inches off the floor. "I'm enhanced as of yesterday. If I find out anyone betrayed me again to Carne or the Ring, I'll return with death in mind."

She dropped Trev and strode around him, heading for the shielded heat outside and a waiting Junior. He leaned against his battered skid-car, as if the filtered sunlight didn't bake the sweat onto his forehead. She made a beeline for him, ignoring the gathering audience.

"What's this about?" Junior asked, his shuffling feet casting up miniature dust clouds in his nervousness.

"I want to sell Millie's to your pa. Ma left the deed to me when she died. I don't think she trusted..." Vic grimaced, unable to call her father Pa or by his name. Just trying pooled bile at the back of her throat. "How much are you willing to offer?"

"It's worth fifty," he said.

"It's worth a hundred, but I'll sell it to you for ten."

"What, why?" He threw out his hands as if to decline a too-good-to-be-true, once-in-a-lifetime deal, as if she swindled him.

"You were honest enough to start at a decent amount, expecting to barter upward. I want the blood price my...the Ring gave my..." She leveled a glower on Junior. "Take it or leave it."

"I'll take it, shit, hell yeah." He fist-pumped the air like a juvenile.

While waiting for Junior to activate his band, she did the same, holding it out for him to swipe his arm across hers and make the payment. A buzz up her arm confirmed receipt. She scanned hers over his, transferring the deed. "Good. I have one more favor." She cast a longing glance at her sol-cycle. "She's yours if you give me a ride to Armstrong Station and deny ever taking me there."

"You're going off-world?"

She arched an irritated brow. Junior paled and hurried to clip her...*his* sol-cycle to the back of the skid-car. She jumped into the car and stowed her carry-all at her feet while he took the driving seat.

"Can you handle city traffic?"

He frowned but powered up, shooting across the sand at a steady clip. His destination wasn't to the city but the highest point in the dunes. It had a different name many years ago, but they called it Stubborn Rock now. He hid the sol-cycle in its shadow and turned them for Armstrong Station. The sky-tower rose as a white beacon on the horizon.

"At the bottom of the deed is my lawyer's details. He'll handle any issues my p..." She grimaced. "He's expecting your call."

Junior nodded and nibbled on his bottom lip as if he wanted to say something but wasn't confident enough. He drew in a deep breath and pushed out the words. "Leave Earth, just like that?" He sliced a glance at her, his brown eyes boring into hers. "They'll juice you with nano-creatures and...what if you're tossed out of the ship for insubordination, Vic?"

"Then I die," she said, with a shrug. It wasn't as if she hadn't faced life-and-death situations in the arena.

Junior hitched a thumb behind him, gesturing to Deadweed. "Why do they think you're dead?"

"Makes it easier for them to hunt me down. I'm reported as alive? That's big news, cheap publicity. If they find and kill me, then no one's the wiser."

His Adam's Apple bobbed. "You ain't scared?"

"I was when they bought me." She looked away, preferring to feast her eyes on the last glimpses of pale dunes and miles upon miles of butterfly panels blurred by the skid-car's shield. The scenery changed to shoreline, housing structures, and solarized buildings as Junior navigated the manual-drive lane with some skill. He spoke no more, which she appreciated. She suspected she had a tracker inside her, so that would be the first stop. Just in case the Ring or Carne had placed her face and sol-cycle on the sec-scans, she'd bribed Junior for a ride. She didn't need them sending bounty hunters into outer space.

He pulled up at the drop-off, and she hopped out before he'd drawn the skid-car to a stop. She grabbed her carry-all and waved him off, trailing her gaze up the white structure of the space station. Too busy for her liking, with travelers hindering escape routes and sec-guards on high-vigilance, she kept her face down and hurried toward the docking bay elevators. Returning her appearance to the natural state might not be enough. She glanced at her soiled heat-res suit. It wasn't her usual red faux-leathers but would that matter if these hugged her just as well? She grimaced and walked into the first boutique on her path.

The A.I.-bot rushed to greet her, and Vic barked out requirements. "Feminine, immediate with no time for fittings, and easy movement."

"Right this way." The A.I.'s smile was stiff, designed to be polite.

Her graceful sashaying made Vic feel like a galumphing Ande. She gestured to a rack of dresses Victorious would never be caught dead wearing. Perfect. When she chose one with pink and peach sashes, the A.I.-bot pointed to the changing booth. Vic grunted and disappeared into it, dropping her carry-all before holding up the dress. How was she supposed to put it on?

She hung it on the hook provided and stripped off her suit and tank. Demagnetizing her breeches, she peeled them off and stood there in her boots, scowling. "Assistance required," she said, and the door opened.

She handed the dress to the bot, and within minutes it was on. The A.I.'s hands blurred as she pulled it on over Vic's head and activated the fastener on her left shoulder. The bot set the booth walls to reflective. Vic faced her image. A band circled her hips from which strips of various lengths fell over her backside to entangle between her thighs. Sashes crisscrossed to cover her breasts and, despite her boots clinging to her calves, she looked like a sensual woman. Faint scars marred her exposed skin, each one a near-death experience she didn't want to remember or the new augmentations.

"I'll take it." She glided her band over the bot's wrist.

"Release at your shoulder to remove the garment," the bot said.

After tossing the heat-res suit and stuffing her old clothing into the carry-all, she slipped it onto her shoulder. She stepped into the crowds, conscious of her bare legs, and did her hips sway with more allure? Having wanted to blend in, the sashes between her thighs irritated even as the garment drew attention from most men. Worse, it drew the focus of the sec-guards. She tested out a bright smile and a playful finger wave. One responded with a wink. It boosted her confidence, and she imitated the A.I.-bot's sashay with renewed determination.

With a scan across the pay-panel, she entered the elevator carrying her to the launch bay. From there, the shuttle would blast off, destination Lunar Base orbiting the moon.

An A.I.-bot greeted her and gestured to her to choose a tube. "Welcome to Lunar Base shuttle voyage Echo 2 Lima 15009. Estimated time to departure is two hours. Docking with the base in eleven hours. Please select a tube and the duration of rest required."

Vic placed her carry-all in the farthest one from the door before grabbing the handle and sliding herself onto the bed feet first. Straps shot across her, securing her to the tube. Reinforced glass wrapped around her, allowing for a farewell view of Earth as the shuttle traveled, as well as an escape pod should she need it. Not that she'd be awake for the journey. Selecting a sedative, she activated it and the sol-cleanser. She'd awake refreshed and waste-free. Ignoring the smile splitting her cheeks, she stared at the padded ceiling of the tube, waiting for the sedative to take effect. It wouldn't be long...

CHAPTER TEN

DRAFE GRUNTED AS HE paced the bridge, waiting for his males to receive clearance. "Is this wise, Aehort?" He spun on the uz.

Despite his servant status, Aehort was more intelligent than all the Qaldreths on this ship combined. Because of him, they'd navigated many galaxies to locate this tiny planet, the home to the strange corpse at the Senate.

"It is. My instincts, as untested as they are, led us here." The orange male did not look away from the approaching space station orbiting the planet's moon.

Drafe grunted again and resumed his pacing. Crossing the galaxies, they'd stopped at several ports, asked one or two questions, and left with the destination revised. Aehort's success had removed the uz stigma. The Qaldreth warriors onboard now trusted that this Ivoy would lead them true.

As an unknown species to these Earthians, he had hoped to step onto the moon's station without fanfare. That was not to be the case. They'd have to play the ambassadorial role as decided by the Qaldreth Command Council. Since Drafe had observed Vadril Ot's behavior, they believed he was more than capable of mimicking him. Drafe doubted it. He didn't have the patience for diplomacy. It wasn't a natural skill for a Qaldreth warrior.

"I shall play the Q.C.C.'s role, Drafe. You be what you are." Aehort's ability to sense his inner turmoil was due to the sharing of his symbiotes.

Their shuttle descended to the docking bay, suction panels extending to hold the ship in place.

A hiss followed when the cabin pressurized, and the door slid open. Before them stood a delicate Earthian female, no taller than his shoulder. Her black hair cascaded down her back, similar to some Qaldreth females, except it hung from her head and wasn't growing along her spine. Behind her stood two males, gripping their useless weapons as if Drafe intended to attack. He smothered a chuckle. If the Q.C.C. decided to decimate, these weak Earthians would not foresee it nor survive it.

"Greetings, and welcome to Earth's Lunar Base. I am Cynthia de Beer, a human woman from Earth. Please forgive my guards; it's protocol to come prepared for aggression."

She held out a gloved hand.

Drafe stared at it jutting out in front of her without purpose.

Beer laughed and shifted it to grab his, giving it many shakes. She dropped his hand to step back. "This is how we greet each other."

"Thank you for sharing this with us. I am Vizen Aehort Uz, Cynthia de Beer," Aehort said, his Earthian language stilted. He offered his long-fingered hand.

She accepted it with a bright smile. "Please, call me by my first name, Cynthia."

Their first names were at the beginning of their full names? He wasn't to call her Beer? That mannerism felt wrong and offensive. He curled his upper lip.

"Please address me as Aehort Uz. I will accompany you for diplomacy. My Qaldreth warrior would like an escort to your most populated areas. We wish to learn about your species and observing is best."

Drafe twitched, surprised at this detour in their plans. Aehort gestured to Zuphayr aac Caah behind him. He tensed with growing fury as Caah trailed Aehort and Cynthia. A guard hovered, waiting for Drafe to acknowledge him. He shoved out his arm, feeling stupid doing so. The guard flipped his visor back and grinned, accepting his hand for a shake. It was an odd custom but so were some of the Qaldreth's.

"The name's Tyler," he said.

Wincing, Drafe shortened his name and applied human protocol. "Drafe."

"I'll take you to Moonstar. It's the best bar here." Tyler hesitated, running his gaze over Drafe's body. "Is there anything you can't consume?"

"I do not know," he said. "I can scan it with a bio-dev to see if it is safe."

Tyler led him down the tunnel and into an open space. High above arched the building's ceiling with Earthians in various shapes and colors crowding the causeways. Many paused to study their passing.

Tyler tossed a smile at him. "They can't decide if you're alien or from Africa," he said. "We have such dark skin tones too."

Earthian females slathered his body with their avarice gazes, as if mating for pleasure was the norm. Their attraction to him made him uncomfortable. On Qaldreth, the warrior approached a female and only when the scent of her deepened, indicating she was fertile. Drafe wasn't certain he liked the roles reversed.

Tyler led him into a crowded room. The thick air hit him first, various scents—some biological, others artificial—assaulted his nose. He grimaced, fighting the urge to cover his face.

"Sit here. The air is cleanest under the vents." Tyler must have noticed Drafe's discomfort.

Folding his long legs to do so, he sat on the soft bench. He leaned back to study the comings and goings of the Earthian species. Random conversations reached his sensitive hearing. A few males attempted to attract a female's interest. One male owed another tokens—their form of currency. Images and lettering flickered in holographics above the bar, suggesting moments of normalcy and hinting at their home planet.

Tyler held out a container. Drafe accepted, sniffing it. Water; chemically cleaned but safe. He thanked him and settled in for the long pointless watch, ensuring his eyes recorded everything. Males propositioned females, vice versa, or same gender, but intimacy was high on the agenda.

"You like this place?" he asked Tyler.

"It's better than most," he said, his blue gaze tailing a female striding into the bar.

Drafe admired the sway of her hips and the appealing softness of her light hair. Her garment enticed, fluttering around her pale limbs and curves. Her gaze surveyed the room as if she analyzed for threats. A slight relaxation of her shoulders meant she hadn't found anything of concern. She slipped onto a seat at the bar, exposing muscled, scarred legs. The urge to run an unarmored finger along her skin gripped him, and he scowled at the strangeness of the attraction.

"Who is she?" he asked Tyler.

"Never seen her, although I'm not sure I want to. There's something lethal about her."

"Lethal?" Drafe knew what Tyler meant but wanted him to share his impressions.

"She scans the room, lingering on those I know to be dangerous. Her posture is coiled, as if she could kill without hesitation." Tyler sipped his dark beverage, licking his lips before continuing. "That's premium water she's drinking, so tokens aren't an issue. She's waiting for someone she cares about, glancing around every few minutes."

Drafe ran his gaze along her form. There was an eagerness every time she looked at the door. Her body stiffened, and the smile spreading her plump lips shot a dart of need to his groin. She leaped off the seat, throwing her arms around an Earthian male. He was huge in comparison to the other males in the room, his skin almost as dark as Drafe's. She flashed a bright smile and gestured to him to join her. Ordering him a beverage said she knew his preference.

"He has arrived." Tyler slurped his water. "They're not lovers, though."

Drafe sliced a glance at his escort. Not lovers? Tension he hadn't acknowledged eased from between his shoulders. Urging his symbiotes to improve his hearing, he eavesdropped on her conversation.

"What do you mean you're not coming with?" Anger stiffened her spine as her cheeks flushed pink. He liked the color on her. "Why travel to get here then? Why not just send me a message?"

"I want to at least say goodbye, brat," the Earthian male said, grumbling something under his breath that was too low for Drafe to decipher. "I needed to meet with your future boss."

"My what?" she asked before taking a long draw of her water.

"I called in a favor. You start within the hour." He pressed his wrist to hers, but she didn't look down. "That's the details. I'll see you in two years when my service is up."

Her shoulders slumped—her understanding of his situation clear. "Fine, Ande. In two years, we meet here. No excuses."

"Glad you see it my way, Vic. Now try and find a young buck to breach you. No need to go into space still a prude."

"A prude." She hit him on the arm. Drafe relaxed further. They had a sibling relationship. She flicked a dismissive hand at the bar. "Like I could find someone here to share sex with me."

"I'm going to try," her Ande said, surveying the room.

She chuckled, the sound husky and alluring. "Only you would travel here to have sex with a random stranger."

"True. If you don't find anyone, Dieter the mechanic will do."

Her answering grunt brought an unexpected smile to Drafe. She reacted like he would. If he understood the interaction correctly, she wanted to share sex with someone. If they were compatible, he would oblige her.

"Tyler." Drafe removed his bio-dev from its holster strapped to his thigh and ran the device over the Earthian male.

He stiffened, his hand hovering above his antique weapon. "What are you doing?"

"Scanning to see if our species are compatible," Drafe said, though why he answered the male, he didn't know. Eagerness to spread the female's thighs had him ignoring his usual self-inflicted boundaries.

"And?"

Drafe blessed the male with a bold grin while he re-strapped the bio-dev. "Good." He shifted forward on the seat to rise, wanting to approach the female now. Her male friend had said she had one hour. Drafe grunted, wondering if it was too short a time to satiate his needs.

Ande pressed his cheek to hers and left for a group of males at the back of the room. There were such males in Qaldreth who preferred each other's company. Drafe didn't focus on that; instead, he watched her.

She spun the seat and studied the room with bold interest. Nervousness teased a corner of her mouth, revealing how uncomfortable she was. Her gaze flicked over him but returned, settling on him with admiration and an arched brow. She assessed his physique. Bolts of fire traversed his nerves, as if she caressed him where her gaze lingered.

He rose to his full height and strode toward her. She too slid off her seat, meeting him halfway across the room. When they were a hand's width apart—her height reaching just above his shoulder, he paused. Her scent hit him, enflaming his senses, and shaking his control. Ozone and sunbaked rock infused the sweetness of her femininity. Closing his eyes to inhale again, he groaned. He unarmored his fingers and gripped her arms, running his hands up and marveling at the softness of her skin. Her tiny scars beneath his touch whispered of her skills as a warrior who'd survived many battles.

"My name's Drafe." He forced the words through clenched teeth and ignored the gruffness of his voice. His arousal urged, burned, and throbbed, eager to explore this Earthian female.

"Vic," she said, her voice lyrical and breathless.

"I am not Earthian, does this bother you?" He shifted closer to bury his face in her hair. She clasped his biceps, arching into his body. He liked that, how she fit against him.

"If we're not genetically compatible, you're wasting my time," she said.

He stilled at her bold response, then chuckled, liking her bluntness. "We are well-suited."

"Good." She crowded him and latched her lips onto his. He jerked away, stunned. Confusion feathered across her features. His senses caught alight, reminding him of the feel of her lips on his, the nectar of her taste lingering there, tantalizing him.

"What was that?" He had envisioned removing her garments, spinning her, and plunging into her sweet depths wherever they were. Being unprepared for this didn't bother him. He'd assumed she'd be his teacher like he would guide her in what pleases him. Not this thing with her lips. Though, it had been enjoyable.

"A kiss," she said and did it again.

This time, he held himself firm, granting her the right to taste him, to share his breath and soul. He looped his arms around her and crushed her against him, lifting her off the ground. Something leaped in his chest, pounding his heart, and stealing his ability to breathe. His symbiotes reacted to her with uncharacteristic eagerness.

She buried her fingers in his mane, and his senses exploded, merging into a ball of intense need. Tightening her arms shot fiery darts to his arousal, dragging a growl from him. She was his, and he would have her many times to appease this craving.

"Ambassador Vizen Aehort Uz has summoned you to the ship," Tyler said, holding out his hands to show he meant no harm.

Drafe groaned and released the female with reluctance while trailing his fingers along her curves. She blinked at him, lust clouding the soft brown of her eyes. Understanding dawned, and she stepped back to cup his cheek, her thumb brushing his now-sensitive lips.

"It was a pleasure, Drafe," she said and left the room, her strides confident. Not once did she glance back.

"I waited as long as I dared," Tyler said, throwing Drafe an apologetic look.

He ignored the Earthian male and dropped into the seat, leaning back to stare at nothing but the flickering images of the holographics.

"Give me a moment," he said, his voice still hoarse. A familiar face crossed his vision, and he focused on the holo. "Is that her?" he asked Tyler. The flickering image of a female had hair of fire and red eyes, but the face was the same. Those were the lips he'd tasted. "What does the lettering say?"

"Shit." Tyler gaped, switching his gaze between the holo and Drafe. "It says she was an arena champion who died."

"Arena? You endanger your females?" Fury gripped him, and he bounded out of the seat to grab the Earthian male's shoulders.

"They battle women...females. We never pit them against males."

"Her name?" Drafe released the male and raised his gaze to study her face. Hence the scars. Each was a badge of honor, proving her ability to survive.

"Victoria Harper," Tyler said, shuffling out of reach.

Drafe grunted. The poor male didn't know how fast or lethal a Qaldreth could be. "Return me to my ship," he said, striding from the room. "Send me the data you have on her."

"Why?" Tyler's fear irritated Drafe, burning his nostrils with its acrid stench.

He sliced Tyler a warning glance. "I intend to finish what she started."

Chapter Eleven

Year: 2219

Lunar Base

VIC COULDN'T WALK STRAIGHT, as if her knees had liquified, and her lips tingled in unison with her taut nipples. Drafe. His voice had rumbled, growled, reminiscent of a grizzly's chuff. It had brushed over her skin, raising the hairs all over her body.

The moment her gaze settled on him, her heart rate spiked. His intense focus snagged hers, and when he rose, the physique of a warrior in molded metallic scales had snatched her breath. His presence dominated, demanding attention and admiration. His graceful yet efficient movements aroused her instincts, flooding adrenaline through her body—warning of a predator. Playing with him meant teasing the tiger, and the appeal of it delighted her.

Drafe. He had darker-than-midnight skin, yellow-brown eyes, and his cologne smelled of fire and something addictive. His lips were dry, his taste salty, making her mouth water. She'd kissed a stranger. Every muscle and nerve thrummed with pulsing energy as if she was empowered, invincible, and yet, he'd left her aching for more. No wonder Ande did this often.

Farg, Ande. She'd forgotten about her friend. Stopping to collect her carry-all from the locker, she scanned the details he'd sent her. Position: security officer. Ship: the *Mula Pesada* docked in bay 39E. The contact: Themba Masuku.

Darting through the crowds, she headed for the lower level '39.' The display vids listed the ships and their docks above the elevators, making it easy to find. In the steel tin, the stench of sweat assaulted her, but she held firm, watching the red numbers count down the levels. Each stop swapped the travelers for workers and crowded her deeper into the corner.

When the elevator stopped on her level, she squeezed past a few 'affectionate' men, repaying their fondles with sharp jabs of an elbow and one knee to the groin before stepping onto the causeway. She grimaced, twitching her nose against the myriad of smells, and ignored the cursing coming from the elevator behind her.

Weaving through the workers to reach the balustrade, she raised her gaze to the rows upon rows of ships going left, right, then up, and down. Their sizes and abilities varied from the massive hauler dominating the bays, to the loaders, cruisers, couriers, and military shuttles.

Since the *Mula Pesada* wasn't easy to miss, she headed left down the causeway, dodging scurrying workers while admiring the shapes and colors of the ships. The military was solid black, with mounted cannons stating their purpose more than the shimmering letters marking their designation.

Against this, lay the hauler. There was no rhyme or reason to its design—an elongated rectangle, with pieces jutting off as if they'd used metal scraps to fuse holes. The front end of the ship had a little curve to it, but the back end was open-aired and box-like, a warehouse for ice.

She kept away from the railing, not wanting an eager worker to knock her over with his pallet rig. It meant meandering around the food stalls and spice dealers, crossing alleys, and dodging filth swept into the corners.

"I swear, I don't have it. I promise." A man's sobbing plea pierced the din of blurred announcements, hawkers selling their wares, and the greeting cries between workers.

She paused mid-stride and peered into the long alleyway. A blast of air stinking of rotting waste blew her hair back when she faced the group of men. One pressed a skinny runt to the soot-and-poster-lined steel walls.

"You don't? Well, that's a shame." The tallest man chuckled, a mane of brown hair haloing his head. He folded his bulging arms across his massive chest, his forearm catching his stitched name tag—Nikko. He'd spread his legs in a stance that was far from casual.

"I love breaking knees, Webb," Nikko continued, a smirk twitching the scar above his eye.

With his skin drenched in sweat and moisture pooled on his lip, the weaselly man squirmed before the snap of his finger drew a scream.

Her lips curled in distaste at the unmatched fight with Webb the weakest. A quick scan of the other men crowding the alley had her arching a brow. A woman stood to the side, her hands clasped behind her, legs spread wide in a military stance. One side of her hair was shorn, revealing a beautiful skull. Her name in worn white lettering on her dark blue overalls declared her as Leah. Another stocky man hung back, leaning against the wall with his leg bent, his booted foot planted firmly. He toyed with a steel toothpick, rolling it across his bottom lip. The lettering on his uniform was illegible.

A slim teenage boy tapped on his smart band, stilled and met Nikko's gaze. An almost imperceptible shake of the head doomed the weasel named Webb.

Vic's shoulders slumped when her soft heart insisted she intrude. She held still, not wanting to get involved, but her conscience wouldn't shut up. Air rushed along the back of her neck, raising the hairs and tightening every muscle in her body.

"Is this necessary?" She kept her steps light, having learned not to reveal her approach within the first year at Carne.

As one, they stared at her strolling along the alleyway toward them. Leah's posture stiffened. Toothpick-man pushed off the wall, his hand resting on his hip above his blaster. Nikko unfolded his arms. Fury darkened his features as he shoved the boy behind him. Noble of him but unwarranted.

She unhooked her carry-all, hung it on a jutting drain pipe, and met Webb's wide eyes.

"Sell your wares somewhere else," Nikko grunted and ran a dismissive appraisal over her.

"It's my off day." Vic grinned, flicking her skirts aside to flash a thigh. She rolled her shoulders while his crew gathered in front of Nikko and his victim. "I love a fight as much as the next whore, but I suggest you rethink this. I'll let you off with a minimum amount of pain if you free the weasel."

"Farg off, and mind your own business." Nikko shook Webb once then tossed him aside.

"Why do they never listen?" She tutted, then burst forward, landing her heel into toothpick-man's chest and sending him flying. He bounced off the wall, denting it. Sprawled on the floor, he tried to rise but collapsed.

Nikko threw a punch.

She dodged and counter swung with an uppercut while smirking at him. Her enjoyment must have irritated Leah since her face mottled. She entered the fray, swinging a punch.

This one Vic caught with her hand. The impact of Leah's fist striking Vic's palm radiated along her cybernetic arm. Closing her fingers, she crushed Leah's hand. The woman paled and screamed, then pleaded with Vic to release her.

"Stop." One word in Nikko's baritone made Vic pause.

She faced him, prepared to take him down. On par with Ande's bulk, she wasn't intimidated, and thanks to Ande, had practiced fighting such a sizable man.

To his credit, he didn't so much as twitch. With a hand clamped on Webb's shoulder, Nikko met her gaze. From behind him peered the boy, his eyes wide and flickering, as if he filmed her.

Farg. She hadn't thought of that.

"You best delete that, boy." She waited, squeezing Leah's crushed hand to draw a whimper.

The boy nodded, flopping his hat, then raised his wrist to tap the keys. "It's...done. I swear."

A woman of her word, she unwrapped her hand and freed Leah. She staggered back, slammed into the wall while cradling her hand, and slid to the dirty floor. The boy darted to her, running his wrist over her disfigured fingers.

"Webb owes us for delivered cargo." Nikko pursed his lips, as if he hated having to explain himself to Vic. "Without his tokens, we'll run out of fuel halfway to Europa."

"What about other buyers for your product? Does it have to be him?" She gestured to the weasel, his skin taking on a greenish hue.

Nikko scowled and released Webb with a shove. The man stumbled to the side and wretched.

"Take back whatever you've delivered and blacklist him." Vic folded her arms across her chest, mimicking Nikko's earlier stance.

"It's not as simple as that." His gaze shifted to Leah who reached for her blaster with her good hand.

"I wouldn't if I was you, Leah," Vic smirked. "I can kill your boss where he stands."

Nikko jerked back, his eyes widening.

"So make it simple," Vic continued.

The boy unholstered Leah's blaster and tucked it in the back of his pants. Wise.

Webb tried to run past her, but she caught him by the throat and pinned him to the wall. His feet dangled inches off the floor. The stench of vomit hit her with his every puff.

"Is Nikko's request for payment unreasonable?" Vic studied her human hand then nibbled on a broken fingernail.

Webb shook his head.

"Spill it. Why can't you pay?" She sliced a glance at Nikko leaning his shoulder against the wall beside Webb.

"I...I lost my access pass, and it will take a day for a renewal."

This was but a petty squabble? She pointed at Nikko. "So pay the man's docking fee."

"I offered, but he declined," the weasel whined, not endearing himself to her.

She closed her eyes with a deep sigh. "Do you have to be on the station to receive your access?"

Webb gulped. "No."

She released him and met Nikko's deep blue gaze. "Take him with you, and once the payment is through, drop him off at the next way station."

Unhooking her carry-all, she slung it over her shoulder and sauntered off. "Accommodate him at his expense," she tossed without looking back.

When she merged with the crowds, relief flooded her like a shot of sweed hitting her stomach, warming her from the inside out. A new beginning for her shouldn't have to start with someone dying at her hands.

It took longer than expected to reach the ice hauler. Because of its looming size, she kept climbing off the wrong elevator. At last, she strolled toward a burly man guarding the hauler's loading dock.

Pausing in front of him with the toes of her boots brushing the metal ramp, she endured yet another lurid appraisal. Well, tit for tat. She studied him too. The way his grease-stained pants clung to muscled thighs. His brown vest—that had once been white—molded a carved torso only hard work could build.

"Hi." She fluttered her fingers in a wave, hitched her shoulders, and rocked on her toes.

He grinned, then wiped off his smile. "Get lost."

"That's rude. I was told to report for work." Farg, if nothing came of Ande's instructions, she didn't know what she would do. She didn't need tokens, but traveling between planets was a sure way to avoid running into anything to do with Carne Corp. "Contact is Themba Masuku."

"Ah." The guard's grin returned. "You must be the new security."

She winced. Sure, security, but alas, it *was* up her alley. She could fix things too, although sol plates from a decade ago couldn't compare to the current technology. "I am." She squared her shoulders.

"I'll escort you in." He tapped buttons on his smart band and gestured to her to follow. As soon as she stepped onto the ramp, wands rose from the corners, and a white beam hummed into existence. It took a few seconds to scan her. "Sorry. We take security seriously, what with the high price of water. Name's Dieter." He offered his hand, which she accepted.

This was Dieter? She could see why Ande thought he would do. The mechanic's touch was gentle, and perhaps he would be as cautious when he fucked her. She followed him along winding passages patched with strips of mismatched metal. The lighting flickered. Nothing other than groaning machinery reached her ears. A mixture of oil, burned rubber, and ozone saturated the air.

"I'm taking you to the captain. Ande said you would be along." Dieter glanced at her, his gaze lingering on her almost-exposed breasts. "He didn't say where you're from, though."

She grinned. Farg, she loved her best friend. "Here and there."

Dieter tapped on a dented metal door that looked like it came out of an ancient submarine. Winking at her, he leaned his shoulder against it and shoved it open. Behind a metal desk sat a fat man, dark-skinned, dreadlocks to his shoulders and cybernetic eyes glowing silver.

She knew that face.

Before her, with a bulging stomach, sat the legendary Maz the Massive.

He nibbled on a chicken leg—the real bird—licked his fingers, then wiped his hands on a dirty rag. With a flick of his wrist, he instructed Dieter to close the door.

Alone in the room, she studied the unmade bunker bed, antique books scattered across the floor, hundreds of sketches on the walls, and a bonsai tree stashed at the back of an empty shelf.

"Victorious in my quarters?" He rose, strode to the vendor, and filled his cup with...she sniffed, coffee—the good kind. "Victoria Harper, in the flesh."

Harper? No, she wanted nothing to tie her to the Ring and her pa. Her ma's maiden name would have to do. "It's Victoria Barnes now." She slid her carry-all off her shoulder and caught the strap with her fingers before easing it to the floor.

"If you're dodging Carne, then yes." He sipped his black coffee and blinked at her. "I don't doubt your skill, gal. It's why I agreed to Ande's offer." He settled behind his desk. "You'll work hard, keep your head down, and not start fights my crew will lose."

"Fair enough."

He paused, ran another gaze over her outfit, one she was beginning to regret buying. Drafe had damn near devoured her with his yellow gaze, but the lecherous glances she was getting tainted the enjoyment she'd found.

"No sexual relations allowed on my ship."

She jerked back. Farg. Now what? Ande must not have known about it or else he wouldn't have recommended Dieter. "Only on your ship, or are way stations included in that?" If there was time, she might be able to convince Dieter to take a hotel room with her before they departed.

Themba pursed his lips, a hint of a smile in the corner of his mouth. "You're smart. I'll give you that. What happens on dock leave is not my problem. Word is, you didn't finish your bon voyage so to speak, and are still the property of Carne. You're lucky, gal, that what I owe Ande is huge." He muttered about harboring a fugitive as he flicked through an abused paperback—a massive sandworm on the cover. By the state of his quarters, it looked like he never left it. "I'd appreciate you not mentioning...my past. No one on board knows."

"Ditto."

"Security is ex-military. They'll rib you in the beginning, give you the shitty jobs, but it's par for the course. Don't take it to heart." He drained his coffee but held onto the cup, his gaze hooded. "I heard Erv died. No details are known."

She winced, remembering the macabre scene that had greeted her. How she felt about him was ambiguous at best. Sometimes, he'd been the father she never had, despite knowing his 'care'—ensuring medical treatment, good food, and rest—protected Victorious, the asset. Mostly, he'd been an ass with his smirking, training, kidnapping more children, and convincing many to upgrade their limbs to cybernetics.

She gritted her teeth. Her pure-human status was no longer. In the end, Erv and Carne had won. "A single shot with the blaster, execution-style."

The door swung inward without warning, with Dieter leaning in. "Got a problem, boss. The crew called for an evac."

Themba leaped to his feet. "What the farg?"

"Not to worry. I dispatched Tiny." Dieter's gaze didn't stray from Vic's chest, not even when Themba circled his desk to grip Vic's arm and tug her to the door.

"Show Vic to her quarters, and stop ogling her. She's not ice, y'know." Themba waddled to his desk.

"Sure, boss." Dieter pressed his palm to her lower back to slip past her, heading deeper into the ship. She sucked in a deep breath to catch the familiar and nostalgic smells of grease and sol.

Behind her, Themba roared into his wrist, "Farg it, Sarg, I asked you to keep a low profile…"

As Dieter led her along kinked pathways with too many doors, she said nothing. He had a lovely ass, but other than that, she reeled from the interview. Maz had accepted all manner of implants. She doubted her captain had more than thirty percent human left in him. Which meant, she might not be able to take him. She grinned. A challenge wasn't a bad thing, per say.

Up a ladder she and Dieter climbed, the bulkheads closing in, the metal grating beneath her feet worn, and with stickers and posters personalizing submarine doors. In front of a plain door, the name slot blank, he paused. "My room's the red door…if you need *anything*."

She frowned. "Captain said—"

"What Themba doesn't know can't hurt him." Dieter caught a lock of her hair and tucked it behind her ear. "When you're settled, just call me on the system. Computer, this is Vic, grant her permanent access to room '403.'"

"Access granted to Victoria Barnes," a semi-feminine voice crackled as the door swung open. "Room sterilization complete. Security restricted to Victoria Barnes."

"It's just Vic." She flashed a smile at Dieter while closing the door in his face. "Computer?"

"Yes, Vic."

She felt like an idiot with her face raised to the paneled ceiling. "Is anyone else allowed access to my room?"

"On this ship, Security personnel can override access."

Vic sighed. As she had thought. So her room but not hers. Yet another place she couldn't call home. Scanning the four-by-four-meter cube, she studied the markings on the walls indicating the hidden toilet, basin, table, and closet. The sol-bath was a sliver of glass embedded in the wall. The bunker was single, and she almost missed staring at the rungs of Ande's bed above it.

This was freedom, no Carne, no Pa, just four walls on an ice hauler heading into space. She was far from the childish dream of working her ma's sol farm. This was her life, the embodiment of freedom, for now.

No one had ever accused her of lacking patience.

Chapter Twelve

Year: 2219

Lunar Base

TRUE TO HIS WORD, when Vic summoned Dieter, he left his room, closed his red door, and loped over to her waiting in the passage. "Ready to see the ship and meet the crew?"

She gestured to him to lead the way. "What happened? Why the evac?"

He shrugged. "Not sure. Tiny's still in the med bay with two of the crew. Sarg is with Captain, no doubt rehashing what happened. I'll find out soon enough. No one died, so that's good."

He was too cavalier about the people he worked with.

From the lack of wrinkles, she would place him in his mid-twenties, yet he acted as if he had been a mechanic for a decade. "How long have you been hauling ice?"

"Years." He grinned. "On *Mula Pesada*, only two. I like it so far. Captain's a fair man, and those are rare in the far reaches. Employees get a decent bonus too."

He entered a round room, counters wrapped the walls, a circular table dominated the center, and a few walls held plants. The UV lighting drew her, and she paused beside one, running her fingers over the green leaves while absorbing the 'sunlight.'

Her chest expanded when she drew in a deep breath, as if for the first time in a while she could breathe freely. "Any chance I can have one of these lights installed in my room?" She opened her eyes and met Dieter's gaze.

"Sure. I'll do it after dinner." His ogling implied something a little more intimate.

"Thanks." Not that she would spread her thighs because Ande recommended Dieter, but she was open to it. She did like the smell of the man.

"This is the mess. We take turns at cooking."

She jerked back. "What?" The Ring's canteen was fully staffed. Living on protein bars and hydro-gels was the extent of her pre-arena life. "I don't know how to cook."

He cringed. "You'll learn."

"Great." She huffed. "Wait, as in real food? Not just gels and bars?" Themba *had* been eating chicken.

"Yup, we have a stocked storeroom, animals pens, and hydroponics."

She gaped. "I've never *seen* a live animal, let alone eaten one."

He chuckled. "Well, now you will. Sorry to say, cleaning the pens and feeding them will be your responsibility. That is until you earn the crew's respect."

Taking two mugs out of a cupboard, he tucked them in a vendor. The aroma of coffee filled the air, and she hummed. When she had won her first match, Ande had treated her to her first cup of coffee. The *Mula Pesada* crew drank it without a thought to its expense.

Dieter offered her a mug. "Cream? Sugar?"

Gathering her scattered wits, she nodded. Having never had either in her coffee, she wasn't sure how to respond. He poured a dollop of white liquid, plopped a cube of compacted white powder, then stirred with a steel teaspoon.

Taking a tentative sip, the roasted, bittersweetness coated her tongue. She groaned, casting a smile at him. "I usually drink it black."

He chuckled. "I can tell."

She laughed and cupped the mug with her hands. "This is better."

"I like mine sweeter. Sarg likes his as black as sin." Dieter whipped his head to the side when stomping along the grated flooring reached them. "Time to meet the crew."

She downed her coffee, in case she was forced to abandon it, and rose, not liking the vulnerable position of sitting. The first person through the doorway shot bolts of ice down her spine.

"What the farg," Nikko growled, striding toward her, his shoulders squared, his fingers curling into fists.

"You've met?" Dieter sliced glances between them. "This is Vic, our new crewmember." He shifted, as if he wanted to come to her defense.

With a tiny shake of her head, she held him back.

"Why the farg is the bitch here?" Leah sidled closer to Nikko, pressing her bandaged hand to her chest.

Vic sighed. "There's still time for me to disembark. It was lovely to meet you, Dieter."

"Stop." There Nikko went again, using his authoritative voice to calm her instinctive reactions. "Captain has explained your presence. The debt has been canceled." His lips curled in distaste. "As much as I hate having to deal with you after the stunt you pulled, your contract states a minimum of two years. Should you leave before then, the debt-paid will reverse."

"What? Two years?" From one prison to another. Slamming her fist into her palm, she gritted her teeth. She would fargen kill Ande when next she saw him. Sure, it kept her 'safe' until he won his deca-match, but still, he could have told her, or better, allowed a loophole. She glared at Dieter. Perhaps if he hadn't interrupted the captain she might have learned more about her 'service.'

Leah's cheeks flushed pink, but her anger couldn't hide the fear in her eyes. "I ain't working with this bi—"

"It's out of my hands, Leah." Nikko glanced at her over his shoulder.

"She did take us down." Toothpick-man pushed past Leah to reach the vendor, helping himself to coffee. His gray gaze warmed when he peeked at Vic's legs. "Cybernetics?"

She clenched her jaw and took a moment to calm her resentment. "Without my permission."

"Y'know, you *do* look familiar." The boy weaved around everyone to pull a hydro-gel from a cooling drawer. In tight black pants and a matching sweater, the only thing large about him were his boots.

"That's Grunt. I'm Trent. Welcome to the *Mula Pesada*." Toothpick-man raised his mug in a salute before sipping from it. His black hair flopped over one brow.

"Grunt, get me the surveillance of that alley, and strip it from all databanks." Nikko's barked order silenced the mess.

"On it." The boy grabbed something out of the cupboard and left.

Nikko stared after Grunt until his footsteps faded. "Now, I see you both admiring our newest crewmember's remarkable assets. You know the rules."

Trent's shoulders slumped. "No fucking our crew."

"Good. If you think you can sneak into Vic's quarters without me noticing, Dieter, you don't know me as well as I thought you did." Nikko's words wiped off Dieter's smirk. "Victoria Barnes is here to stay." Nikko flicked his fingers, and as one, the crew abandoned him, leaving him alone with her. "Sit."

She pursed her lips, pinning her shoulders back as tension coiled in the pit of her stomach. "I prefer to stand."

"I won't attack you, Vic." He drew in a calm breath and slid onto the bench, resting his elbows on the table. "What you did in that alley, though impressive, was without provocation."

"Was it?" She arched a brow. "Look at you, all muscle, towering over a weasel of a man." She sat, mirrored his stance, and met his gaze, challenging him.

He didn't back down, didn't glance away. "I wasn't hurting him."

"I don't tolerate bullies, and if you know who I was, we wouldn't be having this discussion."

He grimaced. "No, I don't know your history. I do know the debt owed."

Well, he knew more than she did. What did Themba owe Ande that was worth this much? "Since we're laying the cards on the table, I'm a fugitive." She raised her fingers to study the fine lines marking the healing process post-implantation. "I ask nothing from you other than a haven. You've seen what I can do, so earning your respect isn't something I give a farg about. I do need one thing."

Nikko's scowl softened when he ran an appraising gaze over her cleavage. She doubted he was aware he was checking her out.

"I'm a virgin. For years, I fought to keep my innocence, in defiance, but I need...physical contact." She winced, not appreciating having to divulge this to a relative stranger. But, she had to have his permission to disembark, if he'd allow it. Then again, what did the state of her untried nethers mean to him? Nothing. She folded her arms across her chest. Keeping her mouth shut and solving this on her own might have been the better approach. It's just that...after that kiss with Drafe, her body hummed with an addictive energy she was too intrigued about to ignore.

Nikko's breath hitched as he jerked back.

"I'd like the opportunity to find someone dockside to relieve me of said innocence. Dieter was suggested, but since Captain mentioned the rule, I have no other options." She frowned. *Why didn't Ande know about that rule?* Not that she could reach out to him, take him to task for the bullshit he'd landed her in. Carne monitored all correspondence. They'd find her within days.

Nikko's cheeks darkened. "Just like that? Can't Tiny...um, remove it?"

Vic grimaced. "I don't have my hymen anymore." The rigorous exercise she was put through had robbed her of that. "I should at least experience fucking before I die hauling ice."

He stared at her for a minute. "I can delay departure for a few hours."

She chuckled, splaying her hands on the table. "I didn't expect you to agree to help me."

He pinched the bridge of his nose. "You're part of my crew, my responsibility, and that includes your wellbeing."

"I appreciate what having me on board is costing you." She smiled. "If I'm delayed for whatever reason, the *Mula Pesada* can depart without me. I'll hire a skiff or a hopper and find you."

"Right." He didn't believe her.

"I'm a fugitive, Nikko, but not without means." She pushed herself to her feet. "Now, all I need to do is find a specific man. Can anyone on board help with that?"

"Grunt's our tech guru." Nikko raised his face to the ceiling, summoning another smile from Vic. She had thought she was the only idiot to do that. "Computer, patch me through to Grunt."

"Patch complete," the computer intoned.

"Grunt, Vic needs your help." Nikko jumped up to order a coffee.

"Shoot." The boy chewed on something as he spoke.

Instead of staring at the ceiling, she watched Nikko while he sipped his black coffee. "Grunt, can you locate a man dockside, goes by Drafe?"

"Is that all you have?" Tapping of keys followed.

For a moment, she closed her eyes to better envision Drafe striding across the Moonstar's dance floor to reach her. "He's dark-skinned, wears nanotech armor, has yellow eyes."

Nikko mouthed 'yellow.' She ignored him.

A shiver rippled along her skin, sparking an intense heat to settle in her core. If Drafe was still on the station, she might be able to find him and suggest a few hours of pleasure. Dieter would have sufficed, Trent at a push, but who she wanted was Drafe in all his masculine glory.

Used to seeing men fit, strong, and virile meant she needed more than that. There was something dark, seductive, and exotic about Drafe.

Something that sent a frisson of excitement along her nerves and raised the hairs at the nape of her neck. Finding him was her last chance to experience intimacy before heading into outer space for who knew how long.

Chapter Thirteen

Year: 2219

Lunar Base

DRAFE MET AEHORT'S GAZE. The Ivoy knew and saw too much, as expected of a symbiote transfer. In the ambassador lounge, Drafe hovered behind him, studying every person eager to intrude.

"I apologize, Drafe, for not forewarning you." Aehort bowed his head.

"She was...unexpected." Drafe didn't want to discuss Victoria Harper when he had just cooled his ardor. A slither of sadness remained though, as if he had lost an opportunity, missed out on something momentous.

"True connections are rare." Aehort smiled at a passing server carrying a tray of colorful beverages. "If she were to appear before you now, what would you do?"

Every muscle in Drafe's body tensed. His symbiotes sparked to life, rippling along his skin and receding his armor, leaving parts of him, for a moment, bare. He laughed. No, she wasn't a threat, despite having seen her fight on the holo. Foq, such a woman had passion, strength, and self-discipline., Yet softness lingered in her hair, her skin, and the pliancy of her lips.

"I cannot abandon you a second time, Aehort." Duty called. He scanned the room, watching twitching fingers and the pseudo-happiness offered with false flattery. "How much longer?"

"We have breached the humans's database where they store their video footage, communication, military strategies, and stockpile locations."

"Good." Drafe rubbed his fingers along his thigh, needing to burn through this pent-up energy. The texture of the armor pressed into his bare skin. Sighing, he willed his symbiotes to calm but not to recede. A naked male in an alien station would not go down well.

Tyler strode toward him, his excited expression the most honest in the room. "I found her. Well, it has to be her. A Victoria Barnes signed up today on an ice hauler."

Drafe beamed. "Excellent, Tyler."

"Only thing is, they're departing in a few hours. They've logged a delay. The station allows a few hours pro bono, but after three, they will be charged."

Drafe didn't care about costs. There was time to find her, to form some sort of communication path with her. Not that he knew if human technology was compatible with Ivoyan. "How do I reach her?"

Tyler grinned and waved a black strip. "Smart band." He snapped it over Drafe's wrist.

A buzz ran up Drafe's arm while he studied the device.

"It's powered by your body's energy and connects with the closest available communication port." Tyler raised his wrist to his lips and spoke into his matching band. "Meorri aac Drafe Arrak."

Drafe tensed when a bolt shot up his arm. He gripped the band, preparing to rip it off him when Tyler's voice emanated from it. Pausing, he uncapped his hand and tapped the flashing star. "Drafe." He felt like an idiot and raised his gaze to meet Tyler's.

"As simple as that. You mention her name on this, and it will try and find her."

Excitement sparked a shift in Drafe's posture, and he faced Aehort. The male inclined his head and strolled to the exit, trailing his Qaldreth warriors.

Drafe paused and pressed his lips to the device. Before he could say her name, a flash of color amid the grays and blacks of the guests caught his focus. Striding across the vast hall was Victoria, her gaze fixed on him, her garment baring more than covering.

Foq. His cooled ardor exploded into life. His symbiotes bounced and reverberated, exposing and armoring him. His hair rose, no longer draped down his back.

"Farg, Drafe, your eyes are glowing." Tyler searched the room and chuckled. "Right, that's my cue."

Drafe spared him a glance. "Thank you for the assistance, Tyler. I am in your debt, and this should not be taken lightly."

"Glad I could help. I'll fall in with your warriors to ensure Aehort Uz is well-guarded."

Drafe lowered his gaze to rest on the human male. "You are honorable and have earned my respect."

"Drafe." Vic's rasping voice snapped his attention to her. "Am I intruding?"

"I need to escort my uz to the ship. Join me."

She hesitated, sliced a glance at Aehort, then shifted closer to Drafe. "Are you sure you want me with you?"

"One warrior is good, two are better."

She gasped and rested her hand on his chest for a moment. Color splashed her cheeks, but she said no more, just fell into step beside him.

"I am told you have a few hours to spare." He scanned the crowds as they cut through them. Aehort's arrival was unexpected, so Drafe didn't anticipate an attack. Still, a Qaldreth warrior prepared for all scenarios. The sun-drenched scent of her teased him, and he snuck a glance. He had not planned to meet her.

They crowded each other in an ascending box. Her arm brushed against him, and a thousand sparks exploded outward. With all his strength, he kept his gaze forward, his arms by his side. Soon enough, he would have her beneath him, her sweet essence engulfing him.

"This?" Ulvus gestured to Vic as they approached.

"None of your business," Drafe growled, his glare warning Ulvus to back off.

"We will await your return. Meorri aac Ulvus Sava, escort me to my quarters." Aehort met Drafe's gaze, then captured Vic's hand, pressing his palm to hers. His eyes rolled back. He hummed. To her credit, she didn't react and didn't break the connection. "You are most welcome, Victoria," Aehort dropped his hand and strolled into the *Aroagni*.

"What was that?" She leaned against Drafe's chest.

With eagerness, he looped an arm around her to keep her there. "Ivoyans are clairvoyant to some extent." He buried his fingers in her silky strands tumbling down her back and tugged gently. "Where to?"

"I booked a hotel room." Pulling out of his embrace despite his efforts to restrain her, she caught his hand and gestured to a double-door twenty meters away.

He didn't look at the crowds or at the stalls. They could not hold his attention, but the sway of her hair brushing her ass... "I am pleased you found me."

She cast a smile over her shoulder. "I was lucky to arrange this. My new employer surprised me by agreeing to help."

"Help?" Drafe furrowed his brow.

"Yes, I want you." Her laughter wrapped around his chest, squeezing the air out of him.

She hurried him through a predominantly red lounge and into another ascending box. Once it climbed, she dropped his hand and pinned her back to the side, watching him. Her stance was casual, not like her appraisal.

The urge to use her kiss on her was tempting, but if he started in this box, he doubted they'd make it to the room. Stepping onto the level also carpeted in red, she strode ahead, paused outside a numbered door, and swiped her smart band over a white panel. The door clicked open, and she sashayed in. When he followed, he did not expect her to lift a leg to undo a boot. Doing so exposed first a smooth thigh, then a scarred one. Her tiny feet were delicate. Exposing them made her vulnerable. That she did so freely meant more to him than she could know.

He growled and hurried to strip off his boots. Naked, his symbiotes retracting his armor, he burst forward and pinned her to the bulkhead. He pressed his lips to hers, savoring her flavor. When she swiped her tongue across his, his control crumbled.

Gripping his shoulders, she wrapped her legs around his hips and clung to him. A groan tore from him when she pressed her sex against his. Foq, he wasn't strong enough to handle the temptation of her.

"Garment off, now." His voice wasn't his, sounding more like the mating call of a vasquva.

She laughed and tapped her shoulder. The garment dropped, pooling where their hips met, and revealing her breasts. "You don't have nipples."

"Males do not nurse babes." He cupped a breast, relishing the peak of her nipple stabbing his palm while surrounded by exquisite softness.

She moaned, arching her back. Grabbing her ass, he hoisted her against him and strode to the bed. With one knee at a time, he crawled onto it, sprawling her beneath him. She reacted so foqing beautifully to his every touch.

"I want to please you, little one, but I need to learn how to." He clenched his jaw when she rubbed her hot core against his hard koq. "Do not touch me until I have done so."

She blinked at him, then nodded, lowered her legs, and raised her hands above her head. He wished he could remember her like this forever, laid before him like a blessed offering from Osnir. His hands trembled where he stroked her neck, over and around a quivering breast, along the hard yet silky dips of her ribbed stomach to the apex of her thighs. So far, she was similar to a Qaldreth female.

"Allow me."

"What?" she squeaked, resisted the nudge of his thumbs for a second then let him spread her legs.

He shifted back until he could nestle between her thighs, his nose an inch from her exposed sex. "Foq, Vic, your human sex is like a cucooya blossom. Petals circle a tight bud holding the tree's water. I wonder…" Using his tongue, he parted her petals to reach the bud—as he would to a cucooya to capture a few droplets of dew. The untamed, exotic taste of her burst across his senses. "So good." When he found the bud, he suckled. Her cries and pleas drenched his ears. She thrust her hips to meet his tongue, her breath fluttering.

In his life, few things had brought him this much joy: the summer feast after a stark winter, when he had first held his father's sword, securing his sister's future, and this…this female. He ached to bury himself in her, but unfamiliar with her species, he needed to explore a little more. Not willing to cease suckling, tasting her, he slid a thumb along her thigh and under, encountering the slickness of her arousal. He slipped a finger into a hole a little higher than a Qaldreth's.

She moaned, gyrating her hips further.

Withdrawing his thumb, he extended his forefinger, testing the depth. Osnir have mercy, she was tight…too tight, perhaps? Inserting a second finger, he paused to smile. She stretched, and with the additional stimulation, was rushing toward her pleasure without him. If he judged the clamping along his fingers correctly.

Pulling away, he flipped her onto her knees and positioned his koq at her entrance. As he pushed into the silken heat, how well she squeezed him, was bliss he'd never imagined nor experienced.

"Foq, Vic, you are breathtaking."

Chapter Fourteen

Year: 2219
Lunar Base

VIC COULDN'T BREATHE. JUST by touching her, Drafe had roused so many emotions she couldn't begin to identify. She ached, her skin flushed, and deep within her, something twanged, making demands she prayed he could assuage. When he buried his face between her legs, she wanted to squirm away. Nudity was one thing, but exposing her sex was new to her.

Yet, when he sucked on her, stars exploded behind her eyes, the colors awe-inspiring, the sensations ricocheting through her. This was amazing. Why had she taken so long to find out? Had it been out of principle when Sebastian Carne had implied it was her prized possession?

Writhing under Drafe's skilled tongue, she thought this was it. Something built inside her, rising, growing, until she expected to break in two. Then he dipped a finger inside her, and new sensations assailed her. He could do anything to her now, and she would let him.

Finding her face buried in the linen, her ass in the air, wasn't what she expected. He'd flipped her without a word of warning. Not that she minded when he pushed into her, expanding her, introducing her to an intense need, an ache so deep she whimpered his name.

"Foq, Vic, you are breathtaking."

His sincere compliment settled on her arid heart.

Arching her back, she silently pleaded with him to hurry. Never had she felt this good. Never had she been complete, as if the connection between them had come full circle.

"Drafe, please."

He growled and layered his chest to her back, pulling his cock out to thrust in.

Overwhelmed by a burning need, the fire in her core, and her mind bombarded with thoughts of him, she screamed into the linen to smother her cries for more. As he sucked on her ear, thrust in and out, he splayed his fingers over hers. Tingles began in the very depths of her and spiraled out and upward, until with his deep thrusts, she exploded.

Shivers assaulted her. She coiled, riding an explosion of pure pleasure. He roared, slipped an arm around her waist, and bit her shoulder, summoning another intense crescendo. He collapsed on the bed, taking her with him, yet kept her close. His labored breathing and pounding heartbeat merged with hers.

Tears pressed against her eyes. They made no sense, and still, she had chosen him. He had delivered beyond what innocent her could have imagined. Yet despite the sense of rightness, she couldn't help but feel she had lost a part of her. Her very soul was no longer hers alone.

Feathering his lips across her ear and along her jaw, he tilted her head to snatch a kiss, grumbling as he did so. "Amazing, Vic."

She nodded, unable to speak past the lump in her throat.

"May I search for you when my mission is complete?" The sincerity in his golden-yellow eyes tore at her. He was sweet for such a warrior.

She twisted to cup his cheek, brushing her lips across his. "I would be honored."

"Ah, Vic..." Dieter's voice sliced through the moment. "You best hurry. Nikko just told me to fire up the engines, but I know for shit, you're not on board."

She stilled, groaning at her inability to see Nikko as a lying sack of shit. "I'm coming." When she tried to wriggle free, Drafe tightened his hold around her.

"No," he growled.

She chuckled past the darkness of goodbyes squeezing her chest. "Duty calls."

He released her but watched her scoot across the bed to yank on her dress. When she bent to tug on her boots, he snatched her into his arms and pinned her to the wall again. His kiss was heaven, the taste of him, and the heated dominance of his tongue. For someone who hadn't known what a kiss was, he'd learned fast. Hoisting her legs up, he plunged into her. Too close to her last orgasm, she exploded, riding pure pleasure that left her disinterested in returning to the ice hauler and what Nikko had done to her. Instead, she clung to Drafe as he fucked her hard enough to bounce her off the wall. Sweat glistened on his obsidian skin, and when she buried her fingers in his mane of hair, he bellowed, his body twitching. He arched, keeping her in place with the power of his hips.

"I mean it, Vic. Ten minutes to departure."

Drafe staggered back, his cock still hard and a delicious black and cream color. She would love to explore the ridges on the top, and the pointed tip of his cock too. On trembling knees, she managed to don her boots. With a last lingering kiss, she slipped out of the room, then burst into a run, taking the stairs instead of waiting for the elevator.

Sprinting and weaving through the crowds, she bounced her leg when she had to take the one elevator to the docking level. Dieter waited on the ramp, his brow furrowed as he searched for her.

Grinning, she strolled the final few meters. "I'm here."

His shoulders slumped. He beamed. "Cutting it fine, Vic."

"You're not going to garner any favors for helping me. If Nikko wanted me off, he won't appreciate this."

"Captain's my boss, and he told me to call you." Dieter pressed a red button as soon as they stepped into the cavernous bay. The mechanical whine of the ramp retracting merged with the squeal from the lowering bay door.

She had hoped Nikko hadn't sold her out. Why had she thought she didn't need to guard her back as she had at Carne? "Yeah, I think we have a 'who's boss' problem."

"Want to finish the tour now?" Dieter flicked his gaze over her. "Might as well get your uniform too." Walking backward along the passage, he studied her. "What took you dockside?"

"Oh, just had to see a man about a promise I made," she chuckled.

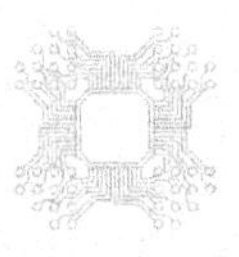

Drafe stared at the closed door then sat on the edge of the bed. Holy Osnir, he was bereft, still aching, his symbiotes zinging along his veins in tormented bliss. As explosive as this had been, it hadn't been enough. He needed more time with her, more of...her. While snapping on his boots, he relived her kisses, the addictive sounds she made that caught in her throat, and the feel of her engulfing him. Never had he been this energized. His symbiotes reacted to her in ways he struggled to understand.

In his village, there were too few females for mating, especially for pleasure. And traveling to other villages for such a task was done only once a season. The males who did so had to accept that their symbiotes recorded their dalliances for all generations to witness. He was not such a male.

He licked his lips and savored her flavor, better than the sweetest of water, the freshest of vasquva, or the fragrance of the morning sun hitting the Nadaar dunes. Summoning his armor, he strolled out of the room but not before he drew in a lungful of their union. He wanted to capture the moment. Growling, he stomped into the descending box and across the lounge. His glower silenced anyone curious enough to glance his way.

The *Aroagni* was close, not that he cared when he cut a wide path through the crowds.

"What has you so miserable?" Vaen guarded the entrance, his scowl a deterrent as well.

"I...lost something." How else could Drafe explain the darkness enshrouding his soul?

"Oh?" Vaen studied Drafe. "You have your blaster and a strange black strip around your wrist."

Lifting his hand, Drafe twisted his wrist. He could talk to her, so that was something. She said he could find her after they had learned who killed the Ots. He need only focus on that.

"Ulvus is most displeased with your departure." Vaen fell into step beside Drafe. "Aehort awaits you in the command room."

"I know where it is. You need not escort me." Drafe glared at Vaen. He was hoping for a moment alone, to gather his focus, and remember the honor of Qaldreth came first.

"Aehort was most specific." Vaen grinned and thumped Drafe on his shoulder.

"Fine." He shrugged, trying to dislodge Vaen. "Cease touching me."

Vaen drew in a deep breath. "You smell...good, like Qaldreth sunlight baking the rocks around the Aguura salt plains."

Fire exploded inside Drafe and across his vision. "My..." His what? His scents? His personal space? His...Vic? He'd lain with her twice. She wasn't his but was a free female, without filial responsibilities, alone... Yet, she had said she would be honored. The perfect response. His armor hardening should have warned him, but instead, he threw Vaen off.

"Whoa." Vaen held up his hands, stepped back, and allowed Drafe to enter the command center first.

Aehort met Drafe's gaze for a minute before nodding. "So it has begun." He gestured to the circular table in the center of the oval room. Holographs rose, building a three-dimensional representation of the star system around their location.

"The data shows these carry the explosives." Thousands of blue dots popped into the model, moving as they traveled outward. "They have no predetermined destination. A few collide with meteors, asteroid belts, debris, a few are collected by astro-hoppers—what the humans call those who mine the asteroid belts. A few of these pods encounter planets, habitable or otherwise."

"Do we know what's inside them?" Drafe spun the model as dots blimped out of existence.

Aehort zoomed into a dot, analyzing the pod-shape of it. "No, which is why we need to capture one."

The corpse was discovered in such a pod. Drafe flicked the dot aside and chose another, hoping any difference would reveal more information. "Wouldn't that mean opening ourselves to the same outcome?"

"Indeed." Aehort squeezed his shoulder as if it bothered him. "I considered this conundrum. Not if we study it on an asteroid or desolate moon."

Drafe traced a dot's trajectory in reverse. "Where is the source of these pods?"

Aehort touched the model and blue lines formed, pointing to a planet nearby. "This is what the humans call Jupiter—to them it is but a ball of compressed gas. They have no knowledge of what lies on its surface or if it has one."

"Yet, the pods originate from here? What about one of its moons?" Drafe spun the model, touching the closest moon to expand it. Details popped up: iced oceans, a silicate-rock mantle, and an iron core.

"It is possible." Aehort tapped the model, and seventy-nine moons aligned from largest to smallest. "We'll investigate everything to do with this planet. Monitor all communication in and around it. Mark future pod deployments."

Aehort had a plan. The confidence crossing their bond bolstered Drafe's flagging spirits.

"Leave us." Aehort met the gazes of the males in the room, then waited for them to obey. Once they were alone, he faced Drafe. "She is yours. You need only be patient."

Drafe winced. "Am I that obvious?"

The uz cackled, his laughter jarring his narrow shoulders. "Only to me. She is part of the solution to this, Drafe."

He clenched his jaw at Aehort's cryptic words—cursed Ivoyan intelligence granting the species a preternatural foretelling. Regardless, no way would Drafe endanger Vic.

"Be at ease." Aehort patted his shoulder with his elongated fingers. "Now, bathe, you stink of mating."

Drafe stumbled to his quarters, a little dazed as he unraveled and analyzed Aehort's words. Stripping off his armor, commanding his symbiotes to unmask, he stepped under the water's spray. While washing, he touched parts of himself she had, and when he rubbed his koq, renewed sensations bombarded him. If he didn't resolve this mission soon, memories of her would be the death of him.

He snorted. When next he traveled home, all would know how he had lost his soul to a non-Qaldreth. If he had his way, Vic would be with him when he stepped onto his homeworld.

Chapter Fifteen

Year: 2219
Mula Pesada

"Dieter, this is amazing." Vic stood in chicken shit, with the stench of pigs and cows burning her nostrils. The chickens had two legs they scampered on but six on their backs like the spines of a dinosaur. The pigs were many and ravenous, whining when she neared. There were two cows, large rectangular beasts with eight udders each. The snorts, grunts, squawking echoed off the hull, sounding more like alien whales than farmstock.

"Yup, you have to feed them. The chickens get from this bag." Along the wall was a row of bags, all beige. Someone had painted a 'CH' on it, for which she was grateful. "Spare feed is in the storeroom. The pigs get our kitchen scraps. About once every three months, we slaughter one. This is why we have so many. The cows you need to milk. Take turns, though. They get cranky if you milk them daily."

"Farg. I've never milked a cow."

He laughed. "It's easy. I'll show you in the morning. If your chore is to tend the animals, you have to rise earlier than the crew, as well. Might as well make breakfast while you're at it since you would've gathered what eggs the chickens have laid." He waved his hand at the strange peephole houses to the rear of the chicken pen. "Once you've done this and made breakfast, there's the itaya to take care of."

More for her to do? "The what?"

"An alien parasite that lives off sol, so tend to breed close to the engines. They're space-worthy, territorial, and will attack if provoked. Spraying them with nitrous oxide is considered an act of aggression." He grinned as if he hadn't shocked the shit out of her. "Not to worry. You'll be suited up, tethered, carrying the nitro gun and a blaster. You'll do fine."

She gulped. "Out there?" Pointing a finger, she indicated the outside of the ship, in space, no oxygen... No problem.

"Yup. The tether's strong. I'll show you, of course. I can't send you out there not knowing what to look for. So once we're out of the neutral zone around Lunar Base, we'll suit up."

"Sure," but her voice quavered. "When do I get to see the engine room?"

"Off-limits to new employees for obvious reasons."

"Farg." Her shoulders slumped. "I used to repair solar plates when I worked my ma's sol farm. I miss the smell of it, the steadfast presence of the machinery, their drones and twangs as if they offered comfort and companionship."

He blinked at her as if she'd lost her mind. "You have maintenance experience?"

She bit the inside of her cheek lest she spewed nonsense again. One session with Drafe and her wits were scattered. "It's been a while, but I am handy with a welding torch."

He beamed. "Those are different with no oxygen, but I can do with your help. I'll run it past the captain. Might be able to split your time."

He loped to the door leading out the pens. "Let's get you a uniform." He jog-walked along the passages, spinning to check she followed until they reached a locker room of sorts.

"Here's the replacements. The first set is free, anything else comes out of your cut." He thrust a shirt, cargo pants, a jacket, and boots at her. She couldn't help but remember when Ande had done the same so many years ago.

Sighing, she placed the stack and unhooked her dress clasp.

"Wait." Dieter gasped and spun on a heel, showing her his back. "I didn't... You shouldn't..." He chuckled. "That was unexpected."

"Sorry." She stripped off the dress and her boots. "Where I come from, nudity's a non-issue."

"Where is this place? Can I join?" His attempt at humor to disarm the tension in the air was appreciated.

"Trust me, you don't want to experience or live through what I had to." The pants had numerous pockets, the shirt was a sleeveless T-shirt in white, and the jacket had a place for a white name tag, just like Leah's. The boots were too big, so she shuffled around Dieter to find a smaller pair. Once those were on, she stomped to ensure they fit well, then tapped his shoulder.

He faced her, his cheeks glowing. "Tiny will add your name. Speaking of which, you need a full medical. It's protocol. She can't fix you unless she has a baseline understanding of your health."

"Sure." Vic grinned. At the Ring, they had medicals after each battle and at least once a week before that. Carne took great care to protect their assets.

Grabbing her dress and old boots, she hurried after Dieter. He marched past the mess, the food storeroom, and a command center. A quick peek in showed Grunt stuck in front of a massive console with an extensive holographic map of their solar system. The sharp medical odors of the med bay made her grimace. Twitching her nose, she hoped to ease the sting of sterilizing agents.

Tiny wasn't tiny. No, she was a short, plump woman with purple hair. When she smiled at Vic, she appeared to be the sweetest person. "I thought Dieter would never bring you."

"Had to see the chickens first." Vic chuckled. "But we saved the best for last."

"Wait outside, Deets." Tiny rose from her chair to approach Vic, gliding her hand along the steel counter.

"I'll check on lunch." He ran his gaze over Vic, blushed, and bumped his shoulder as he scrambled out of the med bay.

Tiny giggled. "I see you're making an impact...again."

"Sorry about yesterday. I saw bullies scaring the shit out of a weakling." Vic winced, getting tired of having to explain herself. Would she do it again? Farg, yes. Where was the weasel? She'd ask Dieter later.

"I can believe that. Nikko's scowl is quite intimidating, or so I'm told." Tiny pointed to the threadbare gown. "Please strip, and put that on."

"Nudity doesn't bother me."

Tiny met Vic's gaze, but the solid white of her eyes made Vic twitch. Was she blind? Stripping off her newly acquired uniform, she stood before Tiny.

"It may appear as if I'm intruding on your personal space, but I see through my hands. I apologize if they're cold." What followed was similar to a full body massage but without the relieving of tension and aching muscles.

Vic gritted her teeth, enduring the constant stimulation, especially after Drafe touched her.

"Mm, you are in prime condition. The implants are new and well done. I've never felt such a masterpiece of craftsmanship." Tiny grinned and stepped back.

"How do you know about the implants?"

Tiny held up her hands, and embedded in her fingers were sensory chips, no doubt to enhance touch. "Cybernetics respond differently to flesh. Yours are almost imperceptible, along with the barest of scars. Your new limbs must have cost a fortune."

Why would I need your tokens? Sebastian Carne's knowing smirk flitted across her thoughts.

"Yes." A grin formed. Injuring asshat Ramirez was a bonus.

"I've documented everything. You may dress." Tiny paused as she sterilized her hands. "Be gentle with him. He's a sweet man."

Vic pulled on her pants and clipped the magnets in place. "Who?"

Tiny took a while to respond. "Dieter."

Ah, now Vic understood. "I'm not interested in him." She tugged on her shirt and snapped her boots on. "Does he know?"

"Know what?" Tiny didn't look up, choosing instead to keep her gaze downcast.

Vic smiled. The poor girl pined. "That you like him?"

Tiny gasped and sliced a glance at the door. "No," she whispered.

"Why not?"

Tiny dropped her chin to her chest as she straightened the tools in a metal tray.

Women were fools. Then again, Vic had done everything she could to survive. Avoided relationships with everyone but Ande, fought for her innocence, her freedom, and her life. "You're beautiful as you are, Tiny. He would be a fool not to see that."

She snorted, her eyes shimmering with unshed tears. "Right, and now that you're here—"

"Tell him I have someone." Drafe's obsidian chest, his pale-yellow eyes, his roar when he orgasmed, followed by his promise to find her... Yes, she had someone.

"You do?" Tiny's white eyes widened with pure joy.

Vic smirked. "In a way."

"Is that the man I smell on you?"

Vic laughed. "What does he smell like?"

"Sunlight, hot rocks, sheer masculinity?"

"Yes," Vic rasped, wishing she'd had the time to bury her nose in the curve of his neck.

"I'll send you the results of your bloodwork." Tiny tapped a vial.

Their session was ending. Sadness dampened the lingering lust in Vic's heart. She cast a glance at the door, as if beyond it lay a life of loneliness. Perhaps, if she took the first brave step toward friendship, a warmer world awaited her. "Mind if I visit you?"

"Sure." Pink splashed Tiny's cheeks.

"You're the only one without a hidden agenda." Vic drew in a deep breath, finding that step had been easier than she'd anticipated. "Here I can be myself."

"You're welcome anytime, Vic. I'm alone for the most part."

Clasping Tiny's hand for a quick squeeze, Vic hit the button on the door, opening it. "See you later?"

"Sure." Tiny waved at Dieter hovering in the doorway. "Bye, Deets."

As Vic and Dieter strolled to the airlock, Vic exaggerated a sigh.

Dieter's gait faltered. "What's the matter?"

"If I wasn't already in love, I'd tap that." She hitched a thumb at Tiny. His reaction would reveal much.

He jerked to a halt. "What? In love?"

Vic gritted her teeth. That's all he took from what she said? "My heart belongs to another." Well, it wasn't a complete lie. "Is Tiny dating anyone?"

He frowned. "Not that I know of."

Farg did she have her work cut out for her. In the airlock, he helped her climb into a spacesuit. As soon as she was in, he closed her up, touched a blue button on her shoulder, and similar to vacuum sealing, the suit hugged her like a second skin.

"Makes it easier to move, especially when you're hauling ass away from vengeful itaya."

Right. Survive the Ring, all its combatants, to be ravaged by space parasites? Oh. She couldn't wait. Helping Dieter into a suit, she earned a nose full of groin, chest, and armpit before she too zipped him shut and hit the button. These suits were older than those Carne supplied, though the functionality remained the same. But she didn't have the heart to tell Dieter she'd done this before. Just not on the *outside* of ship.

"Tap your heels together to activate magnetization." He balanced a helmet over her head and tapped the top until it was a snug fit. Her breath fogged the visor. He flipped it back with a chuckle while clipping the suit to the helmet.

She did the same for him, except the tapping. As tall as he was, she couldn't reach. He had no problem doing it himself and clipping the suit to the helmet.

"Comes with practice." He handed her a blaster and strapped one to his thigh. She did the same. After flipping her visor down, he hit the airlock release. As the door slid open, he unhooked two silver guns that had the look of bazookas of old. "You can't pick these up with gravity activated. They're heavy."

She wasn't paying him that much attention, not with the vastness of space before her and the dwindling Lunar Base orbiting the moon. Behind that was Earth, happily spinning on its axis as if her life wasn't in peril.

"Computer, extend tethers." His voice filled her ears.

Something snapped onto Vic's shoulders, but before she could spin to study his back, he pushed himself out the door. At the last minute, he caught the door's edge and swung himself. He vanished from sight. Fear strangled her throat, and she thrust herself at the door.

"Hurry up, Vic. This is a time-waster of note, and I have pasta sauce on the boil." His voice in her ears calmed her erratic heartbeat. Moving in the cumbersome suit didn't bother, not when anti-gravitational fighting had been part of Carne's training. In a tank, the chance of floating off was zero. She shuddered. Would Dieter fetch her if her tether snapped?

She caught the edge and mimicked his maneuver, tapping her heels at the last minute. The thud-thud reverberated up her legs when the boots pinned her to the outside of the ship.

"The longest part of this is the walking." He pointed with his nitro gun to the stern where plumes burned with bright light.

At each thud, she grew accustomed to the task of strolling with space around her, mostly by pretending it wasn't there. He recited his pasta recipe he hoped she'd like. Yeah, there had to be something on the intra on how to cook old school. Protein bars on a plate with hydro-gel in a glass was all her struggling brain could envision.

"Sometimes I have to suit up to repair a panel or exchange fuses some idiot engineer installed on the outside." He paused and gestured to the lumps of mustard yellow clinging to the side of the ship. She was so close to the engines, the sol heat dewed sweat on her brow, and the white plumes burned shapes into her retinae.

"How can you see?" She blinked to clear her tearing eyes.

He chuckled. "It's always the little things I forget. Computer, activate the sunvisor for Vic."

"Sunvisor activated."

When her visor tinted, she sighed. Gazing out to space, there was a sense of peace amid the lethal beauty. She didn't feel as alone as she thought she would, just as long as her boots stuck to the metal beneath her.

"Okay, on the count of three, hit the switch on the side and aim for the piles." Laughing, he called out three and fired.

She joined him, blasting the yellow lumps. They popped off like hydro-gel caps. The momentum launched them into space, toward the Lunar Base.

"They'll catch a ride on another ship." He stepped to the side and aimed at the next pile.

One by one, they cleared the itaya. It was satisfying work. No creature was harmed, and her relief at that meant she might not be the one to slaughter a pig when the time came.

CHAPTER SIXTEEN

VIC GIGGLED AS THE chickens swarmed her, bumping her with their additional appendages. More legs made sense. Last night, Leah made roasted chicken and salad. Vic had never tasted anything that good. Well, besides Dieter's pasta. Her raving drew a blush from Leah, though, at this point, Vic couldn't say whether it was from embarrassment or if their vendetta was ongoing.

Computer had awoken her to tend to her task. As soon as she unhooked the bag, the chickens gathered around her. Sprinkling the seed garnered a little breathing space. She hooked the bag and chose the next, the one with 'P' on it. The contents made her gag. Rotten food, something she wouldn't have wasted to begin with, had to be poured into the troughs. The cow bags were closest to them, marked with a 'C.' She stuck in her hand and pulled out pale-gold strands. A deep inhale filled her chest with...she couldn't say. There was something deeply organic about the smell, like sand, dead grass, sun, and dew.

"There's hydroponics just for the cows. Captain loves his cream and cheese."

Vic cast a grin over her shoulder. "Morning, Dieter. Thanks for my UV light."

He shrugged. "Did it while you were dockside." His fingers twitched as if he longed to ask about her unscheduled trip. Instead, he scooped a metal bucket off a shelf and strode to the farthest cow. He stroked her nose, taking the time to greet her before kneeling to place the bucket under the udders. "Come, Vic."

She mimicked his greeting, with an added scratch behind the cow's soft ear, then kneeled on the opposite side of Dieter. The cow twitched away from her, shuffling on her feet.

"Mm, seems I need to do this a few more times before Spots is comfortable with you. Watch my fingers." He wrapped his hand around an udder, and with a gentle tug, squeezed from top to bottom. A jet of white liquid hit the bucket's bottom. "Do this until you reach the black mark on the inside of the bucket. That's all we ask of them each day."

"All right, and what's this one called?" She rose and rubbed the cow's nose.

"Moo," he grinned.

She chuckled. "You named her, didn't you?"

"Yup." He carried the bucket to the door, expecting her to follow. "Captain said I could since it was my chore for a while."

"That was sweet of him."

"Sweet?" Dieter laughed. "Captain wouldn't give a damn if I named her Blessings, as long as she supplies his milk and cream. Hungry?"

"Starving." Vic checked the pens were properly shut, then hurried after him. "I could kill for a coffee."

"Same. Nikko's making breakfast so prepare for a feast: bacon, eggs, hashbrowns, mushrooms, and fried tomato." Dieter hummed as he lugged the bucket. It wasn't heavy but cumbersome. "We'll decant this in the kitchen, sol-ray the bucket, and return it to the pen after breakfast."

"Then what's your next task? What's mine?" She trailed him into the mess, the delicious aroma of coffee and bacon enticing her to savor each inhale. Grunt sat at the table, sipping black tea.

"You're with me as a new employee," Nikko answered as he cracked an egg into the pan. "Later, Tiny will show you how to make butter and cheese."

Vic bounced on her toes, excitement flooding her body with pre-battle adrenaline. "It's like I'm on a farm."

Nikko sliced a glance at her. His lips twitched before he lowered his gaze. "I'm happy you approve."

"I do. I'm like a kid in a tech store."

"Hey," Grunt called out, looking up from his tablet.

"Thanks for yesterday, Grunt. I owe you one." She sat on the bench beside him. "Victoria Har...Barnes pays her debts." *Shit, that was close.* She had to practice saying her new name.

"Excellent. My evil plan is working." He rubbed his hands together in fake glee. "Next time it's my turn to muck out the chickens..."

"Deal."

He grinned. "That was too easy. What's the catch?"

"There is none." She smiled at Dieter in thanks for the coffee he offered her. Taking the cup, she took a sip before placing it on the table before her. "Well..."

"I knew it." Grunt waved his hands. "Give it to me, woman."

She laughed. "Recipes. If I'm to cook, I need to learn how."

"Oh, I can have fun with that." Grunt laughed like the teenager he was, finding too much joy in his own sense of humor. "Cake anyone?"

"Cake?" Tiny hurried in, her hair unbound, and her cheeks flushed. "Am I late? What cake?"

Vic laughed. "It's my birthday, so Dieter's going to teach us how to make a cake." It was all lies. She'd seen an image depicting a multi-colored cylinder with tiny fireworks on top. Not that she'd ever tasted one.

Dieter met Vic's gaze. "I am?"

"Oh, how sweet of you, Deets." Tiny patted his shoulder.

He blushed and ducked his head. "Yeah, couldn't resist the urge to bake. What man can?"

"Idiots, the lot of you," Nikko grumbled, despite the warmth in his voice. He placed a plate of eggs and bacon on the table, then followed it with brown circles and dark gray bulbs.

"Isn't Leah joining us?" Vic shuffled along the bench to allow someone else to squeeze in.

"She's delivering the captain and Webb's meals." Nikko sat beside Vic, pressing his side to hers. Before she could say anything, a fried egg, two strips of bacon, a brown circle, and a pile of bulbs landed on her plate. "Toast?"

She blinked at Nikko. "I don't know."

"How the farg did you survive, Vic?" Grunt smeared butter on a golden square and slid it onto her plate.

"We had meals, I just don't know what went into them. Growing up was mostly hydro-gel."

"Can you use these?" Dieter waved his knife and fork, only to wince when Tiny jabbed him in the ribs.

Vic laughed. "I'm not uncivilized." She gathered said utensils and cut a piece off the egg. Not that she had eaten anything like this, but she had seen it served to Erv. "We had a white-gray glop."

"Boiled oats?" Tiny squeaked while scrunching her nose. Dieter bopped her on it with his forefinger. She blushed at his attention.

Vic scanned the table. Did no one see how Tiny felt about the man?

"We had slabs of what might have been reconstituted meat. Once a week, they served sugar buns." Shoving her forkful into her mouth, Vic groaned at the explosion of salt across her tongue. "Delicious." Her fingers trembled when she grabbed the circle and bit into it. "What is this? The crunch, the gooeyness?"

"A hashbrown, and these are mushrooms sauteed in butter." Grunt pointed with his knife.

Vic's moans filled the room as she devoured her first breakfast. At lunch and dinner last night, they had been as entertained.

When Leah strolled in, the laughter died, and everyone focused on their plates, as if they were guilty of fraternizing with the enemy. She sat next to Tiny and packed her plate.

"Where's Trent?" Vic asked before biting into a squidgy gray mushroom.

"On duty, manning the bridge. One of us must be on guard at all times." Nikko scooped a hashbrown and a spoonful of mushrooms onto Leah's plate. "It's what I'll be showing you after breakfast...once you've had a shower." His nose crinkled.

Tiny giggled. "I wasn't going to mention it, but you and Deets smell of cow."

"Oh." Vic placed her utensils beside her plate and sniffed her sleeve. The stench of Moo lingered. "Oops. I'll take a sol-bath before meeting you on the bridge?" At Nikko's nod, she wiggled off the bench. "Thanks for breakfast."

Rushing to her quarters, she left the door open while she stripped in front of the sol-bath, letting the plate beneath her feet spin as the rays scanned her. While basking in the UV light, she studied herself in the reflective surface, confirming her hair was still braided and hadn't yet begun to unravel. Not wanting to keep Nikko waiting, she threw on her uniform and jogged to the bridge, hoping they would have a heart-to-heart. It had been a dick move on his part to pretend to help her.

Trent rested his boots on the console, gripped a tablet in hand, and chuckled at a vid.

"Morning." She stepped into the room, then sidled to the right to lean against the bulkhead. There wasn't seating other than the chair in front of the console, which Trent occupied. She hoped she didn't need to learn the purpose of the acronyms beneath the many flickering buttons.

"Hey, Vic." He flicked his gaze at her but paused to appraise her from the boots to the tank top. "How was breakfast?" Without breaking eye contact with her breasts, he touched the tablet and slid it into the side pocket of his cargo pants.

"It was amazing." She beamed then frowned. "I'm sorry, should I have brought you a plate?"

"No worries. Someone will." He folded his legs and rose, prowling toward her.

Like she hadn't seen that done a million times. A kick to the knee, and a punch to the gut and throat would incapacitate him for good.

"If you value your life, Trent, I suggest you accept the no-sex rule and use your hand instead."

He winced and held up said hand as if in surrender. "Fair enough."

"Now that that's resolved..." Nikko strode onto the bridge and hitched his thumb at the door. "Leah's holding breakfast for you." Once Trent left, Nikko faced her. "Captain's a little old-fashioned."

"I gathered that, and it does minimize drama." Which put paid to her untried matchmaking skills with Dieter and Tiny. "What if two employees married?"

"Married?" Nikko's brows hit his hairline. "He might agree to that. Now, what's with the Vic Har-Barnes?"

She stilled, having hoped no one had picked up on her faux pas.

"Part of your fugitive persona?"

"Yes." She fluttered her eyelashes and swung out a hip as she'd seen Fortuna do for her fans. "All right, I'll tell you. I had a stage name, but when the emperor fell pregnant with my baby, I had to run, y'see."

Nikko's lips twitched. "Onto business." He tapped the chair, asking her to sit.

When she did, he rested his hands on her shoulders, pinning her in place as Erv had done for every meeting she had with Sebastian Carne. She squirmed in the chair.

"Any of these lights flash red, you call me or Grunt." Leaning over her, Nikko touched the wide screens running the length of the console. Billions of stars blinked in greeting. "If a red circle appears on here, call me." He spun the chair and forced her to meet his gaze. "If something flies past the screens, you hit this red button." He pointed to the massive rectangle button at the top of the console.

"Okay, so red is bad."

He grinned, softening his features into rugged attractiveness. "Yes. Any questions?"

She shook her head.

Trent returned, balancing a plate on his hands while reading from his tablet. He stumbled when he saw them, slipped around them, and waited for her to vacate the chair. She did so, jumping up and almost bumping into Nikko. Since when had she become this clumsy? Thankfully, she halted before she touched him. After Tiny's medical assessment, she needed a little space.

"With me, Vic." Nikko marched off the bridge and along the passage, taking turns randomly. Not wanting to have to ask the computer to direct her, she stuck to his tail. She would never live down getting lost. When she entered a room behind Nikko, the stench of old sweat filled her nostrils. She laughed, surprised to realize she had missed it.

"Let's see what you have." He stripped off his uniform jacket and hung it on a hook.

She did the same and met him in the middle of a five-by-five meter training mat. "You're not ready for this, Sarg." She raised her fists, rolled her weight onto her front foot, and winked at him.

He lunged and landed on his back.

She'd swept him off his feet by directing his momentum to where she wanted him. "We don't have to do this, y'know. Although, I do appreciate the exercise."

Each lunge, parry, punch, and duck sprawled him on the mat. His grunts became heavier, his resilience less enthusiastic. Not once did he manage to touch her.

"Where the farg did you learn this?" He wiped sweat from his brow with the hem of his shirt, exposing a lovely set of abs.

"A decade of training against the finest, Nikko." She fell into a defensive stance, her fists in front of her face, hoping to hide her grimace. This crew was slipping under her guard, getting her to reveal tidbits of who she was and what she had endured.

"How good are you?"

She shrugged. "Without breaking a sweat, I can kill. I choose not to."

"So you were going easy on us?" Grunt slipped into the gym and settled on a padded bench to watch them.

"Death isn't the only solution." She smiled. "It is often delicious to consider though, especially when someone wishes me harm."

"You're an assassin?" Grunt's eyes widened.

She laughed. "No."

Nikko rocked on his toes, forming fists as she did. "Then how do you know the captain's son?"

Everything within Vic stilled as realization dawned. "Ande?" A twang shot her as loneliness settled like a deep ache in her bones. If only she could hear his voice, but contacting him would alert Carne.

Nikko nodded.

"We trained together." Farg, so *that* was the connection. Ande had asked dear old dad to hire her. Or was there more to this? In all these years, when she had spoken of her pa, Ande had never once mentioned that he had a father or that said father was a Ring legend.

"Ande's as good as you?"

She shrugged. "Better with his strength and bulk."

Nikko struck, his punch hitting her chest. She stumbled back, not feeling anything, as if he had shoved her aside. *What the farg?*

"How much of you is cybernetics?" He huffed, shaking his hand.

"My arm and leg." Touching her chest, she gasped. Her fingers recognized the feel of armor, like Drafe's. Hurrying across the mat, she stopped an inch from the floor-to-ceiling mirror. A pearlescent shimmer rippled over her skin. As she rubbed her sternum, the armor faded to her normal skin before rippling into place again.

Facing Nikko, she burst forward, pausing in front of him. He blinked at her. "Punch me as hard as you can." She threw her arms out wide and waited.

"Are you sure?" His brows knitted even as he curled his fingers into a fist.

"My chest, please. Let's not bruise my face, shall we?"

He spread his thighs, pulled back his fist, and punched her. Again, the force pushed her back a few steps, but she'd felt nothing.

Closing her eyes, she listened to the incoherent whispers in the reaches of her mind. Screaming at them to remain there, she ran, ignoring Nikko calling her name. Tiny would know what was going on since she had taken a blood sample yesterday. Bursting into the med bay drew a yelp from the blind woman.

She clasped her chest, panting for breath. "Vic, you scared the shit out of me."

"Sorry, Tiny. Did you get the results from my bloodwork?" Every muscle in Vic tensed, waiting, ready to explode into action.

"Yeah, but they make no sense." She raised her face to the ceiling. "Computer, explain Vic's bloodwork results."

"Victoria Barnes's blood contains an overabundance of nanites. This is to be expected with her recent implants. However, these nanites are not decreasing in number and dying off as designed. In addition, an unknown organism has merged with them and may be the reason for the nanites' extended life."

"What?" Vic squeaked.

"There is no clear indication of how they entered your system. Removing them will be impossible since they have fused with your DNA," the computer continued in her monotone voice.

"What?" Vic slumped onto a bunker, gripping the metal railing.

"It is unusual. The nanites encourage your body's healing process and are integral to post-implantation. It now appears that they will remain indefinitely."

"Thank you, computer." *Farg.* Vic gazed at Tiny. "What doesn't make sense?"

"The existence of these organisms, Vic. When you enter a public area on the Lunar Base, a sterilization spray neutralizes all manner of bugs. Yours are...foreign. I can tell you that." She waved a plastic model of a worm. "They carry the memory cells we find in human brains."

"Right." That explanation didn't help. Vic drew in a ragged breath. "Am I dying?"

"No, they're not harming you. They're commensalistic since I can't see what they gain in this symbiosis. They're repairing minor damage to your liver and kidneys—the natural decay from a diet with insufficient hydration and nutrition."

So much for Carne's expensive medical team. "Okay, fine, great, but can this explain the shimmer?"

"The what?" Tiny furrowed her brow. "As in glitter? You're glowing?"

"Kind of. Nikko punched me, and I didn't feel it."

"Oh, dear." Tiny giggled. "That must've irritated him."

Vic hadn't checked his reaction, too focused on her Drafe-like armor. She would have to chat with Drafe. Excitement coiled in her stomach, and those whispers rose in a crescendo, as if urging her to reach out to him. He had a smart band, and if it was possible, perhaps she could hear his rasping voice again.

Pushing off the bed, Vic rose. "According to you, I'm well, and I don't need to panic."

"Yes, and I'll have to inform the captain." Tiny typed on a small console, then paused. "Only the captain. Medical results are considered confidential."

"Good to know." Vic liked that, when at Carne a yeast infection was open for discussion and ridicule.

"We are traveling to the best medical facility in the galaxy.... Well, past it." Tiny's hurried words sparked Vic's instincts. Why would they, an ice hauler, visit a medical facility? Unless they bought ice from the source.

"Thanks, Tiny. I'll find Sarg, and let him punch me again, as a peace offering for abandoning him on the training mat."

"Enjoy." Tiny waved at the bed even though Vic was at the door.

She strolled to the gym, slipped inside, and raised her hands as if she approached a rabid animal.

Nikko waited, his arms folded across his chest. "What the farg was that?"

"An expected issue with my nanites." She wasn't about to reveal that a little of Drafe had found a home in her. That was for Drafe's ears, though how she would reveal that with the fargen ship listening in was beyond her. "Go ahead, Sarg, punch me again." She smirked. "You know you want to."

CHAPTER SEVENTEEN

Year: 2219

Aboard the Aroagni.

DRAFE LEANED OVER THE holograph, tracing the pods' paths to the origin. The *Aroagni* circled Jupiter shrouded, not wanting other research or cargo vessels to spot them. The planet was truly a ball of gas. Nothing hovered close to its center or survived the gasses, and even though Ivoy planned to mine it, Drafe was nowhere closer to finding the source of the pods.

"Focus on the moons." Aehort paused beside him. "A few are inhabited by humans. One of them might have more than meets the eye."

"Like a secret base?" Drafe tapped the console and ordered a deeper scan of each moon as they traveled past it. He settled his gaze on the closest warrior. Awayar aac Caah Taed knew only of water and ice, his white hair and eyes blaring his origins. "Listen for communications not on the expected frequencies and crafts landing where they shouldn't. Send a shuttle to capture a pod. Do not open it."

"Acknowledged, Drafe Arrak."

Drafe straightened and rested his hip against the table. Something felt odd, the whispers of his symbiotes were quieter than usual.

"What bothers you, Drafe?" Aehort studied him. Though, what went on in his brilliant mind was far beyond Drafe's understanding.

"I cannot say." He closed his eyes and imagined himself on Qaldreth, the sunlight on his face and the hardpacked salt plains beneath his feet. On his hip hung the familiar weight of his water pouch, and in his hand was his father's sword.

"*Gevatia*, is this a cucooya?"

He lowered his gaze in his vision and smiled at Vic leaning against the tree. With suitable reverence, she cupped a blossom. She wore Qaldreth breeches and a tunic, and on her side was a water pouch marked with his symbol. More than this, she called him 'beloved.'

An electric charge shot up his arm, whipping him out of the vision. He blinked at his smart band. Bringing his wrist to his lips, he answered, "Meorri aac Drafe Arrak."

"Drafe?"

His breath froze in his lungs, and he grinned, too pleased to speak. Aehort nudged him out of his daze. "Yes, Vic."

"I...I was going to ask you something, but I can't put it into the right words." She paused. "It's good to hear your voice."

"You are well?" Foq, she better be, or else he would hunt her down and save her. Human medicine had to be primitive, although, the work done on her mechanical limbs was almost on par with Ivoyan technology.

"I'm fine. Enjoying my job, and the food's amazing." The joy traveling with her voice saturated his heart. "How is your...task going?"

"Frustrating, but I am determined to finish this." *Then find you*. He didn't say the words but hoped she heard them anyway.

"I can't wait."

Foq, this was worse. He ached to hold her, to bury his nose in her sun-drenched hair and kiss her soft lips.

"I'm sending you my medical results. I hope it helps with your decision. Implants can be good and bad and can carry *organisms* if not properly handled."

He frowned at his smart band. *Organisms? What decision?* "I look forward to reading it." *Why is she speaking in riddles? Is someone eavesdropping?* He cupped the band and faced Aehort. "Can we secure this connection?"

"Not at the moment." Aehort touched the console and tapped the buttons. "The weakness is on her side."

Foq. Drafe released his breath on a whoosh. "When and where will you be docking, Vic? I could meet you there."

"You can?" She laughed. "I don't know. Probably not for a long time. After all, I saw you days ago. Farg, it feels so distant." That last bit she whispered. "Did you get my file?"

He glanced at his smart band at the document flashing. "Yes. Thank you for sending it."

Then before she disconnected, she said, "I wish I was with you."

He wasn't sure he heard right but chose to believe he had. Before he could respond, she ended the call. He gritted his teeth, not liking how she'd left him with all these questions.

"She is not safe." Aehort gestured to the smart band. "Share the file."

Drafe did so while battling the urge to command the *Aroagni* to chart a course to her ship.

"Mm," Aehort hummed while he scanned her medical results. "I see."

Drafe narrowed on the document hovering in the middle of the galaxy model. It held jargon he couldn't understand. Facing Aehort, he waited, folding his arms across his chest to better control his barbaric impulses. His armor shimmered on and off, revealing his agitation. His woman wasn't safe, and that didn't sit well with him.

"She has your symbiotes."

"What?" Drafe slumped, splayed his hands on the table, and peered at the document. "How the foq did that happen?"

"You have to ask?" Aehort cackled as he pressed the call button. "Send a maed to the command center."

Drafe frowned. "What are you planning, Aehort?"

"If she has your symbiotes, then you have hers."

Drafe gasped and held his hand in front of him, twisting it to study it from all angles. "She has symbiotes?"

"The humans call them nanites, meant only to heal for a time. They have built-in self-destruct mechanisms that prevent them from overwhelming the body. Except hers aren't dying and have fused with your symbiotes."

"Healing?" Drafe withdrew his dagger from his belt, unsummoned his armor, and sliced his palm. The pain was negligible. Before his blood could breach the gap, his skin knitted together with an odd prickling sensation. *Foq.* He ran the dagger across his forearm, and again he healed without spilling a drop.

Nenn rushed in and waited.

Aehort nodded at him. "Take a sample of Drafe Arrak's blood. Test it extensively."

"Yes, Vizen Aehort Uz."

Sighing, Drafe held still while Nenn pressed a gun to his neck. It pinched for a moment. Nenn studied the clear blood in the capsule, then rushed out.

Drafe couldn't see the point. "This will only confirm it, Aehort."

"Yes, but perhaps we can neutralize her nanites in you, but your symbiotes cannot be extracted from her. As I said, Drafe, she is yours."

Drafe hid how his mind reeled. What flooded him with warmth was that she had called him and sought his guidance. She had no idea what this meant to him, that she had lowered her pride, her self-reliance, and asked for his help. Without hesitation, he would offer his aid. For she had a part of him in her and, he hoped, left a piece of her in him.

CHAPTER EIGHTEEN

Year: 2219

Mula Pesada

BY THE SIXTH DAY, Vic had managed to milk Moo without a problem. Handling the udders, or as she liked to call them, elongated nipples, was trickier. All it had taken was crooned compliments while she stroked Moo's ear. Now, after many attempts, she waddled down the passage to the mess with a full bucket.

"You did it?" Dieter cheered.

"Sure did. Moo's a sweet cow." Vic placed the bucket on the counter beside the butter tub. She flicked a finger through the lump of butter Tiny had shown her how to make. While she licked the yellow goodness, she hoped they didn't tackle cheese next. Mastering making that delicacy was far harder with its many steps.

Leah glared at her while stirring the eggs Vic had collected that morning. Scrambled eggs and jacks were on the menu. Even though Grunt, Tiny, and Trent let Vic hover while they cooked, Leah hadn't once allowed her in the mess. The bandage was off, and the stitches had faded, but Leah cradled her hand as if it bothered her.

Not that Vic would apologize. She hadn't survived by going around saying, 'sorry, this will hurt.' "Need anything? More eggs?"

"Parsley," Leah clipped.

Vic jerked back and sprinted down the passage to hydroponics, happy to visit it. She couldn't explain how much she loved her job. The lab held the most accumulated water she had seen in her life. Scanning the plants, she searched for the label 'Parsley,' then plucked a few leaves like Tiny had shown her.

Vic's braid whipped from side-to-side when she jogged to the mess. She placed the gathered leaves beside Leah. Hesitating, Vic half-expected the woman to chase her away. When she didn't glance her way, Vic grabbed a coffee instead.

"What are those?" She gestured to the golden circles between sips of smoky goodness. Farg, she was addicted and happy to be.

"Jacks, made from ground flour, eggs, and milk." Leah met her gaze as she flipped one. "Pinch of salt, some sugar, and a rising agent."

"They smell incredible." Vic drew in a deep breath. "The sugar sweetens the air."

Leah offered a stiff smile. "Set out the plates. I'm sure the crew will be here soon."

Vic did as asked, eager to eat. While she placed a fork to the left of each plate, and a knife to the right, she snuck glances at Leah. Her friendliness had Vic on the backfoot. Zebras didn't change their stripes, or so the saying went.

With his nose buried in his tablet, Grunt barreled in, almost colliding with Vic. He whispered an apology and settled onto the bench. All had their spots, and Vic had inadvertently stolen Leah's at the first breakfast. Now, Vic sat next to Tiny and on the edge of the bench. As far as Vic was concerned, Leah could squeeze between Grunt and Nikko until doomsday.

"Tomorrow, we reach Europa." Trent bounded in, sliding into Nikko's spot since he was manning the bridge. "Can't wait to show you the ropes, Vic."

"A moon?" She rose to order him an orange juice—his preference.

"Yup, and an endless source of ice. We can't mine it fast enough." He grinned when she offered him the glass.

"Why aren't there more ice haulers?" She drained her coffee and rose to pour another.

"An unexpected storm on Jupiter impacted the haulers positioned on Europa at the time, cutting the numbers in half. They're frozen relics on the surface." Leah scooped scrambled eggs onto each plate, followed by stacks of jacks.

"Did I miss it?" Dieter strode in with Tiny close on his heels.

"Miss what?" Vic asked, then bit into the jack. She groaned, closing her eyes to savor the doughy sweetness.

"That." Leah laughed.

Vic paused, her mouth gaping on the verge of taking another bite. "Oh. I'm so sorry. I can eat in my room—"

"And we miss out on your reactions? Nope." Leah squeezed between Trent and Grunt.

"Did you want a coffee, Leah?" While chewing on a jack, Vic hitched her thumb at the vendor.

"Please, black with sugar."

"Mine and Tiny's are the same as yours," Dieter called out, throwing an arm across Tiny's shoulders for a hug. Her cheeks flushed pink again.

With her gaze resting on Tiny, Vic swapped mugs as the vendor poured the coffees.

She served the mugs, then joined the crew, diving into her scrambled eggs with gusto. After this, she planned to teach Tiny defensive strikes. Then Dieter would fetch Vic to, at last, show her the engine room. Daily, she went out on the ship with him to check panels, fuses, or a leaking seal. Today, she would go alone because he had to prep the ice riggers.

She was a little nervous, but the butterflies in her stomach weren't half as bad as her debut Ring match. Nikko told her to nap in the afternoon since her first bridge duty was that evening while everyone slept. Her life was settling into one of relaxation, laughter, and good food.

Still, in the quiet hours alone in her quarters, she longed for arms to hold her, cradling her against his obsidian chest. Silly, that's what she was. She'd met and fucked Drafe in a day. To harbor any affection for him was crazy.

Then there were the dreams, of deserts, of the sweltering salt plains, of a sky with two suns. When she awoke, the fragrance of morning dew and warm sand filled her senses, as if she recalled memories. No way would she mention her madness to Tiny, not when endless dunes reminded her of home.

Rising, she stacked her plate into the washer. Sol-rays would clean the dishes, leaving whoever cooked next to pack them away. She was scheduled to do breakfast next, with the crew thinking frying shouldn't be too hard. Farg, she hoped so.

"Meet you in five, Tiny?" Vic squeezed her shoulder.

Tiny nodded, her purple curls bouncing. All looked at her, curious as to the reason behind the meet-up. "I messed up a test, so Vic agreed to let me scan her again."

At that, the conversation renewed.

In the gym, Vic climbed onto a suspended machine that supposedly mimicked swimming. It gripped her around the waist and allowed her to propel herself forward. It had taken her an hour to figure out what exercises worked, not that she had any idea if she was doing them right. Still, she loved the sense of freedom it gave her, as if gravity no longer limited her movements.

Dieter called to her, his face raised. "What's going on? Tiny never fargs up."

"Just teaching her a few defensive moves, Deets."

He winced. "She's blind. You know that, right?"

"Even more reason to help her." Vic rolled onto her stomach to gaze at him while she 'swam' in what the computer termed 'froglike.' She had to scour the intra to find out what a frog was—a cute little creature with its big eyes and long tongue.

"If you hurt her..."

"You don't care for her, Deets. She's just another crew member to you. One day, a man's going to see what a treasure she is and lure her away from the *Mula Pesada*."

"The farg he will." He paused mid-rant. "What man? She hides in her med bay."

"Because she knows it well. Move one thing out of place, and she'll bump into it." Spinning down until her feet touched the mat, Vic met his gaze. "She's not happy. Yeah, I know, I'm an outsider, but I see more than you do stuck in a familiar environment with the same faces. She's lonely, Deets."

"Don't call me that."

Vic chuckled. "I can call you anything I damn well please, and there's nothing you can do about it. Now, as I see it, you can help me bring her out of her shell and find her a good man to love her. For that, you need to step aside."

He paced, his fingers twitching when he ran them through his hair.

"Oh, am I bothering?" Tiny stepped into the room but no farther.

He spun and gathered her hands, leading her to the center of the mat. "Are you sure you want to do this?"

"Yes. I'm an easy target. It's why I don't leave when we dock."

He scowled. "I can protect you."

She smiled and cupped his cheek. "What happens when you want to find companionship? Why would I play the third wheel?" She grimaced but lifted her chin. "I need affection too, Dieter." She offered him her back and faced Vic. He raised his hands as if to stop her, then dropped them by his side. "Shall we, Vic?"

"Sure." She unclipped the machine, hating the drag of the ship's artificial gravity after the sensation of weightlessness. "What I'll teach you can only be done if they touch you." She clasped Tiny's wrist. "I have you, now, try and get away."

No matter what Tiny did, Vic held firm. The woman's struggles had no impact on Vic's footing or grip.

"Okay, stop." Vic squeezed. "Register where my thumb is. Can you feel it?"

Tiny nodded.

"Good, now, instead of yanking, curl your wrist inward and tug down."

When her wrist slipped free, Tiny squealed, swaying her hips in a happy dance. Dieter chuckled, having chosen to stay and watch, as Vic had hoped.

"Now, I'm going to breach your space. Don't be alarmed. Register where my breath is, that will tell you the location of my face." Vic crowded Tiny, almost touching her from chest to knees.

"I sense your breath. Your chin is about here." She touched Vic's jaw.

"Good. Can you guess the location of my upper arms?"

Tiny thrust out her hands and caught Vic's arms.

"Great, you're doing well. Slowly, lift your knee."

Struggling to balance on one foot, Tiny wobbled.

"Tighten your grip on my arms. Use me as leverage." Vic grinned. "Raise your knee."

Tiny did so, nudging Vic's thigh.

"Good. When someone tries something you don't like, do that, and knee them in the groin. It hurts just as bad for a woman. Leap back though, because they will double over." With a shove to her chest, Tiny stumbled and fell, landing on her ass with a gasp.

"What the farg, Vic?" Dieter was beside Tiny, his hands hovering over her, not sure where to touch.

Vic folded her arms across her chest, trying not to smirk. "She could be bumped while crossing a bar, Deets."

"Vic's right." Tiny reached out to sense her changed surroundings and encountered his hands, arms, shoulders, and neck. She clung to him while she rocked onto her knees, her face in line with his, and her lips but a breath away from his chin.

"Why the farg would she go to a bar? The men there are assholes." Dieter leaped to his feet and scooped Tiny into his arms. "Stop giving her these ideas, Vic. You're done. This is...done."

Smirking, Vic waited until Dieter's footsteps faded, wishing she could eavesdrop on the conversation to follow. She'd been right. He *did* care. The good old jealousy trick had worked.

Dusting her hands, she sauntered out of the gym to the airlock. Time to get to the boring part of the day. She chuckled. Peaceful was what she meant. After suiting up, she holstered her blaster, tucked an all-tool into her belt, and pressed the button. "Computer, activate tether."

"Tether activated, Vic." The thump on her back confirmed the successful attachment.

She vaulted out, caught the edge of the door, and clicked her heels, landing with a gentle thud-thud before striding to the bow of the ship. Each inch by quadrant had to be checked. Some days, when she finished early, she'd find a ledge to sit on and stare into the endless ocean of stars.

Today, she tightened a loose panel, exchanged a few fuses, and informed the computer of a busted light. Then she squatted and ran her gaze across the galaxies. There was something timeless about it all. She was but a speck of dust and as meaningless. Often ships traveled near enough for her to read their branding. Unless it was military, then a moving void marked their passing.

This ship was closer than usual, painted a bright red instead of sleek gray. When the Carne logo blazoned, she gasped and snapped to her magnetized feet. Nikko was manning the bridge, surely he wouldn't ping Carne in greeting? She leaped across the *Mula Pesada's* side, sticking to the shadows while aiming for the airlock. Adrenaline and the deafening roar of panic masked the fear of her boots not sticking.

"Computer, patch me through to Nikko." She huffed as she tried to jump farther, her momentum hindered by the catch and release of her boots and the tether whipping behind her.

"Patch complete."

As she rounded the aft, Nikko answered, "What's up, Vic?"

"We have a not-so-nice ship passing by. Don't ping it, don't hail it, just let it fly by."

Nikko paused. "Is it military?"

She hesitated. Why would Nikko worry about a military vessel? "Worse. It's Carne."

"So? They often do pleasure cruises to the moons of Jupiter." He laughed, but it sounded odd, as if he was trying for casual. "Besides, if we don't ping them, they might think it curious."

She winced. "What do you normally do?"

"Ping away."

"Farg, first get Grunt to hide my details and life marker, Nikko. I'm on my way and will explain it all." She slipped into the airlock and hit the depressurize button, waiting those precious seconds for the door to seal and air to return. As soon as she could, she unclipped the tether, flipped her visor back, and ran.

"Am I hidden?" she asked the second she careened onto the bridge.

"Yup, now spill." Nikko leaned his ass on the console and folded his arms across his chest.

She tugged off the helmet. "I'm Victorious, former champion of the Carne Ring."

Nikko scoffed.

"Picture me with red hair and eyes." She waved a gloved hand across her face. "Whether you believe me or not, it doesn't matter. They wanted me to serve more time. I refused."

"If what you claim is true, you won the deca-match and your freedom."

She had been so naïve, believing that was all she needed to do. "If I owe them, I serve."

"What debt could you have incurred?" He straddled the chair and rested his arms along the back, spinning it side-to-side as if she was telling him an entertaining story.

"They caused an accident that took my arm and leg, then replaced both with cybernetics. State of the art, so expensive that there was no way I would ever be able to repay them."

He paused in mid-swing and ran his gaze over her. "What did you do, Vic? What aren't you telling me?"

"I may have pretended to kill their representative." She shrugged, remembering peering out the shattered window to the balcony below. The poor man's legs were twisted into odd angles.

"Farg, you're not kidding, are you?" Nikko tapped on the console, summoning past arena wins. Her face dominated the screens, confirming her words. Swearing a blue streak, he slammed his fist into his palm. "What the farg? I should've been told." He glanced at her, his expression hardening. "You were right to warn me. We don't want trouble with Carne." He worked the keys—their colors lighting like a fireworks display. "We got your back, Vic." He tossed a tight smile her way, though, not quite meeting her gaze. "Says here," he tapped the console, "you found a broken light. Can't have that. Best fix it, before Dieter shows you how to work the ice riggers." Nikko hitched his thumb to the outside of the ship. "Once you've mastered the riggers, you can spend the day as you see fit."

Relief soaked her, and she allowed her shoulders to slump.

"I'm just going to have a little chat with the captain," he gritted out.

She grabbed her helmet. "Thanks, Sarg, for listening and saving my ass." If he lied about hiding her and Carne boarded the *Mula Pesada*, she'd be ready.

"Anytime," he called, his focus once more on the console.

Striding to the storeroom, she hummed a jaunty tune that might have been Ande's theme song at one point. She found the required light fixture and returned to the airlock. Clutching the part between her thighs, she checked the oxygen in her suit, clipped the helmet in place, and slid the visor closed. Once the computer attached the tether, she smacked the button to open the door. Out on the ship, she strolled to the light and replaced it. With the broken part in hand, she took giant steps, leaping across the back of the ship to the aft. She was eager to learn about riggers, imagining them to be like a forklift meets a crane. Red arrows marked the location of the airlock. Catching the tether in hand, she swung, using it to launch herself over the edge of the ship and into the airlock.

Except when she vaulted off, a tug across her back jarred her, and a sickening sense of dread poured ice through her veins. Glancing over her shoulder, she gaped at the retracting tether while she traveled out to space, past the ship, and the gaping maw of the airlock.

"Computer, emergency." Her panting peppered the silence. "Farg, Nikko, Dieter, someone?" With a scream, she tried to slow her trajectory, scrambling or swimming like a frog. A frenzied laugh rose to choke her. "A week on the job, I die by accident?"

Or was it? Why would this happen after she revealed who she was to Nikko? Here she'd hoped he'd forgiven her for how they'd met, put it behind them. Farg it, she should have known better. It was too late for recriminations. Hindsight more than kicked her ass. The box-like ship in its rust metals grew smaller the farther away she traveled. Not even Carne's ship was in sight. At least she was close to the shipping lanes, right?

She slapped her wrist, hoping to activate the smart band through the thick suit. "Drafe?"

Silence.

She swallowed a sob, then forced herself to calm. Wasting oxygen was foolish. Tiny or Dieter would notice she was missing. *Farg. Farg. Farg.* She should have stayed with Drafe and let the *Mula Pesada* leave Lunar Base. Another wave of tears leaked, forming droplets to float away then splatter against her visor. The blurring of her vision urged her to wail at the unfairness of it all.

She'd always believed she was a survivor. Never had she thought she would die by asphyxiation.

Closing her eyes, she quietened her breathing, heartbeat, and riotous emotions. Someone would find her. They had to. She refused to die this way.

CHAPTER NINETEEN

Year: 2219

Aboard the Aroagni.

DRAFE SWUNG HIS LEGS off the bed, rested his elbows on his knees, and rubbed his face. Exhaustion remained, sinking through his spine until all he longed to do was sleep. Rest was elusive. Whenever he closed his eyes, he tested the bond between him and Vic, whether the symbiotes shared as they did with an Ivoyan. A few emotions trickled through, the strongest being happiness. Without the medical minds on Ivoy and the guidance of the Q.C.C., he wasn't sure what to expect from this... Osnir help him, he didn't know what to call it. Some would consider it an abomination. What mattered to him was the how, why, and if it would harm a human.

If he managed to get Vic to Ivoy, would they treat her like a specimen to be studied? Her life was meaningless if the anomaly she was served the greater good. He needed to find her, to seclude her on Qaldreth. The warrior in him wanted her safe. As a male, he ached to hold her, as if having her in his arms would bring him the peace he sought.

Pushing off the bed, he crossed to the shower, hoping the hot water would soothe the tension in his shoulders. Being able to use water as if it wasn't a precious resource hadn't changed decades of caution. Three minutes was all he allowed himself. He closed his eyes for the jet of soap, then the rinse before the timer shut off the spray. A blast of air dried him.

Clipping boots on and summoning his armor, he left his quarters and strolled to the galley, eager for tulsig or the Ivoyan version of it. None compared to Larya's, though.

He paused at finding Ulvus enjoying an early breakfast. The male arched a brow mid-bite. Drafe crossed to the replicate and ordered a plate of tulsig. While he waited, he poured a jar of water.

With both in hand, he slid onto the bench at the same table. "Morning."

Ulvus didn't say a word but tapped his plate with his regrown hand.

Drafe shrugged and bit into a tulsig cake, savoring the pseudo-saltiness.

Ulvus leaned back and sipped his water. Smacking his lips, he forced a smile. "Rumor has it, you mated with a human."

Mated? Perhaps, Drafe had. Qaldreth warriors dreamed of returning home to find someone from their tribes. No female at his village, or those the hunting parties visited, had tempted him. Mating required the successful transference of symbiotes, which meant... He grinned. As Aehort had said, Vic was his.

"Unconfirmed at this time." He finished his cake and reached for another.

Ulvus's face hardened as he pursed his lips. "I would ensure it's a no. Meorri do not dilute our bloodlines."

"Oh?' Drafe chuckled. "Who will you mate when we return home?" He could count the available females on one hand.

"A weakling from the Ki'irinzi Mountains is preferable to a lesser species."

Drafe laughed. There was nothing lesser about Vic. Nor did he mention that the female to choose Ulvus for a mate was a fool. Then again, his family did have the oldest symbiotes.

"I cannot recall you being this entertaining, Ulvus."

The male growled and slammed down his jar. "This is no joking matter. The reputation of our tribe is at stake. The symbiotes remember."

"That they do. If you had our tribe at heart, you would not have stolen my water pouch." Drafe licked his thumb and reached for his jar. "The symbiotes do remember, Ulvus Sava."

"Kreta curse your arrogance, Drafe."

Drafe grinned. "Osnir protects me. Perhaps you serve the wrong god?"

Ulvus leaped to his feet and stormed off.

Appearing unphased, Drafe devoured his last cake. Dread or anticipation burned in his gut. His knee bounced, and his symbiotes barreled along his veins. An event was coming, one he needed to pay attention to, whatever it was.

"Good, you are awake." Gusin grinned as he strode into the galley. He hitched a thumb behind him. "What is wrong with Ulvus?"

"Many things." Drafe glanced at Zuphayr aac Gusin Taed with his shocking blue-lilac hair and eyes. From the sky tribe, against a pale obsidian skin, they were a striking tribe to behold.

"Well, Caah and Vaen are returning with a pod." Gusin shuffled from foot-to-foot as he waited for his food, a white gooey substance eaten with a scooped utensil.

"Excellent." Drafe closed his eyes and conveyed with emotion to Aehort that it was time. Pushing off the bench, he slapped Gusin on the shoulder. "Man the *Aroagni*. Caah will be traveling to the chosen site."

Gusin nodded, carrying his bowl to the table.

Drafe strode to the bay, patting his stomach.

"Good morning," Aehort glided into the passage. "Today will be momentous for you, Drafe Arrak."

He gazed at Aehort, hoping for a little more insight. His uz continued without saying another word or conveying across their bond an emotion Drafe could understand.

The shuttle, sleek and as organic as all Ivoyan crafts, skimmed into the bay, carrying the captured pod. Caah leaped out as soon as the door opened.

Vaen trailed him. "Took some skill to capture it."

"I masked its beacon as soon as Vaen guided it inside." Caah grinned, gripping Vaen's forearm. "A task well done."

"Good. Our destination is a dwarf planet the humans call Ceres." Drafe nudged his chin, and his males climbed into the powering down shuttle. Aehort glided across the bay and stepped inside, the high ceilings of the Ivoyan shuttle more than capable of handling his height.

"Ceres?" Vaen raised a brow as he and Caah returned to the shuttle, with Caah assuming the pilot's seat.

"A rock with massive craters. Humans mine it for water, but the site we chose is far removed from the nearest colony." Drafe ran his hand over the dull, gray pod that was nothing more than a tube. Resting on a hoverbed, once they landed, maneuvering it would be easy. That was smart thinking on his males' part.

The door shut a second before Caah piloted the shuttle out of the bay. Spreading his legs, Drafe clasped his hands behind his back and watched the space whizz past the front screens. Aehort sat on a mounted chair, staring at the pod, his wide mouth pursed in displeasure.

Minutes later, they descended and touched down on a marbled-gray landscape. With a tap to their throats, they activated their shields and filed out of the shuttle. Vaen directed the hovering pod meters away from the shuttle. All five of them studied it.

"The last one detonated after a few hours of breaking the seal." Drafe met each male's gaze through his shield. The shimmer was slight, not hindering his ability to see. The air trapped between him and the thin shield would last no more than two hours. They didn't have much time.

"Work fast. Gather what information you can, and do not disturb me." Aehort extended his arm to hold his palm above the capsule, his eyes rolling back.

Drafe gestured to Vaen to pry open the pod. He held his breath when the lid edged up. With a shove from him and Caah, it slid off, revealing the corpse of a woman. Drafe frowned. He'd expected it to be a man, as per the last time. Drawing near, he studied her unmottled skin carrying a tinge of gray. She hadn't started to decay yet.

"Mm," Aehort hummed. "She endured great pain." He winced. "Even in death, her cries for mercy fall on muted ears."

"Her body has been enhanced." Nenn scanned her, holding his arm over the gaping pod. "Every inch, including her organs has been altered. What remained human was removed."

Caah frowned, the flop of his white hair ruffling his shield. "I don't like this. Some of her enhancements have been stripped from her." He gripped the side of the pod, careful not to touch anything but the edge. "The pod has been fitted with an explosive device. I would need to remove it to study it." He tapped the holographs on the model shining from his arm. "If I hazard a guess, once the sealed pod is opened, there is a time limit to reseal it before it explodes."

Drafe gritted his teeth at the logic of it and the arrogance of the Ivoy and Qaldreth not to test for explosives. "That makes sense. If they have to open a pod, they need a bypass."

"They expect these pods to be destroyed upon impact." With shielded fingers, Vaen caught a lock of her brown hair, as if he tested the texture of it. Drafe had done the same when he first met Vic, relishing the softness of her hair. "Why do this? Why not burn or bury the bodies?"

At Vaen's words, they spun as one to Aehort still in an Ivoyan trance, all hoping the Ivoy would answer or complete his assessment.

"Burying would require soft soil, a mine, or cavern." Nenn pinched his lips, his red hair rising and falling the faster he typed. "They would need immense fuel reserves."

"This close to Jupiter?" Drafe waved his hand at the looming giant. Nenn shrugged and deactivated his arm.

"Hydrogen gas is volatile, and mining it would be hazardous." Caah as a tech expert, a Taed, traced a thin line across the woman's skin.

Drafe's symbiotes rippled in alarm. He leaped across to study the crisscrossing scars. "What the foq?" He'd seen those before. How was Vic tied to this? He closed his eyes, willing his racing heart to calm. There had to be a logical explanation.

"Place the sensors, Caah. Let us have done with this rock." Vaen scanned the surrounding hills. "We have an Ivoyan in the open."

Drafe grimaced. "We wait for Aehort Uz. Spread out." His males obeyed, halting ten meters away in perfect synchronicity. Drafe remained by Aehort's side as he should have done with Luharp Vadril Ot.

Time passed, the silence calming, yet his symbiotes leaped and bounced, as if warning him of impending danger. He clenched his fists, willing to endure all manner of pain to protect Aehort. Having failed the Ivoyans, he wouldn't do so again.

His males were better trained, remaining still with only their heads turning from side-to-side as they scanned the horizon.

Aehort gasped, stumbled back, then spun on his heel and marched to the shuttle. Drafe's males closed in. He waited until the last male stepped inside before he shut the door on the pod and this desolate gray rock.

"Caah Taed, hurry." The steel in Aehort's voice straightened Drafe's spine. He met the Ivoyan's gaze, waiting for something to cross their bond, something more than a deep-seated urgency.

"What is it, Aehort?" Instead of answering Drafe, Aehort shook his head.

Frowning, Drafe focused on their bond until the intense dread became his, like a solid weight in the pit of his stomach. The more he assessed the symbiotes' reaction, the more it didn't flow from Aehort. Sadness and longing leaked through. Vic was in danger.

Drafe tapped his smart band and whispered her name. The shuttle's droning engines and the muttering between his males highlighted the silence from her.

"Drafe Arrak, we have a problem."

Drafe touched the implant in his neck. "What is it, Gusin?"

Aehort slumped, his skin fading from amber to orange. "It has begun."

Foq. Luharp Vadril Ot had been as secretive with his motives. Drafe should have expected the same from an uz. Ivoy was Ivoy.

"We have collected a stranded human." Gusin hesitated. "Ulvus Sava intends to interrogate."

"Foq." Leaving anyone in Ulvus's hands would be murder. "Caah, get us back now." Drafe lunged to the front of the shuttle, slamming his hand into the power lever. The shuttle shot forward, the full-pulsed engines bringing it in hot.

Caah's fingers flew across the console, the male laughing as he steered the shuttle with admirable skill.

"The bay is prepped for landing. Ulvus Sava has the human trapped near the airlock."

"I will return to my quarters." Aehort rose to his four-toed feet. "No escort is needed."

The shuttle tinkled when Drafe disembarked. He didn't spare it a glance. Instead, he bolted. All knew the wickedness of Kreta lurking in Ulvus's mind.

Drafe sprinted around the corner and into the airlock prep room, then skidded to a halt. He gaped, disbelieving his eyes.

Chapter Twenty

Year: 2219

Aboard an alien ship.

VIC SQUEEZED HER EYES shut. With space laid before her like an endless graveyard, she couldn't bear to look at it. Nothing whizzed past, no matter how she squinted or glared until her eyes watered. Her suit beeped the second warning. Across her visor flashed the quarter marker. Twenty-five percent of the oxygen remained. It took all her control and discipline to calm her breathing.

Every ten minutes, she tried calling out, hoping someone would pick up her frequency. Hell, she'd face down Carne if it meant she lived.

She wanted to snort at her stupidity. In the vastness of space, she was but an infinitesimal speck.

"Drafe," she whispered, letting a tear slide free. Sparkling like a diamond, it floated in front of her and collided with her hair, darkening the wayward strands. Exhaustion bombarded her mind. She was so tired of staying calm, of surviving, of succeeding despite the odds. If she drifted off to sleep, could she die without waking? Not that death had scared her before, but she hadn't been this alone. Ande was on the outskirts, watching and waiting, ready to bolster her flagging spirits, to rush her to medical if needed.

Another tear slipped free.

She had wanted her freedom, but never like this and at this cost. Well, she was free now. A hysterical bark of laughter escaped her, but she tamped it down, not willing to waste the oxygen. If she survived this, by some incredible miracle, she would return to *Mula Pesada* and fargen kill everyone. Well, maybe not Grunt, Dieter, and Tiny, but the rest of them would die a slow, torturous death.

Squeezing her eyes shut again, she tried to roll over. Nope, she had nothing to push against. This was the view she would die with. She breathed in and exhaled slowly. What she should have done was kick Pa off the farm and harvest sol. Out on the ocean beds, she would have spotted visitors from miles away.

No, space had offered the freedom she had so desperately needed. Love might have blossomed with Drafe if she'd been afforded the chance to find out. Sorrow, as she well knew, was like a thick blanket: hot, wet, heavy, sucking on her heart, soul, and her ability to think.

Since the fifty percent oxygen beep, she'd studied her situation from all angles. Without access to communication, she couldn't call for help. Nor could she slow her trajectory. The last time she had tried had spun her out of control, 'landing' her on her back. Jupiter loomed to her right, so large it appeared close enough to touch. To her left was the Kuiper Belt.

Would her corpse be pulled into orbit around Jupiter, would she splat on a moon or an asteroid? Millions of years from now, an advanced species would run tests on her and assume humans had mechanical parts. They'd call her by the name imprinted on her titanium bones: Carne.

She splayed out her arms and legs, as if she floated on the surface of an ocean, swept away by the tidal currents. She'd imagined so many times what that must have felt like. Some training vids had touched on how-not-to-drown. Living on a dried-out sea bed, the irony of it had tickled her sense of humor.

Just like that, she drifted to sleep, lulled by the beauty of uncharted galaxies and twinkling lights.

A beep jerked her awake.

Ten percent oxygen remained. The letters flashed red.

She closed her eyes again, unable to deactivate the irritating message.

"I know. Stupid suit," she muttered. "Farg off."

Another beep intruded on her snooze. *Five percent oxygen remained. Replace canister now.* "Sure. Let me take the spare one out of my pocket. Oh, wait, it's in my other pants." Drawing in a calming breath, she tried one more time. "Mayday, mayday, woman adrift, taking the scenic route around...fargen space."

Right, sure, that worked. Look, a ship. Oh, wait, no, more stars. She giggled then pinched her lips. Laughter bubbled in her chest as the tears rolled free.

"Ande, I wish I told you. You're the family I always wanted."

She cried, drenching her visor and saving her from the darkness smothering her.

"Drafe, you had such promise. I miss you, like a piece of my soul had crossed this endless void to you." Her chest swelled with emotion, and something rippled along her skin. Visions of worlds and people she didn't know flitted across her mind. They told stories she'd never have the time to sift through.

A shadow traveled from the bottom of the visor to the top, engulfing her in black. Death wasn't what she'd expected. Most spoke of a white tunnel calling her to pure love and light. Perhaps this was hell, a place reserved for killers, haters, and those who defrauded on their taxes. Exhaling, she arched, offering herself to the shadow and the gentle nudge, as her life left her body.

She hit something hard, shooting a bolt of agony from the back of her head to her fingertips.

What the farg? She opened her eyes and squinted at the distorted faces filling her vision along with the fargen message warning her that two percent of her oxygen remained. The squiggly species were demons? She laughed. No wonder they tormented humans, who were, as a whole, prettier. Also, hell lacked fire and color in general. Gray geometric shapes marked the ceiling high above. Lights flickered in blue.

"Is it human?" The words were in English.

She grinned. Good. Spending eternity trying to get a demon to understand her was her definition of hell.

"Yes. Open the visor." Fingers covered her face and flipped the visor back.

Fresh air cooled the tears on her cheeks. She blinked at the faces, all with obsidian skin and brightly colored hair flowing down their backs. Brown, green, blue, and black matched their eyes, for the most part. Farg. Did her version of demons look like Drafe dipped in a kaleidoscope of hair dyes?

"A female." A man with blue hair and eyes smiled at her. "Welcome to the Ivoyan ship, *Aroagni.*"

He held out his hand, but she stared at it. This was insane. She'd gone and lost her mind, something she hadn't anticipated. Maybe she was re-inhaling carbon dioxide, triggering hallucinations. The man dropped his hand, a frown knitting his brow.

"Juunn, take care of our guest. I need to check on the shuttle." The blue-man jogged through a door, disappearing.

Juunn, the green-haired man, crouched beside her, his eyes glowing like brilliant peridots. "You are safe. We mean you no harm."

She chuckled. Now that was funny. They wouldn't harm her. She would make fargen sure of that. Scrambling to her feet had them stepping back. She unclipped the helmet and tossed it aside, relishing the satisfying thunk as it landed on the metallic floor. When she climbed out of her suit amid snaps and zips, it was under their vigilance.

"What does it matter if you harm me? I'm dead, after all." Now that she was free to move, she tapped her chin while studying them. "Or will I bleed in hell?" She had moments ago been in pain, so bleeding was a possibility.

"She has lost her mind," a black-haired man growled. He gripped his blaster. "I say we kill her. Whatever she has could be contagious."

Kill her? When she was dead already? Maybe she had to fight her way to heaven? She nodded. That would be the most probable. "Try it, big boy." She grinned, raising her fists in front of her as if she could dodge a blaster shot. A tingle raced across her skin as it hardened then shimmered like armor. Right, Drafe's gift to her. She wiggled her nose, willing her silly tears to fade. All her hope for a future with him was gone. She'd wasted that opportunity for a position on the *Mula Pesada*. What a fool she'd been.

"This is nonsense, Ulvus. She is a guest." Brown rested his hand on Ulvus's shoulder.

"She could explode, Igar. What do we know." Ulvus glared at her with yellow eyes so like Drafe's.

The moment Ulvus reached for his blaster, she struck, taking him to the grated floor. Juunn and Igar jumped back, then lunged forward when Ulvus groaned.

She tutted. "Oh, no, you don't. Come closer, and I *will* kill him." She wiggled her foot pinned to his throat, barely able to resist his squirming attempts to rise.

Igar held up his hands. "We mean you no harm. Ulvus was jesting. He would never have killed you."

Ulvus garbled words, but the fury in his pale-yellow eyes was incongruent with Igar's soothing tone.

She sighed. "I have killed before. I had to, you see. Twice I wanted to, but every time was to survive." She leaned an elbow on her knee and peered at Ulvus. "If I free you, will you promise not to attack me?"

He narrowed his eyes while trying to shove her off him. Had she not used her cybernetic leg to balance her, he could have. She *was* far lighter than him.

"Foqen agree, Ulvus, or die like this." Juunn threw his hands in the air.

Lights flickered, and all raised their gazes to the ceiling.

"Aehort Uz's intervention will bring dishonor on your tribe," Igar growled at Ulvus.

With a roar, Ulvus punched her thigh, buckling her leg and bringing her knee down onto his chest. No pain radiated outward from his hit, as if a child had patted her. He grunted and shoved her off him, then rolled away from her. Juunn hoisted her up and shoved her behind him. Thinking this situation resolved, especially when Igar and Juunn formed a muscled wall between her and Ulvus, she lowered her fists. A fresh ripple of tingles preceded the fading of her armor, and she splayed her fingers to better admire the pearlescent light display across her skin.

Leaping to his feet, Ulvus barreled between Igar and Juunn. Their reaction was impressive but not swift enough. Ulvus swung a fist, catching her across the chin. Her head snapped to the side. Pain exploded to the rear of her skull. Her vision spun as a deep agony pulsed in her jaw. While chuckling, she staggered back but caught herself before falling to a knee. A champion never showed weakness. Her armor spread like a bolt from a taser blast. *Too fargen late.*

While she massaged her jaw with a thumb, she poked the area with her tongue. "It's been a while since I've tasted my blood." All lies, but confidence planted doubt and fear in her opponents. A habit she had yet to break.

Ulvus struggled against Igar and Juunn, who flanked him.

She smirked. "Why, thank you, gentlemen."

Bursting forward with her cybernetic speed, she kicked Ulvus in the gut, driving him back. Such force would have taken down a human. Ulvus stumbled but righted himself. She didn't hesitate. Using his knee to launch herself into the air, she flung out her arm to collide with his throat. She landed in a roll, vaulted to her feet, then faced him.

He clutched his throat, gasping and fighting for air. Dropping to his knees, then his hands, he gagged like a robo-cat coughing up a fake furball.

"Relax, he won't die. Just minor asphyxiation." She pointed to her inhuman arm. "If I'd hit him with this one, then yes, he'd be dead. Now, where the farg am I?"

Juunn and Igar blinked at her, gaping like whale skeletons. The lights flickered again. Juunn dipped to help a glowering Ulvus to his feet, whose cheeks had paled to a dark gray.

"We good? Or do you want me to kill you?" She grinned. "Let me know, and I'll schedule you in." She was being too sassy, but farg, she was tired, thirsty, and wanted answers.

Blue-man burst into the room, but that wasn't what snagged her attention. Behind him was a man she had intimate knowledge of. *Farg, hell is mean.* Her heart swelled, and she hurried to calm it. He was a figment of her imagination. By no means was he the real Drafe.

He jerked to a halt, his mouth widening into a bright grin. "Vic?" Striding toward her, his gaze scanned the room and settled on Ulvus. "What the foq happened here?" Instead of waiting for an answer, he arched a brow at Vic. "What did you do?"

She rested a hand on her hip, thrusting it out for good measure. "Nothing. Defended myself. Survived. The usual."

"Ulvus, Juunn, Igar, we will discuss this later."

A familiar orange alien hovered in the doorway. "Bring her, Drafe Arrak, when you are ready."

She frowned. *Huh?*

Drafe closed the distance between them, pausing when he was an inch from touching her. "It is good to see you, Vic."

"This is the human female with whom you have sullied our tribe's reputation?" Ulvus rasped, massaging his neck.

"Sullied?" She peeked around Drafe's wide shoulders. "Do you want to die? Is he always such an asshole?"

Drafe laughed. "Yes." He laced his fingers through hers and tugged, leading her down a narrow passage. "How did you come to be on my ship?"

"My tether snapped, launching me off the hauler. Not sure yet if it was an accident." She grimaced, having been minutes from death. That hadn't been a pleasant experience, and if she found who'd flung her out to die, she'd kill them without hesitation.

He paused mid-stride and faced her, gripping her upper arms. "Who would want to do you harm?"

She forced herself to unfurl her fists. "My question exactly."

His eyes paled to sunshine yellow. "Why is your mouth red?"

She wiped her split lip, smearing blood across her hand. "Blood."

His fingers tightened when he tugged her closer to him. "Did Ulvus—?"

"The asshole thought I carried a deadly disease."

He jerked back, dropped his hands and spun, as if to face Ulvus. "Kreta curse him."

Vic caught Drafe's wrist. "He also thought I would explode. Does that happen often?"

Drafe frowned, narrowing his eyes into a brooding stare that sparked heat in her core. Her breath caught, and butterflies skittered from her ears to her lower spine. *Oh, wow.*

"Come, let me attend to your injury." He sliced glances at her while they marched along passages before pausing in front of a seamless door. It opened at his touch. "Your blood is a magnificent red. So unusual."

She smothered a giggle at the odd compliment. "Um, thanks, I think. Wait. What color is your blood?"

"Clear," he said, as if her question was silly.

Pure plasma? Did that even make sense? She studied her blood-stained, armor-shimmered fingers. Only when the door sealed behind her did she realize where he'd taken her.

His quarters had the look of carved rock. His bed was a shelf with furs draped across it. The lighting shifted and filtered as if sunshine leaked through.

She tilted her face to bask in its pseudo-warmth. "Your quarters are amazing, Drafe."

"Ivoyans learned centuries ago that a little bit of their homeworld calmed the minds of the warriors." He tapped the surface of a table.

She climbed onto it, shuffling on her ass until the underside of her knees pressed against the edge. The texture beneath her fingers was smooth metal, so the rock was an illusion. "This is what your home looks like?"

He nodded as he gathered items from a hidden cupboard.

"It's amazing, Drafe."

"Recede your armor," he said.

"Right. Like I can control it," she scoffed. "Damn thing forms whenever." As if to make her out to be a liar, her skin shimmered amid weak tingles. In an instant, the heat from his UV lights hit her, and she moaned, relishing the heat.

His touch was gentle when he clasped her chin to run a strange box an inch over her mouth. He smirked. "You have healed already."

She shrugged. "I still have nanites in me."

He arched a brow while opening the flat packet, sliding out a sheet of thin white fabric. With it, he dabbed her mouth. Cool, it soothed as he wiped her chin and lips. His movements slowed to a caress. He shuffled, spreading her thighs wider. His nostrils flared, and his yellow eyes darkened to amber. He tossed the cloth aside, cupped her jaw, then brushed his lips across hers.

She gasped, sucking in his sun-drenched scent. Her heartbeat leaped and danced. Gripping his hips, she tugged him closer to wrap her legs around him.

He groaned and deepened the kiss, sweeping his tongue across hers. A tremor rippled through her. She needed his body against hers, the heat of his skin warming hers. He grunted when she crushed him within her embrace.

"Drafe," she whispered when he broke the kiss to nip her ear.

He jerked back, met her gaze, then pulled away from her. Not willing to blink, she ogled him when his skin undulated, exposing every inch of him in a breathtaking obsidian and gray. Off went his boots. He stood before her, naked, his muscles rippling with any movement he made.

"Farg, am I in heaven?" she rasped.

CHAPTER TWENTY-ONE

Drafe blinked at the woman in his quarters. Foq, he'd almost lost her. How in Osnir's blessed universe had they been the ones to find her? Miracles he believed in, but this...was incredible. His symbiotes rippled under his skin, preemptively forming his armor. If he found who'd wished her harm, he'd kill them without hesitation. She was his to protect. His...

He had dreamed of her being here with him. Not once had he thought his dreams would be realized. As she trailed her gaze over him, his symbiotes leaped to life, sparking excitement and heat through his body. He hardened to his full length, his fingers twitching while he granted her this moment.

She slid off the table and unclipped her boots. With a flick of a wrist, her tunic landed on top of his strewn boots. She shimmied out of her breeches and stood before him in tiny slips of white that did nothing to hide her. Arching and thrusting out her breasts, she unhooked the top cloth, tossing it to the floor. Snagging her fingers into the bottom triangle, she peeled it down then shoved it aside with her toes.

He sucked in a sharp breath. *Osnir, she is beautiful.*

Chuckling, she threw herself at him. He caught her, held her close, and relished the fullness of her in his arms. Too eager, he took a moment to bury his nose in the curve of her neck. He inhaled, drawing deep into his body the scent of sun-heated rock, the tang of salt, and the natural sweetness of his female.

When she dug her fingers into his hair, volatile need exploded, and he growled, crushing her lips with his. He couldn't get enough of her. His vision blurred, but he refused to close his eyes and miss a moment. His chest expanded, filled with heat and longing. His heart pounded a parsec a second. Why did she have such a hold on him?

She panted between kisses, clinging, stroking, and squeezing any part of him she could reach. Perhaps she felt the same? He hoped so, not wanting to be the only one in this madness. He spun her, pinned her to the bulkhead, and reached between them to tease her sex. She whimpered, spreading her thighs wider. Slick, hot, and swollen, her heartbeat pulsed above her entrance. He circled the hard bud, drawing out her pleasure. She bit him, licked and kissed him, unable to remain still under the onslaught.

He grinned. She was so responsive. The taste of her drenched his tongue in memory, and he longed to sample her petals again. Not now, though. He needed her too much to do anything other than bring her to release before plunging into her depths. Just the thought of doing so set a tremble in his knees. He tensed his hips, ensuring she remained pinned to the bulkhead, his koq rubbing her backside. She cried out, threw her head back, and thrashed, tossing her sunlight-colored hair. When her breathing calmed, he removed his fingers, gripped her hips, positioned himself at the heated wetness of her channel, and thrust in.

He stilled. The tight sheath squeezed, pulsed, and rippled, sending shivers outward. Dipping, he caught her lips for a plundering kiss, then lost in her brown eyes, he withdrew. She gasped, her lips parting.

Her eyes fluttered shut. When he plunged in to the hilt, she moaned, her fingers kneading his arms. Osnir had blessed him with her.

Sooner than he liked, she contracted around him, flooding heat along his length. It was too much, too intense. He roared, riding dunes of pleasure, unable to do anything but pin her to the bulkhead. As he held her up, she kept his knees from collapsing when she tightened her legs around him.

"Foq, Vic." Without pulling out, he gathered her against his chest and stepped under the water spray.

She squealed when it drenched her. "What the farg is this?" She blinked at him, her hair darkened and enhanced the glow of her skin. "You waste water?" She licked a droplet off his shoulder, drawing a rumble from him.

"It is a treasure to my tribe, but on other worlds, it is an abundant resource."

She stroked his chest, the slickness of the drops aiding her exploration. He kissed her, tasting her and the water—two things he cherished the most. Breaking contact, he pulled out, lowered her legs, and washed her. Despite needing to touch her, to learn every valley, he used the opportunity to study the crisscrossing scars on her left arm and leg. They were as perfect as the corpse's. How was this possible?

Once he rinsed her off, he guided her to the side to be air-dried while he hurried through his wash. She laughed and spun in a circle, granting the dryer full access.

Joy engulfed his chest in overwhelming sensations, and he paused mid-rinse. He parted his lips to ask her to be his, then hesitated. Not until he understood the connection between her and the corpses. Ivoy came first, as per his oath.

"We need to meet with Aehort Uz." He closed the distance and halted beside her in the path of the air dryer.

She arched a brow. "Your orange friend?"

"I am his guardian. He insisted we rush to the ship. I sensed your distress, but you did not respond to the smart band." He shook his wrist.

"I wasn't anywhere near a communication device." Shadow crossed her eyes. She pursed her lips. "If my crew jettisoned me on purpose, I swear, Drafe, I will hunt them down and kill them." Strength, determination, and anger bolstered her voice, sounding like a true warrior.

He met her gaze, wanting to declare that her vow was his to fulfill, her debt his to settle, her future his to share. Instead, he nodded. "I believe you. Come, dress in your old garments. We will order fresh ones later. For now, we need to meet with Aehort and find your ship."

"Could I have something to drink?" She pulled on her breeches and sleeveless tunic without her tiny strips of cloth. When she tugged on her boots, her breasts jiggled. He closed his eyes and offered his back as he summoned his armor while snapping on his boots.

"Yes. We will stop at the galley." He held out his hand.

She slid hers into his without hesitation. Her hair fell across her shoulders, glowing in good health and appearing incredibly soft. Breaking his focus, he left his quarters and led her down the passages.

Nenn sat at the table opposite Gusin. They gawked, their meals forgotten.

"Vic, this is Giniiri aac Nenn Maed and Zuphayr aac Gusin Taed."

She wiggled her fingers in a strange gesture and sat on the bench beside them. "Those are your names?"

Drafe laughed. "Your family name is last, our tribe name is first. Aac means from, and maed, taed, arrak, uz, and sava are ranks."

Her tempting mouth formed an 'oh.' He shuffled where he waited at the replicate, trying to ease his hardening koq, as if he hadn't just enjoyed her.

"This is a military ship." She studied their armor then chuckled. "You're so colorful. Is there a significance to your red and blue hair and matching eyes?" She smiled at Drafe when he placed a jar of water in front of her and a plate of tulsig alongside browned strips of garak.

"Each tribe has a color. None know why." Nenn grinned then tore into the fleshy part of his charred audinna—a variegated-yellow mushroom that grew inches above bubbling lava. "That's the Giniiri in my name."

"It also means from which clime we stem." Gusin sucked on his thumb after he popped into his mouth his last bite of raw kurru-la—meat from winged creatures Drafe had yet to see. "Giniiri is the volcano tribe. Zuphayr is where the sky meets the water."

"And Meorri?" She picked up a tulsig with her fingers and bit into it. Groaning, she stared at the cake while she chewed. "This is *so* good."

"Drafe is from the desert tribe." Nenn pushed off the bench, gripped Drafe's forearm, then left.

Drafe settled beside her, content to watch her eat.

"Vic." Gusin offered his forearm. She blinked, licked her fingers, then clasped his arm as Nenn had done.

Drafe's heartbeat stilled at the Qaldreth gesture to acknowledge a worthy warrior. Frowning, he stared after a disappearing Gusin.

"I like your friends."

He glanced at her. "Warriors are not friends. We are broth-ers-in-arms."

She shrugged. "Some you prefer more than others, though."

In her eyes, they were his friends, but that term lacked depth. He would give his life for his males and they for him. What he hadn't anticipated was how this adventure into the unknown had brought them closer.

She emptied her jar and pushed the plate aside. "Thank you."

He rose, and so did she, trailing him. Perhaps it was insanity that made him sneak peeks at her. The door to Aehort's quarters opened before he requested access.

"Welcome, Vic. It is a pleasure to see you again. I trust you are well?" Aehort smiled and gestured with a wide sweep of his arm to a chair. "Please, sit. We have much to discuss."

"We do?" She sat and clasped her hands between her thighs.

"A few months ago, we discovered a pod heading for our planet, Ivoy." Aehort tapped his chin. "I am an uz, a servant class, but since Drafe and I survived the pod exploding, killing all of our leaders and many Qaldreth warriors, the council tasked us to investigate the pod's origins."

Her gaze flew to Drafe. She studied him, as if she searched for an injury. At finding none, she knitted her brows. "You were hurt?"

Foq, he needed to touch her, to ease her concern. Instead, he folded his arms across his chest and let Aehort continue. She was here now. He would have plenty of time to adore her later.

Aehort tapped the closest screen, revealing the many ports and waystations they had visited. "All our questioning led to your planet, Vic."

"What?" she squeaked. "Why would we send bombs in pods beyond the outer reaches of space?" She shook her head. "Humans are greedy. There isn't profit in that."

"We located many such pods on trajectories into the unknown, all launched from Jupiter or one of its moons." With a flick, the three-dimensional image appeared on the screen, thin blue lines tracking through the great cosmos, the origin Jupiter.

She gaped then swallowed. "You said pods, as in more than one. What's inside them?"

Drafe dipped his head to hide his smirk. *She is smart.*

"Human bodies." Aehort rested his backside on the edge of a table.

"Dead?" Her eyes widened.

"Yes." Aehort summoned another image, the face of the female from earlier. "We opened one on Ceres, which is why we were not on the *Aroagni* when you were rescued."

"Vic, the body has your scars." Drafe crossed the distance and captured her left hand in his. He ran his thumb over the faint lines, relishing the softness of her skin.

Shadows darkened her eyes. "Was the pod red?"

He jerked back but didn't release her hand. "Yes."

Her eyes fluttered closed while she drew in a shuddering breath before meeting his gaze. "Carne's involved."

"Who?" Drafe ran his hands up her arm when she shivered.

"They kidnap or buy children to train and fight in the Ring, their arena. Injuries happen often, and cybernetic implants are encouraged." She rose, pulled her hand free from his, then slipped around him to pace. "It's possible they test their medical advances on unfortunate souls. I can't know for sure, but I wouldn't put it past them."

One moment, her face was pale, the next, flushed the color of pink wind-hewn rock. "A cruiser flew alongside the *Mula Pesada.* I rushed inside to tell Nikko, and bam, he jettisoned me. Could the two ships know each other? Could the *Mula Pesada* be hauling more than ice?" She pinched her brow. Her eyes shimmered as if she mourned. "I wasn't allowed in the engine rooms. They claimed some bullshit reason like not trusting me yet. Fargen hell. If they have prisoners, then yes, I would've fought to free them."

"We need to locate the source and bring justice to Ivoy." Drafe caught her hand and tugged her against him. She went willingly then rubbed her temple across his chest.

"Find the medical facility Carne is funding?" She yanked out of his arms and held up her hands. "No way. I ran from them, wanting freedom more than vengeance. Why would I bring their attention down on me?"

"You need not come with." Drafe cupped her cheek and brushed his thumb across her skin. In fact, he would prefer she remained safe.

"So hide in your ship?" She pursed her lips. "I'm not a coward."

Aehort rose to his full height. "We are not implying you are, Vic. You have endured much, lost parts of who the naïve girl farming sol once was."

She blinked at Aehort, then sliced a wide-eyed glance at Drafe.

"Clairvoyant, remember?" He smiled. "We need to find the source first before we can decide on anything else."

She frowned. "If what you say is true and if the ice hauler is tied to this, then Europa is where I'd look. A hauler traveling between Lunar Base and Europa wouldn't be suspicious. Then, once we pinpoint the facility, we need to take control of the *Mula Pesada,* confirm the prisoners are on board, then use the ship. Carne's security is tight. They will have checks in place." She rubbed her palms together. "If we're taking the ship, I want in on that part. I have a score to settle."

"Good." Aehort tapped the console. "Now, as to your organisms—"

She gasped. "You know what they are?"

Drafe laced his fingers through hers, unable to resist touching her a moment longer. "Qaldreth have symbiotes that carry the history of our tribe and ancestors."

"Symbiotes?" She mouthed the word.

"It is also what builds the bond between Aehort and me." He gestured with his free hand at Aehort. "When the explosion killed my Ot and the council assigned the mission to me, I had to share my symbiotes with Aehort. The bond between Ivoy and Qaldreth is crucial to our relationship."

She blinked at him, appearing sweet and infinitely feminine. "How do I have your symbiotes?"

Osnir save him, he wanted to kiss her, taste her tongue, and wrap his arms around her. "When we mated, a part of me—"

"Your sperm?" She threw back her head and laughed.

He smiled. "Yes, and I have your *nanites* in me."

She stilled, her laughter dying. "Are you serious?"

He parted his lips to cease breathing her addictive scent into his body. It was driving him crazy to not throw her over his shoulder and return to his quarters. "Quite."

"Fine." With a deep sigh, she settled her hands on her hips. "What's done is done. So what happens now? Can this be fixed?"

"Not on this ship. I would need our medical teams on Ivoy to assess you." Aehort smiled. "*If* you join us on the return trip."

"To Ivoy?" Her voice spiked. "Is it a habitable planet?" She flicked a dismissive hand. "Of course it is." She stilled again. "Wait, as a specimen to be tested, prodded, with parts of me sliced off to be boiled down to its molecular level?"

Drafe couldn't help himself and laughed. "We bonded, Vic. As I protect Aehort, so too will I guard you."

"Oh." She frowned. "If your symbiotes are in Aehort *and* me, does that mean we're bonded too?" She pointed to Aehort and herself.

Aehort's wide mouth curled at one end. "I do like you, human. On our return voyage to Ivoy, I will teach you how to sense emotions not your own."

"I should be losing my mind here, but given that I knew about the organisms, and that they weren't harming me, I have to say, I like that these *symbiotes* are yours, Drafe." She crossed to Aehort, gathered his orange fingers in hers, then squeezed. "Thank you for the offer, Aehort Uz."

Discussion over, Drafe crossed to the door as it opened at his proximity. "Come, Vic, let me take you to the bridge. From there, we can orbit Europa and search for the pod's source."

With a backward glance at Aehort, she trailed Drafe.

Chapter Twenty-Two

Year: 2219

Aboard the Aroagni.

Drafe jerked awake and stilled when Vic curled against him. He grinned and drew her closer to him, taking the time to kiss her temple and inhale her sunbaked scent. As he lay there relishing the softness of her in his arms, he frowned. What had disturbed his sleep?

"Drafe Arrak."

He cupped the device in his neck. "Speak."

"The pod's explosion confirms the timer is set for six hours."

"My thanks." He tucked his arm behind his head and stared at the ceiling, not wanting to slip out of bed or disturb Vic's slumber.

"What is it?" she mumbled, rolling over to press her cheek to his chest.

He nuzzled her neck. "The pod exploded."

She shifted again. "It has a time delay?"

He smiled. "Yes, long enough for the Ots to gather, to observe and discuss."

"The explosion might not be intentional. Just a safety mechanism to prevent what they're doing from coming into the light," she mumbled and rolled over, exposing a perfect breast.

He cupped it, running a thumb across the soft nipple until it hardened. "Planting any kind of explosion is with the intent of detonating it."

She wriggled under his touch. "True. Do we continue with the plan?"

"Yes." He dipped to press a kiss to her tormented nipple, not daring to do anything more. "Once we locate the facility, we can decide on the next step."

She snuggled against him, feathering a kiss across his collarbone. "Can we sleep now?"

He chuckled, squeezed her, then slid out of bed. "I need to speak to Aehort."

"Let me know what he says." She gathered his pillow close and drifted off.

Drafe stared at her, loving the fire-like lighting flickering across her delicate face. She didn't know it yet, but he was keeping her.

Summoning his symbiotes to cover the bottom half of him in armor, he padded barefoot to the galley, thirsty and eager for a strip of hudu. Nenn sat at the table, his face buried in his tablet. He didn't glance up when Drafe entered.

"What has you awake?" he mumbled around charred meat Drafe didn't recognize.

"The pod exploded."

"So I heard." Nenn met his gaze. "Yet, you left the loving arms of your female?"

"Mm, I have a dilemma I need to work through." Drafe filled a jar of water and sat on the bench.

"Care to share?" Nenn flipped his tablet over and pulled his half-empty bowl closer.

"She does not want to involve herself out of fear. Revenge is driving her to take the hauler, but after that is completed, she might...leave me." Drafe sighed. There, he'd said it, his biggest fear.

"You want a way to keep her?" Nenn arched a brow. "Drafe, she is not Qaldreth—"

Drafe growled.

Nenn raised his hand, a strip of white meat dangling from his fingers. "Let me finish. She does not know our ways and cannot be held to our expectations. In addition, she is a warrior who will not be subservient to you. Perhaps all you need to do is ask her, warrior to warrior."

"That *is* our way." Drafe frowned. "To ask."

"No, I mean, explain it to her, how staying with you will impact her life."

Drafe rested his chin on his hand and stared at Nenn. "She knows nothing of our homeworld. It is right that I share this with her."

Nenn grinned before sipping his steaming tisane that smelled of the inside of a garak. "If you are serious about having her as your love mate, then yes."

"Wise, Nenn. Do we have any Ivoyan data vids on Qaldreth?"

"We do." Nenn wiped his fingers on a cloth and splayed them on the table. He leaned back and stared at Drafe. "As wonderful as images will be, memories spoken from the heart have greater impact."

Memories were good and bad, painting him as strong or weak. No, he need not relive those with her. "She has my symbiotes and access to all Meorri history."

"Yes, but she has not learned to commune with them. You are rushing the most beautiful thing to occur to a warrior, Drafe."

"I know." He slumped. Nenn was right. It *was* incredible that he had found a worthy female, more so that she was a warrior. "I want it done. I want her to be mine with no chance of her walking away."

Nenn laughed, his red eyes glowing. "You are feeling insecure. It is not the way of a fearless warrior."

Drafe glared at him. "Foq, Nenn. Wait until you meet your female."

Nenn shrugged. "I hope to be as senseless as you." He pushed aside his empty plate while licking his fingers. "On a more serious matter, her besting Ulvus has enraged the male. I will guard your back."

"Ulvus is predictable." Drafe downed his water. "Thank you for the advice and warning, Nenn." He squeezed Nenn's shoulder, then strode along the passage, debating whether to return to Vic, visit with Aehort, or do a shift. Restlessness consumed him. Spinning on a heel, he headed to the bridge.

Caah Taed flicked a glance at him but returned his focus to the screens. "The scans for the seventy-nine moons are turning up the usual: mining colonies, some on the surface, and others orbiting the applicable moon. I left Europa for last. I wanted to make sure we covered our bases."

"Wise."

Caah grinned and tapped a beat across the console's buttons. "Want to scan the ice moon with me?"

"Sure." Drafe leaned against the bulkhead to watch.

Still in stealth, the *Aroagni* shot into orbit around Europa. It was a beautiful little moon with white streaks carved into its surface. Many boreholes had been sunk to best harvest the oceans beneath the layers of ice. The images showed land vehicles carving chunks of ice and rolling on, leaving cubes behind them as they moved onto the next section. A hovering ship lifted the cube and flew off.

"Where is it going?" He glanced at Caah.

"To the nearest ice base. From there, the ice hauler will deploy their riggers to collect." The taed tapped the screen to the far right where unnatural bumps marred the horizon. The screen zoomed in on the camp with housing structures that looked like capsules.

Drafe rubbed his brow where a headache was forming. *Foq.* "Mm, and nothing else on the scans?"

Spinning the moon's image on the screen, Caah tapped at the bottom of it. "Some heat signatures closer to the southern core. Investigating now."

Drafe squeezed and released his forearm, a silent display of impatience. If the facility was not on Europa, then due to Caah's diligence, they could determine the source was not from anything remotely close to Jupiter. This would also mean no need to retake Vic's ice hauler, nor a reason for her to stay with Drafe.

He gritted his teeth as each precious second ticked by. The tension built in his shoulders, burning down his spine.

"The area is shielded. Adjusting frequency." Caah's brow knitted. "Some sort of structure is underground." He flicked his fingers, and images appeared on the largest screen. "Whatever it is, it is quite extensive, descending a few levels and spreading out more than three lengths of the *Aroagni* combined."

"Is it the facility we are looking for?" Drafe frowned. "Never mind. I will trace the trajectory to Europa." He bolted with a called "thank you," sprinting along the passages to the command center and its three-dimensional space model.

Aehort smiled when Drafe stormed in. "Yes, it is the correct location."

Gripping the table to hide and channel his energy, Drafe took a moment to calm his erratic heartbeat. "Why do you not share your premonitions? Am I not trustworthy?"

Aehort met his gaze. "You know the answer to this. You need not ask questions."

Drafe huffed. "Fine."

"You would attempt to make my visions come true, endangering yourself in the process, and not opening yourself to new possibilities or experiences."

Everything within Drafe stilled. "You knew about Vic." An explosion of joy summoned a grin. "Which is why you insisted I break with protocol and visit Moonstar."

Aehort ignored him. "If I factor in the orbital path of Europa and the average speed the pods traveled, I confirm the source as being the southern pole."

What they needed to do settled in Drafe's gut. The confirmation added peace to the decision to strike. He prayed to Osnir that no civilians were harmed, but he wouldn't bemoan their deaths too much. After all, they knew what they were doing was wrong. Or were the gods the humans worshipped more lenient on such ethical matters? "Good, Aehort. Now what?"

"Vic warned about security." Aehort pressed the blue button. "Caah Taed, monitor communication into and out of the facility. Listen for security protocol we might need to mimic." Aehort flicked his elegant, elongated fingers at Drafe. "Return to your female. Inform her of this, and ask her how she would like to proceed."

"Ask?" Drafe appreciated the respect Aehort showed Vic.

"It is polite." Aehort rasped a chuckle.

Snatching the opportunity, Drafe pushed for a hint of his future. "I assume, in your visions, that she is beside me when we breach the facility?"

Aehort met his gaze, all humor gone. "Wake her."

Drafe sighed and marched to his quarters, but when he slipped inside, his pace slowed, and his frustration evaporated. In the warm light, Vic lay on her back, her limbs outside the furs, exposing the curved lines of her body to his admiring gaze.

"And?" she whispered without opening her eyes.

He grunted. "I made no sound, female."

She snorted. "You breathe like an antique robo-dog." She sat up, swung her legs over the side of the bed, and gathered her hair on top of her head while she stretched. The act displayed the prettiest parts of her body. "What news?"

Drawing in a breath, he forced himself to focus on anything but the temptation of her. "We found the facility."

She pushed off the bed to don her breeches, fresh from the wash closet. He bolted, approaching her from behind to cup her bare breasts before she hid them from him. Massaging and tweaking the tips, he nipped her neck, then soothed her skin with kisses.

"Caah is scanning the security protocols," he mumbled as he nuzzled the hair behind her ear.

"Good." She spun in his embrace and kissed him, claiming his mouth like he would conquer hers. Warrior met warrior, as they had done in the Moonstar. As she had done to fire his blood so.

When she broke away, he groaned, "Foq, Vic, I adore your kissing."

She grinned at him. "I know. After you've fed me, I can show you what else kissing is good for."

He frowned. "I do not have another tongue anywhere on my body."

She laughed as she pulled away to slip on her sleeveless tunic. Shuffling forward, she cupped his semi-erect koq through his armor. He groaned when she rubbed him, sparking a bolt of pleasure.

"Something else can be kissed like you did to me." Pink colored her cheeks. "Although, it will be my first time."

Everything within him stilled. As confident and skilled as she was, he had never considered her to be untried, virginal. "I...am your first?" He struggled to swallow past the lump in his throat. Any female with a brother, cousin, uncle, or father would remain untouched under Qaldreth protection. Perhaps Vic's Ande had served in such a capacity, ensuring the most intimate part of her remained unsullied.

Drafe was indebted to Ande for his diligence. "I am honored, Vic."

She dipped her chin to hide her face as she tugged on her boots. "The pleasure was all mine, Drafe, but I intend to remedy that."

"I found joy." He tried to assure her lest she felt inadequate.

She stroked a finger down his bare chest, summoning a path of tingles and skinbumps. "Yes, but did you roar my name, did you gasp and beg?"

He scowled. "A Qaldreth warrior never begs."

Her smirk was wicked to behold. "We shall see."

Chapter Twenty-Three

Year: 2219

Aboard the Aroagni.

Vic touched the device implanted in her neck. Drafe called it a language implant, but it was far more than that. Tapping it twice activated a shield around her body, granting her two hours of oxygen and the ability to walk suitless across the outside of the *Mula Pesada*. Farg, she couldn't believe she was doing this, not with the alien males beside her, and certainly not for the fine piece of ass that was Drafe. True, revenge was her motivation, but he had needed her to do this. Had he been Ande, she would have agreed without a second thought.

It was, for this reason, she found herself stomping across the ice hauler with her boots activated and without a tether like she hadn't learned her lesson last time. She scanned her team, trusting them. If she fell off the stupid ship, they would rescue her. Thankfully, asshole-Ulvus had remained on the *Aroagni*. She glanced at the sleek ship. Its organic lines were like combined water droplets shimmering as it traveled through space. Drafe had said it was in stealth but, due to some frequency in the neck device, was visible to them. If she squinted, she could make out a static-like shimmer around it.

Inside, it didn't scream a higher technology. Sure, it had a replicate, and soon she would ask it to make coffee. The tulsig cakes were good, and maybe bacon and eggs would be as wonderful. She paused mid-stride. Was she considering staying with Drafe? Returning to Ivoy and Qaldreth? Not like she had other options. Her job on the *Mula Pesada* was a hell-no. Not to mention that the farthest from Carne and Sebastian's influential reach was with Drafe and wherever he went.

He peeked at her over his shoulder and halted, crossing to her without a thought to the men he impeded. "What is it, *gevatia*?"

Endearments, already? Her chest blossomed with unrestricted joy. She smiled. "Nothing, just admiring your ship."

He followed her gaze. "It is beautiful. It is not often one sees it from the outside."

"Yup." She gestured with her chin that they should proceed. "Once we reach the airlock, opening it might trigger an alarm."

"I am prepared." He squared his shoulders, and she had no doubt he'd be formidable. Used to judging men for their ability to survive a battle, Drafe would have received her support from the get-go.

He marched behind his males, checking to ensure she followed. The shield glowed a pale blue and contorted his handsome features. Later, after all was done, she wanted to run her tongue along the length of his cock. How would he react? Would he like it? She giggled then tamped down her laughter. A little breathless, she joined the males alongside the airlock.

"Caah?" Drafe glanced at his tech specialist.

"All sensors were deactivated the moment we were within range, Drafe. I expect no alarms or a welcome party."

She grimaced, having wanted to cause a bit of panic in her attempted murderers. To trigger the door to open, she slid a hidden panel aside and hit the red button. No lights flashed. Still... She raised her gaze to the ceiling, expecting to find sec-cams. Her instincts warned that they weren't unobserved. *Oh, farg, I hope so.* She wanted to rub her palms together, that eager she was for a full-out confrontation with Nikko.

They filed into the room and waited for the door to close. Once the pressurizing completed, she peeked into the hatch housing her tether to study the shorn edges. Gritting her teeth, she tapped the neck device twice to deactivate the shield then glanced at Drafe. "Ready?"

At his nod, she pulled her blaster from its holster and barreled along the passages leading to the bridge. "Computer, where's Nikko?"

"Greetings, Vic. Nikko is in the mess." The feminine voice was monotone, though what had Vic expected... A gushing welcome?

"Who speaks?" Caah gaped at the ceiling.

"The onboard computer." Vic grinned. "Computer, who's manning the bridge?"

"Leah is on duty."

Excellent. Vic bounced on her toes and tossed Drafe a grin. "And Tiny?"

"In hydroponics."

"Hide our presence, Computer. We wish to surprise the crew." Vic hurried along the passages and snuck into the narrow hydroponics lab, turning to usher the warriors in before closing the door. There was no need for anyone to stumble upon them crowding the passage. "Hi, Tiny."

"Vic." She faced the door. "I thought you... Nikko said we'd lost you to some freak accident." Medical scents engulfed Vic with Tiny's crushing hug.

"You did." So the bastard had lied? Which proved Tiny innocent of Nikko's dealings. "My tether was cut."

Tiny frowned. "Cut?"

"Yes." Vic proceeded to fill her in. "Which leads us to believe there are prisoners on board."

"Us? Wait, did you say warriors?" Tiny tilted her ear to listen. "Three?"

Vic gestured to Drafe and his males to come closer. "One at a time, step forward and introduce yourself."

Drafe cast a glance at Tiny but settled his gaze on Vic. His eyes darkened to a rich amber. "I am Meorri aac Drafe Arrak. Vic is my female."

Her breath caught. Swells of delicious heat uncoiled in the pit of her stomach. Dropping her chin to her chest, she hoped to hide the shimmer of tears. Yes, she was his and happy to be.

"Oh," Tiny gasped when Drafe took her hand. "Does that mean what I think it means?"

"More than you can know." Vic threw her human arm around Tiny for a sideways hug. "Nenn, you're next."

"Describe them for me, Vic. Oh, I do love the way they smell. Like I'm in a biodome on Ganymede, filled with rich soils, succulent plants, trickling water..." She paused to inhale through her nose. "Volcanic rock."

Trickling water? Vic glanced at the vats of bubbling water. And her dear sweet Tiny wanted her to describe them? Sure, Vic could wax lyrical over every aspect of Drafe, but she didn't want to share. And doing so over the other warriors would be rude. "Drafe and Nenn are close to you, the others... Besides, we're out of time. Will you help us?"

Tiny folded her arms across her chest and waited.

"Fine," Vic huffed. "They have obsidian skin. Their hair runs from their brows to the base of their spines. All are muscled, strong, and skilled. Drafe's a warrior guardian. Caah's a tech guru. Nenn is like you, a medic."

"He is?" Tiny gasped, raising her white gaze.

"Can you not see me?" Nenn gathered Tiny's hands in his. "Loss of sight is no more where I come from. Allow me to heal you."

She scowled. "With implants?" She shivered. "That's a no, thank you."

Nenn chuckled. "We regrow your eyes and encourage the optical nerves to reconnect. I will return for you when our mission is complete."

Tiny leaned closer to Vic to whisper, "Is he for real?"

"Yes." Vic chuckled. "Now, will you help us?"

"Sure. What you need is access to the engine rooms. Security was restricted, but last night, Captain just up and gave everyone full-access status. He did sound...odd. Anyway, that means I can appoint you as our new captain." Tiny giggled as if this wasn't a life-or-death situation.

Vic arched a brow. "That could work, but won't Leah notice?"

"Why would she?" Tiny scoffed and waved a dismissive hand. "She's probably got her boots up on the console and her nose buried in smut." Tiny faced the nearest console. "Computer, set all crew to staff access, and grant Vic full control."

"Control granted, Captain Vic."

"See. Easy as that. Computer, locate all storerooms." Tiny gestured to the console now flicking through *Mula Pesada's* floor plans. "I would start there." She returned to clipping rosemary and placing the stalks in a bowl. Her movements were so delicate as she snipped by touch. She stiffened and titled her head as if to peer at everyone over her shoulder. "But Vic, what if you're wrong?"

Vic squeezed between Drafe and Caah who studied the ship's diagrams until they found one large enough. Nearest to the engine rooms, it was clear why anyone would ignore the many heat signatures. She trailed a finger from hydroponics to the storeroom, assessing the least obvious route to take.

Realizing Tiny had spoken, Vic said, "Then we leave the ship without bloodshed."

Tiny squeaked. "Don't harm...anyone."

"Especially Dieter?" Vic teased, tossing her a glance.

Tiny's cheeks darkened. "No," she pursed her lips, "go ahead. Kick his ass."

"What the farg?" Vic opened her mouth to ask then snapped it shut. "You're coming with us. Pack what you need."

Tiny gaped. "But—"

"Do you want to stay on the *Mula Pesada* if it's true, Tiny? Wouldn't that make you complicit in whatever the hell Nikko's up to?"

Tiny slumped and placed the clippers in the bowl. "No, you're right. I'll be ready."

Vic squeezed past the males and hurried along the passages, keeping to the least used. Alerting Nikko or Leah of their presence meant killing them, something she wasn't opposed to, but until they knew how to communicate with the facility, Drafe needed them alive.

The lighting dwindled to a minimum the deeper and lower they traveled. They forewent elevators and used ladders instead. She had her ears pricked for any approaching footsteps, finding the lack of activity alarming. Where was Dieter? After all, the engine room was his domain. Sweat drenched her tank and slicked her palm gripping the blaster when she, at last, stopped before a solid airtight door. Using her cybernetic arm, she tried to turn the hatch's lever. It creaked when she bent the metal bar, and still, the door didn't open.

She frowned at Drafe, who threw up his hands with a husky chuckle. "I am not trying."

Nenn squeezed her arm. "Foq, Vic, I need to take a look at you when we return to *Aroagni.*"

She snatched her limb back and glared at the ceiling. "Computer, unlock this door."

The door clunked open.

Drafe and Caah dragged on the inches-thick submarine-like hatch.

The heat hit her, like a wet blanket of stale air poured over her. She bolted forward, trailing Drafe as he sprinted down the passages, checking each door he passed. Upon peering through the forth porthole, he halted.

She expected the worst.

He spun the dial and yanked on the door. His expression darkened. Stacked high and deep were red Carne-stamped pods, confirming her worst fears.

"Find the prisoners," she rasped.

Nenn and Caah hurried along the passage. A 'found them' echoed in her ears via the neck device, she suspected. She stumbled after Drafe, unwilling to believe it. Standing on the tips of her toes, she peered over the edge of the porthole at the many faces staring back.

"Farg," she moaned, dropping onto her heels.

Caah unlatched the door and swung it outward.

"Who are you?" someone called from the darkness of the room.

"Victorious?" a woman gasped, staggering forward to grab Vic's hand. "Did Carne send you to save us?" The Carne logo on the right sleeve of the red-and-yellow bedraggled uniform announced her as a combatant.

"Carne?" Vic shook her head.

She sat cross-legged on the dirty floor to explain what was going on, what triggered their discovery, and what the plan was to set them free. Faces, some sort of familiar, appeared out of the dark and gathered around her as she revealed their dire circumstances. The acrid stench of urine and unwashed bodies coiled nausea in her stomach, but she held firm, willing to suffer to save these people.

"Pods? Explosions?" A man limped closer. As he approached, Drafe shifted from foot to foot.

Vic smiled and squeezed his fingers, hoping to assure him that there was no threat here. "Yes. We located the medical facility they're taking you to. Computer, patch me through to Tiny."

"Patched through."

Vic raised her chin as if it brought her voice closer to the mic, wherever it was. "Tiny, we found them."

"Tiny can't help you, bitch," Leah spat. "Now I'll get the chance to kill you. Jettisoning was too soft for what I wanted to do to you."

"Where's Tiny?" Vic stilled, dreading the answer.

"She'll be dealt with soon enough."

Vic nodded at Nenn, her instruction clear. "If you want me, Leah, come and get me, but then again, you never had the balls. Unable to face your weakness, you cut my tether, didn't you?"

"No, that was Dieter's idea. I wanted to shoot you while you slept."

"Ah, yes, the coward's way." Vic forced a chuckle. "Well, I'll wait for you down here, shall I?"

"I'm on my way, bitch."

Good. In the meantime, Vic had other tasks to focus on. "Computer, end patch. Caah, can you deactivate the engines? I don't want anyone hitting a self-destruct button. Let's break that connection. We might need the engines later, so don't do anything irreversible." She faced the prisoners. "Listen, you know how to fight. Take this ship, help us destroy this facility, and walk away from a life of servitude to Carne. Whatever you salvage from the facility is yours to start anew."

The crowd rumbled approvals, some applauding. Bright smiles glowed from the shadows.

"Might even stay and make it our home if it's defensible," someone called out.

Done. They had an army if needed. "Computer, the prisoners are hereby employed on the *Mula Pesada* as maintenance crew. Grant them full access to all areas on this ship."

"Granted, Captain Vic."

One by one, the prisoners crept from the room, only for their many footsteps to thunder across the grated floor.

"Computer, is Nikko still in the mess?" Vic wondered if Leah had informed her lover the *Mula Pesada* had visitors? With the way the woman had spoken, Vic would hazard a no.

"Yes."

She nodded. "Lock him down. Where's Dieter, Cap…Themba, Trent, and Grunt?"

"In their quarters."

The captain's location was no surprise. "Lock them down too, and replay archival footage of the prisoners to Grunt. I doubt the kid knew."

"Lockdown initiated."

Vic grinned at Drafe. "Now we wait."

He frowned. "For the female who wishes you harm?" Tugging Vic into his arms, he pressed his lips to her temple. "Do not injure yourself."

She snorted. "We are unmatched. I have her at a disadvantage."

He leaned back to smile. "I know."

Naivete rested on Vic's shoulders. She should have known Leah and Nikko wouldn't easily forgive. Carne combatants were vindictive. She had foolishly hoped the rest of the human race wasn't. "Besides, this will be quick and unsatisfying."

Caah intruded with a bounce to his steps. "Done. Antiquated machinery at its finest. Might upgrade her if there is time."

"Why?" Drafe released her to holster his blaster.

Caah shrugged. "For the challenge of it."

Slow, steady steps announced Leah's arrival. Vic nodded at Drafe and Caah to step back. They faded into the shadows, no doubt an easy thing to do when their skin was the color of darkness. She took center stage in the pool of light, unafraid to show herself. Though not a fool, she kept her blaster drawn.

But the silly woman was taking forever to peek inside the cell.

"Leah, do hurry up," Vic snapped.

The woman huffed and stepped through the doorway, her blaster in hand.

"You're an idiot." Vic started with an insult, drawing a groan from Drafe. She didn't dare glance his way. "Despite my obvious skill and my years as a gladiator for Carne, you think you can take me?"

"A what?" Leah squeaked, her cheeks paling under a fine sheen of sweat.

Vic tutted. "Ah, your lover didn't divulge everything."

"You lie. Nikko would've told me." Leah met Vic's gaze, raising her chin, as well. "You're bluffing."

"Right, when I managed to gain the upper hand in the alley?" Vic sighed. "I see, you want your fingers crushed again." She ran her hand along her cybernetic arm. "The irony abounds. You're escorting prisoners to a medical facility that perfects skin healing technology and cybernetics." She flexed her fingers. "Which I now sport."

Leah raised her blaster, preparing to fire. A bolt of white from the shadows shot it out of her hands. She cried out, shaking her fingers.

With Leah disarmed, Vic tossed a glance at the shadows. "Drafe, butt out."

"She dies by your hand. No blasters." His baritone ran over Vic's senses like chilled syrup over a hot bun.

Leah called out, "Who the farg is there? Show yourself." She took a tentative step back, as if to escape through the door.

Vic lunged forward, using her cybernetics to boost her speed. She caught Leah's arm and flung her into the room.

Drafe leaned a little into the light, exposing his face and glowing yellow eyes, and caught her only to steady her. "Hello, human female."

He revealed himself and, with Caah behind him, strode from the room.

Leah blinked, staring after them. "What the farg—?"

"My rescuers." Vic grinned and holstered her blaster. "Times awasting, Leah. Let's get this over with?"

Leah squared her shoulders and faced Vic.

"What did you do to Tiny?" Vic raised her fists and rested her weight on her front foot.

"Knocked her over the head and left her in the med-bay. Let the traitor bleed to death."

"I doubt it." Vic chuckled. Confidence was key, messing with Leah's psyche as crucial, not that Vic needed those tactics, but it was second nature. "Seems like you can't even kill a blind woman properly." *Farg*. Nenn better get to Tiny and save her. Lord knew what Vic would do if she lost the only ally she'd made on *Mula Pesada*.

True to her stupidity, Leah fell for the taunt. She screamed, announcing her attack.

Vic swung a punch at Leah's throat, hitting it with a sickening crunch. As she crumbled to the floor, gurgling for air, and her eyes wide, Vic crouched beside her. "Alas, I don't have the time to pretend to take a hit, to give you false hope, to toy with you. I want off this fargen ship, and if it means killing you, then so be it."

She strode out of the cell as Leah gurgled her final breath. Not once did Vic look back.

Fire lanced through her right bicep, the force wrenching her to the side. The blaster shot came from the engine room. How the hell—? Caah yanked her to the floor as Drafe headed in that direction, weaving in and out of darkness like an apparition.

Fargen hell. She *had* thought it had all been too easy.

When she tried to rise, Caah pinned her down with his arm across her shoulders. He gestured to Drafe, who stalked like a predator, his movements confident and silent. "Let him hunt. He will need vindication for the scent of your blood in his nose."

She bit her lip, fighting the compulsion to help. What if he needed back-up? What if he was wounded too? Who the farg had fired on her? In the deafening silence, nothing reached her. Not Drafe's location or the shooter's.

Just in case, she unholstered her blaster, wincing when her arm burned anew.

"If you shoot him, he will never live it down." Caah grinned, his white teeth bright in the dim lighting.

"Then help him," she snapped.

"And steal his vengeance? I am no fool, Vic."

She shoved at him, ready to jump up and charge forth.

"Please... Remain here. If you are harmed again, he *will* kill me." Caah met her gaze, his white eyes unsettling. "I guard you as I would expect him to do for me had you been mine."

Sweet of him to say but unnecessary. "Fine. I'll give him five more minutes. Can you check in with Nenn?" She peered into the darkness, desperate for some noise to tell her Drafe was okay. "I want to know how Tiny's doing." She chewed on a fingernail, a little worried her friend might die.

Caah tapped his neck. "Nenn, status?" He smiled. "Good, we will find you soon." He whispered to Vic, "He has found Tiny and is treating her head wound."

Relief drained the last adrenaline pumping through her veins. "Tell me, Caah, why didn't my armor stop the blaster shot?" She raised her elbow to better see her bicep, dark with her blood. Already the pain had dissipated.

"Summoning it comes with practice. In the beginning, its reaction to danger is unreliable."

"So I should have had it ready from the start?" *Stops a punch but not a shot? Go figure.*

"Yes and no. As you train, its formation will become swifter, almost as fast as thoughts fly." He chuckled. "Your existence and the symbiotes transferring to you without the ceremony is what will flummox the Q.C.C. I look forward to their revelation. They can be pompous eels."

She blinked. *Did he call his superiors eels?*

What lighting remained, flickered then fizzled out, enshrouding her and Caah in sheer darkness. She stilled, straining her ears to listen. A solid weight pinned her to the metallic grates, then rolled her just as a blaster shot flared white, burning into her retinae. In the flash of light, she'd caught a glimpse of Dieter, the muzzle of the blaster inches from where her head had been. She laughed then swallowed it when Caah cupped her mouth and flipped her again as another shot flew past her left shoulder.

"Computer," she whispered, "switch on all lights."

A scream followed.

In the blinding white fluorescents, she half-expected to find Dieter still in the passage. He'd slithered back to the engine room; night goggles lay where he must have discarded them.

"Good," she muttered.

Across the doorway, Drafe lunged. A thud and grunt had to mean he'd tackled Dieter to the floor. While they grappled, huffing and cursing, she pushed Caah off, careful not to hurt him. He offered her a sheepish smile and helped her to her feet.

"Want to stay for the show?" she asked him.

"Got to. Drafe might need me...us. Best you stay too."

She snorted. When she crept closer to the engine room's doorway, Caah tried to hold her back. She shrugged him off, waved her blaster as proof she was fine, then peered through the door at Drafe with a dagger at Dieter's throat. He growled something she couldn't pick up, but it had Caah nodding as if what he'd said made sense.

"Blood for her blood," Drafe said, plunged the wicked dagger into Dieter's chest, then twisted it. He didn't pause to make sure Dieter breathed his last. Instead, he rose, kicked Dieter's blaster across the room, then strode to her. Sweeping her into his arms, he stole a kiss before leaning back to study her wound. "Already healing."

"Feeling better?" she asked, despite loving his defense of her.

He scowled. "When I can no longer smell your blood, then I will be well."

Computer intoned, "Captain, Nikko is requesting release from lockdown."

"Denied." She chuckled. Poor Nikko, unable to free himself on his own ship.

"Acknowledged."

She rolled her shoulders, slamming her fist into her palm. "Time to even the score." She took the elevator to the mess level, striding with eagerness to the sealed door. "Computer, free Nikko."

As soon as could the door opened wide enough, she vaulted forward, pinning Nikko to the bulkhead.

"Vic? How is this—?" His eyes bulged when he peered over her shoulder at Drafe and Caah.

She squeezed his throat to get his attention. "I found the prisoners, Nikko. Care to explain? And the pods? Curious little things. Why would an ice hauler have either?"

When he struggled and clawed at her hand, she dug her nails into his skin until he ceased his escape attempts.

"No one questions an ice hauler traveling between planets, and Carne pays well," he rasped.

"Mm, and what's the security protocol when delivering your goods?"

He spluttered a chuckle. "I'm not saying."

"Fine." She released him, then punched him with her inhuman fist, snapping his head to the side. Blood trickled from the corner of his mouth. He groaned but glared at her. She grabbed him by the collar and dragged him behind her. "You know Leah, your lover?"

"No, don't hurt her." He slapped at her hand gripping his shirt.

She said nothing, just continued to the airlock.

"Vic," Drafe warned. "We need him, *gevatia*."

Caah sliced a glance at Drafe, his cheeks paling. *Interesting*. She'd ask Drafe about the endearment later when she had him at her mercy.

"Relax, I've got this." Outside the airlock, she tapped her neck device twice, then hit the depressurize button. Nikko cried out and fought harder to free himself. "Oh, and for your information, Nikko," she paused for effect, "Leah's dead."

The man wailed, screaming denials.

Drafe rested his hand on her shoulder. "Vic, please."

"Do you trust me, Drafe?" She met his pale-yellow eyes. They darkened to amber as he studied her. Something whispered across her mind. The deep resonance lingered, gentle and filled with familiar warmth.

"Yes." He stepped back and activated his neck device. Caah did the same.

She grinned, her chest swelling with a profound emotion she couldn't name. "Right answer."

The door slid open. She tossed Nikko into space, then waved as he traveled, his mouth contorted in horror. Punching the button, she closed the door and waited for the airlock to pressurize. After touching her neck device to deactivate the shield, she kissed Drafe, slipping her tongue in to claim him, to relish the taste of him.

Breaking away, she smiled at the ceiling. "Computer, replay archival footage from the bridge for previous security protocols when approaching the Carne medical facility."

"In chronological order?"

She basked in Drafe's grin. "Start from most recent."

Chapter Twenty-Four

Year: 2219

Aboard the Mula Pesada.

VIC UNHOLSTERED HER BLASTER when she paused outside Trent's door. "Computer, remove lockdown ship-wide."

Awake, he sprawled across his bed, wearing nothing but his pants. "What's going on, Vic?"

"Seems like Nikko's been trafficking humans to be used as medical test subjects."

Trent gaped, his toothpick falling from his parted lips. "Legit?" He rose to his feet, his gaze resting on Drafe looming behind her.

She hesitated. Trent's shock seemed real. "I suggest you stay in your quarters until we can ascertain your role in this."

"Sounds fair." He frowned. "As in *real* people, Vic?"

"Women and men, about thirty of them."

"Farg." He stumbled back and sat on his bed. The door closed on his pale face.

"Computer, the lockdown on Trent remains in place." She smiled at Drafe, loving the patience and peace rolling off him. "Now, to Grunt's. Computer, has the new maintenance crew chosen a manager?"

"They have."

"Please send him to Grunt's quarters." Vic paused, pressing her body against Drafe's. "He's a cute kid and doesn't deserve to die."

"You are the vengeance dealer, Vic. I guard you as I promised."

She rested her fists on her hips to hide how much his words delighted her. It took all her discipline to keep her lips from twitching. "Oh, yeah, and what would you have done had I not been here?"

He didn't hesitate. "Killed everyone."

She couldn't fault him. He was who he was, had never lied about it, and had no reason to. "Fair enough."

Following the flickering lights, a man hobbled along the passage to Vic. "I'm Dez, and the computer says you need me?" He'd had a shower and scrounged clothes from somewhere, although, the trousers threatened to fall off him.

"Yes, the kid's a tech whizz and may be of use to you. I'm sparing his life but placing him in your care. Also, I have Trent in his quarters. His shock is genuine, so his sincerity is yours to unravel. Computer, open Grunt's door."

Grunt swiveled his seat and smiled. "Hi, Vic, Drafe, Caah, Dez." He gestured to the floor-to-ceiling screens. His quarters were otherwise sparse. His bed sat in a corner, neatly made. Nothing was out of place. "I've watched everything play out, and maybe helped a little. Yes, I knew about the prisoners, along with Leah and Nikko's agenda." He rose from the chair and crossed to Vic, drawing a swirl over his inner wrist with a forefinger. A badge glowed. "My name's Iain Grant. I'm with Interspatial Law Enforcement. I.L.E. has been tracking these Ring disappearances and pod deployments." He settled his gaze on Drafe. "We couldn't destroy the pod before your scouts found it.

I.L.E. would like to extend an apology from the human race for the destruction, loss of life, and inconvenience the pod has caused." He tapped the closest screen. "Too many attempts to infiltrate Carne has cost us the lives of trained operatives. The *Mula Pesada* was one of many ships departing from Lunar Base that coincided with the disappearances."

Farg. Typical, Vic, sticking your big foot into the middle of things. "And I ruined your operation."

"On the contrary. You were the catalyst. Everything has come to a head." He tapped another screen, revealing Webb sitting on his bed, very much alive. "Nikko didn't kill Dean Webb as we expected. He will lead us to those supplying Carne with test subjects."

"Will I.L.E. intervene in the taking of the medical facility?" Dez strode into the room to stare at one screen displaying his people laughing in the mess.

"We have insufficient forces close enough to stop you, so no. I do request you leave key members alive to be charged for these crimes."

"Do we get to keep the facility?" Dez offered a lopsided smile. "We are without homes."

"That is agreeable. I will also suggest your facility be a safe zone for those Carne has harmed. I am certain I.L.E will allocate the funds to support you indefinitely."

Dez beamed. "We will hold onto the ice hauler as well, to serve as additional income."

Grunt nodded and captured Vic's hand for a shake. "It has been a pleasure to observe you, Victorious." He blushed. "That sounded creepy."

She laughed. "A little."

"It is best you visit with Themba now. He is not...well. If you need anything, don't hesitate to ask for me."

Vic took that as the cue to leave and did so, waiting in the passage for Caah and Drafe. Dez remained to discuss something she didn't need to be privy to.

"One last stop. Themba hired me as a debt owed." She marched to the elevator and took it to the level above.

Opening the captain's door, she drew to a halt. Where his quarters was messy before, now it was chaos. In the middle of it lay a weeping man. His screen was on, looping a video...of the Ring. She narrowed her eyes, focusing on the combatants. That was Ande. Stumbling in, she climbed over the debris to wipe away coffee dripping down the screen.

Ande was pinned to the floor, losing the match. His stats flickered along the side of the screen, all good. Within a blink, he was up, firing blasters from his left arm. Those were new. Devlin dodged and bounded toward Ande, closing the distance. In each other's space, they couldn't throw punches, so they grappled then spun in a lover's embrace.

"Now that the bitch is dead, you won't come to me?" Devlin's whispered words carried to the arena, silencing the crowds. All held their breaths, as she did. The pain on his face spoke of love lost, of aching need, of yearning. "I thought with her gone—"

Ande chuckled. "Vic was a sister to me, Devil. You fucked me over one too many times. There will never be an us."

The crowd roared, stamping their feet while chanting, "Victorious."

"Listen," Ande smirked. "She is still beloved."

"No, no more." Devlin thrust Ande away and forward kicked him, sending him flying. Her friend landed on the sand and glided, digging grooves with his heels.

Devlin vaulted into the air, planning on landing on top of Ande. She had seen this strike before.

"Move," she yelled, but Ande blinked, as if he had something in his eyes.

Devlin hit Ande with a knee to the chest, winding him. "For Carne," Devlin roared, then ripped out Ande's throat.

A strangled cry tore from her, and she staggered back from the image. Her dearest friend, the closest she had to family, was dying... No, this vid was old. Ande wasn't dead. No, no, it couldn't be true. She spun and hefted a sniveling Themba off the floor to shove his face at the screen.

"Is this true?"

He flicked his red and swollen gaze up. Fresh snot and tears leaked out when he blubbered.

"When?" she asked, despite the stamp in the corner flashing yesterday's date. Dropping him, she cradled the screen again to press her temple to it, pleading for it to be a lie. Ande was fine and would meet her in two years like he promised. "I begged you to come with me," she wailed, slapping the screen, and splintering the glass.

"I honored my side of the deal, Maz." Sebastian's face appeared. "But when you hid Vic from me, you intervened in Carne's business." He tapped his fingers on the desk. "That violates our agreement. I have revoked the protection order on Ande. As you can see, he didn't last long. What a pity." The image flickered to the arena, the scene playing on repeat.

Someone yanked her back, and she flailed, throwing out her hands to claw the screen. Strong arms wrapped around her and crushed her against a warm chest, pressing her face into muscle. The scent of sun-soaked skin relaxed her struggle, and she wept for her friend, her brother, and...her inability to save him.

"It's not true," she chanted. "It's a lie. He has amazing promise. Farg. Devlin killed him. I'll gut him, I swear I will." Her ranting fell on a pregnant silence peppered only by Themba's sobs. He'd lost a son. She pulled out of Drafe's arms and slumped to the floor beside Themba, curling around him.

Time slowed as she cried, drenching the poor man who was sopping wet and shivering. When no more tears flowed and those on her cheeks had dried, she lifted her head. Drafe waited in the doorway, silent, his brow furrowed at her madness, no doubt.

Warmth brushed across her mind. The fragrance of cinnamon teased her senses. She struggled to hold onto both.

"Please..." Her voice cracked. She wanted to ask for Tiny, but the girl was injured. Nenn couldn't help either when he had to see to Tiny.

Drafe crouched beside Vic and brushed her damp hair off her flushed and swollen face. "What do you need, *gevatia*?"

She glanced at her captain and the last connection she had to Ande. "Themba's shivering."

Drafe nodded, scooped her off the ground, and set her on her feet. He didn't release her until she had found her balance. Then, as if Themba wasn't a big man, Drafe lifted and carried him to his bed. She darted around him, tugging on the blankets to tuck in the devastated father.

"I'm here, Themba." She patted the man's shoulder as his breathing deepened.

"We cannot stay, Vic, not with a facility to siege."

She met Drafe's gaze. "How long have I been..."

"Hours."

So much time had made no impact on the solid darkness infesting her lungs. She couldn't breathe, it was so heavy, weighing her down, her eyelids, and her arms. "And you stayed? Why?"

"You were in distress." He rubbed his chest. "I feel it, Vic, and cannot bear it. Please... Action is better than being lost in memories and thoughts of vengeance."

"You just want me to strike the facility with you." She leaped to her feet to poke his right pec with a forefinger.

He caught her finger, hand, elbow, and pulled her closer. "Never. It pains me to put you in harm's way. Nor can I abandon you while you mourn."

She winced at the sincerity on his face. "I'm sorry, Drafe. I didn't mean to insult you and imply you had hidden motives. Go, fly this ship to the source. I'll stay here."

He tightened his arm around her. "And when I return?"

She closed her eyes not to see his sadness, but it didn't matter. Darkness engulfed her soul, and she wasn't sure if it was her own or Drafe's.

"I'll be in a better frame of mind." She forced a smile but couldn't keep it in place. "I promise."

He hesitated, then cupped her cheek. "Be careful."

"Me?" She snorted. "I'm not about to take a militarized medical facility. *You* be careful."

He nodded and let the door shut behind him.

She ignored the tear trickling free and faced Themba. "Right, let's tidy this cesspit and get some food into you." As she picked up shards of broken glass, stacked his books on unused shelves, and watered his desperate bonsai, she told herself that she was doing this for Ande. With the quarters clean and Themba sleeping, she lifted her gaze to the looped match.

Ande had fought the same Devlin who had tormented her when she first 'joined' Carne. Now she had a target. Argh, there went any chance of freedom. She would have to breach the Ring, and stroll into Sebastian Carne's domain to kill him and his puppet, Devlin.

To do that, she would need a ride.

Farg. Bolting out of Themba's quarters, she sprinted along the passages and burst onto the bridge.

Drafe raised his head, then closed the distance between them. He gathered her hands in his and tugged her against him, creating a sense of privacy. "What is it, *gevatia*?"

"I'm coming with you."

He shook his head. "We decided it is safer—"

"Carne killed my...brother, Drafe. I want vengeance, and I need an arsenal. Both can be gotten from taking the facility."

He closed his pale-yellow eyes, his fingers squeezing her. "I cannot lose you, Vic."

"How better to guard me when I'm at your side?" She offered him a wide smile, needing to go, to keep herself busy, to vent her anger, to find someone closer to blame.

He grinned. "That is illogical."

"Fine." She gripped his waist, clutching onto his armor-covered pecs. "Ask Aehort."

Drafe huffed. "That is cheating."

She shrugged, rose onto her toes, and stole a kiss. His breath caught, and before she could pull away, he cupped the back of her head. With a sweep of his tongue, her will crumbled. She adored the taste of him, inhaled his addictive cologne, and leeched what strength she could from his embrace.

This was foolhardy. She hadn't wanted to involve herself, but as she saw it, if she helped Drafe find justice for the Ivoy, he might help her return to Earth and kill Sebastian Carne.

Either way, what would follow was her kind of mayhem, and Carne had ensured she was more than equipped to orchestrate their destruction. Oh, the irony was sweet.

Panting for breath, she rested her temple on his chin. "How's Tiny?"

Drafe smiled when he pulled away and gestured to the med bay. "See for yourself."

"Call me when we approach the facility." Without waiting, Vic hurried from the bridge, aware his men had watched them kiss. She should be mortified, but sex and the acts thereof had been bandied about Carne for the last ten years.

Whispering warned her she might be walking into something a little intimate so she cleared her throat before peeking through the door. Tiny sat on the med bunk, her legs spread with Nenn nestled between them as he ran a weird device over her eyes. She stroked his chest and any part of him she could reach.

Vic smiled. "Am I intruding?"

"Not at all, Vic." Tiny raised her gaze to Nenn's, the white of her eyes paler, revealing a little of her green irises.

"How are you feeling?" Vic crossed to the bed and clasped its railing.

"Good. Nenn has a soft touch." Tiny's cheeks flushed. "You've been busy."

"I have?" Vic shuffled on her feet, not wanting to mention who she killed or the latest news squeezing her chest. 'Ande is dead' looped in the back of her mind. Perhaps she was in shock and shouldn't be making decisions? Too late. She gritted her teeth as tension thickened and climbed up her throat, choking off her breathing. Her vision spun.

Breathe, Vic.

"Aehort?" she gasped, expecting to find the orange alien in the room with her.

Right, the symbiotes. Her future spread out before her. Take the facility, destroy the Ring, and travel to Ivoy. All were decided for her, either through her actions or the consequences of what had happened to her. Despite winning the deca-match, her life was not her own, her path not hers to choose.

She had some choice, though. Heading to Europa with Drafe was her decision to make. And he would help her destroy the Ring whether she took the facility with him or not. But her ma had raised Vic to help where she could. If she asked someone to endanger their lives, she had to be willing to do the same.

She flicked a glance over her shoulder, as if she would find Drafe behind her. His quiet support was as precious as water. Farg, she would need to tell him how she felt about him and soon.

"Vic?" Tiny's voice broke through Vic's thoughts. "Are you all right? Nenn, scan her too."

"I'm fine." Vic threw out her hands to stop him, but he ignored her to wipe away the blood staining her arm. As Drafe had claimed, only smooth skin remained. "I know I told you to come with me, but you can stay with Themba. If you want."

"Nenn invited me to travel with him to his home." She pursed her lips, her purple hair bouncing. "I'm undecided. You?"

Vic drew in a slow breath, taking the plunge. "I too will be going to Ivoy." *At some point in the future.*

"Oh. Then, of course, I'll go. I didn't want to be a burden nor the only human woman on board their ship." Her smile was so bright and carefree. Vic had never known such an emotion, not as a child, and sure as shit, not as an adult.

"Tiny, sweetheart, you helped us free the prisoners. You're not a burden." Vic squeezed her shoulder. "Since you're in Nenn's capable hands, I'll return to the bridge. I'm sure there's much to discuss. When you are feeling better, please care for Themba. He's..." she winced, "not well."

Abandoning them to whatever she had stumbled upon, she hurried along the passage to the bridge, sliding in to lean against the bulkhead, her knees trembling. Pretending to be emotionally stable was draining. A dark room, a bed, and time were all she needed.

When Dez spotted Vic, he crossed the room to grab her hand. "Victorious, thank you."

"It's just Vic." She forced a smile, uncomfortable with his gratitude.

He bobbed his head. "Fair enough. Drafe tells me he has the security protocol to breach the facility's defenses."

She grasped the news, needing it to focus her spiraling thoughts. "Good. We must end these experiments and the deployment of explosive pods."

"With Iain's promise of assistance, we hope to find a new home down there. Maybe set up a control base." Dez smiled but sadness lingered in his brown eyes.

He and his fellow prisoners must have endured much, yet he chose to face the future with courage. So too should she. There would be time later to mourn Ande.

She rolled her shoulders, trying to ease a burning ache in the middle of her back. "So, minimize damage is what you're asking for." A shadow pressed down on her again, smothering her thoughts, what her senses communicated, what her purpose was for being there. Her gaze settled on Drafe leaning over the console, chatting to Caah, flashes of a smile between comments. He would be her beacon of light and hope.

Dez chuckled. "Something like that." He squeezed and released her hand, drawing her back to the moment.

"I'll try." That was all she could promise, because at that moment, she wanted to burn Carne to the ground.

CHAPTER TWENTY-FIVE

"We have the security protocol, but there are still two hours before we will be in range." Drafe gripped Vic's arm and ran his thumb over where her wound had been. "I need to speak with you."

She offered a small smile. "Sound's serious."

He nodded. "I need you alone."

She peered around Drafe at a grinning Caah. "Please go with Dez. Make sure the shuttle is ready for departure."

The bridge cleared.

Drafe hesitated to speak after several minutes had passed.

"What is it?" She frowned and captured his hands, running her thumbs over his knuckles.

"Nenn suggested I share a little of my home, of its blazing suns, the endless sand plains, the rolling dunes, the vasquva, the hudu, the garak, the venai stones. But none of those convey the sunbaked scent greeting you in the morning, the crunch of salt beneath your boots, the sweet tang of dried vasquva, or the warm glow of a venai stone across your beloved's face."

"Beautiful, Drafe." He had her at sunbaked scent. "Are we going to Qaldreth? To your tribe?"

"Yes, after we have appeased the Q.C.C. There is more, Vic."

"I don't doubt that. Why don't you start with *gevatia*. Why does Caah find the use of it alarming?"

Drafe's eyes glowed a brilliant amber as he cupped her cheeks to tilt her face to his adoring gaze. "It is Qaldreth for...'my heart.'"

She gaped, then blinked to clear her blurring vision. He couldn't mean... She shook her head as the tears slipped free despite her best efforts. "Is it the symbiotes talking?" They'd only known each other for weeks. Love couldn't stem from that. It was illogical and lacked a strong foundation.

"No." He smiled and snuck a kiss, his lips lingering on hers. "I loved you from the moment you told me not to waste your time and from the second you kissed me."

She laughed through the tears and threw herself into his arms. "I love you too."

Air rushed out of his lungs, and the release of tension drooped his shoulders an inch.

"You were worried?" She ran her hand across his collarbone, marveling at the velvet texture of his armored skin.

"Yes. I feared you would choose to stay." He closed his arms around her. "I would not have forced you to come with me to Ivoy or Qaldreth."

"I do have a quest I need to complete." She nibbled on her bottom lip, debating telling him when it might ruin his opinion of her. "I want to return to the Ring and kill Sebastian Carne."

"A noble endeavor, and one you will not do alone."

Gasping at his unwavering support, she snatched a kiss. He deepened it, groaning when he crushed her against him and slid in his tongue, conquering her thoughts. For that moment, sorrow didn't dare linger. When he drew away, she fought to breathe as lust unraveled in her core.

"We're dating?"

He laughed. "No, Vic, it's much more serious than that." He buried his fingers in her hair, cupping her head to hold her still for yet another plunder she happily submitted to. "We are *vatia sahaar*...love mates. When we step on Qaldreth soil, all will know you. The symbiotes will whisper to you, will record who you are, and what you mean to me, to my tribe. You will be known for thousands of generations to come."

"For eternity?" Many promised to love each other until the stars ceased to exist, but this shit was real.

"Yes. You will adore my sister and her mate, Vic, and they you."

He had a family? "You have a sister?"

"As do you now." He captured her escaped tears with his lips before claiming her mouth. "This is meant to bring you joy," he said into her hair.

"It does. I'm...happy." She hugged him, pressing her cheek to his chest.

"I know. I share it." He nuzzled her temple with his chin. "I wanted you to know, let you decide for yourself to stay with me."

"I will stay with you, Meorri aac Drafe Arrak." She grinned, unable to resist teasing him.

"This pleases me, Meorri aac Victoria."

She jerked back. "My name changes?"

"This bothers you?" He pulled away, frowning. "You are part of my tribe, and all should know this."

It sounded like she was married, like she had found a place to belong. Tears prickled behind her eyes again, as if she hadn't cried herself out an hour ago. "I'm honored, *gevatia*."

A slow smile dominated his lips. *Farg, he is magnificent.*

She snatched a kiss, climbing him like a solar tower. Grabbing her ass and without breaking the kiss, he spun and pinned her to the bulkhead, grinding his hard cock at the apex of her thighs. She moaned, needing more, him, now.

"Please," she whimpered between kisses and gasps for air.

"You better not be doing what it sounds like. I may be blind, but I'm not deaf," Tiny called from the med bay.

Vic broke the kiss, panting.

Drafe chuckled. "Your old quarters?"

"Farg, a closet will do." She grabbed his hand and tugged him behind her. "Good thing my quarters is the size of one." Giggling like children, they hurried to her room. When the door closed, she shoved him against it and unsnapped his trousers.

He rubbed her hands aside, but she insisted.

"Trust me, Drafe." She met his gaze and waited.

When he lowered his hands to his sides, she stroked his hips until his armor faded and his cock sprang free. Heat flushed her cheeks, and she licked her lips, nervous but oh so eager to try this.

She wrapped her fingers around the girth and slid up and down the length of him, amazed at the silky, hot feel. He moaned when she ran her touch over the ridges along the top. She grinned. So, he was sensitive there. Good to know. She followed the path of her hand with her tongue. The velvet heat of his skin warmed her, and a hunger like nothing she had ever experienced burned in her core, urging her to be brave and bold. She wrapped her mouth around the head of his cock and sucked while stroking those ridges.

"Vic," he rasped. "Osnir save me, that feels...incredible." His voice roughened, hoarse, like gravel along her senses. Encouraged, she sucked harder, pulling him deeper into her mouth, relishing how much joy pleasing him brought her.

He stroked her hair, his touch switching between gentle and rough, until he cried out, and tugged on her shoulders.

She released his cock and smacked her lips. "What? You don't like it?" She widened her eyes, adding a pout while stroking the length of him.

"Strip. Now."

"Spoilsport," she chuckled. "Fine." Since she was crouching, she unclipped her boots.

"Leave your boots. I cannot wait, Vic."

He hoisted her to her feet, spun her, and unsnapped her pants, shoving it and her panties down. Then with a thrust of his hips, she toppled, her ass in the air. He grabbed her hips, angled his cock until he rubbed against her entrance, then with a thrust, buried himself. She moaned, arching her back, despite being bent over like a paper straw.

Within a few powerful thrusts, she didn't care as she rode a wave of splintered pleasure so exquisite, stars circled her vision. He wrapped around her, thrusting even as he layered her back with his chest. Releasing one hip, he squeezed her breast while pressing kisses to her neck. Another orgasm barreled toward her. She couldn't hold it back and didn't want to. Screaming, she exploded into a kaleidoscope of shivers, pebbling her nipples, tightening her core, and stealing her breath.

He roared, stilled, and shuddered, panting her name. After pulling out, he gathered her into his arms, crossed to her bed, and sprawled her onto it. Climbing over her, he pressed her into the mattress and spent minutes kissing her, not sparing an inch of her face. He gazed into her eyes between kisses, his pupils glowing amber.

"I love you, Vic."

She nodded, unable to trust her voice. Instead, she wrapped her arms around him and held on tight.

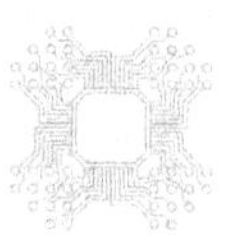

WHEN THEY STRODE TO the bridge with Drafe gripping her hip, he unsheathed a dagger from his boot. "Take this, Vic."

She accepted the weapon and spun it, testing its weight. The handle looked like bone, the blade an unusual shimmering steel. "It's beautiful, Drafe."

"The handle is a hudu tooth, the blade is made from an old star that fell in our territory."

A gift? She sniffed, wiping her nose with the back of her wrist. Only Ande had given her things, and she had cherished each one no matter how small. Most were extra food parcels, fighting lessons with a master, or a vid of her home.

Once on the bridge, she slipped the weapon into her boot then squeezed Drafe's hand. "Thank you." Rising onto her toes, she kissed his chin. Any higher and back to her quarters they would go.

She smiled at Tiny and Nenn manning the console. "Glad to see you two. We're getting ready to take the facility."

"I'm staying, of course." Tiny stilled and didn't glance at Nenn.

"I will be heading moonside with you, Vic." Nenn squeezed Tiny's upper arm, captured a lock of her hair, and tucked it behind an ear. His fingers trembled.

"Good. I like knowing there's someone I can trust on the *Mula Pesada*. How's Themba?" Guilt slammed into Vic, tightening her chest as if a cybernetic hand reached into her to crush her heart. Drafe draped his arm across her shoulder and pulled her in for a kiss. She leaned against him, drawing strength from him.

"I administered a calming drug. It will knock him out for a while. The computer is monitoring his vital signs." Tiny paused. "I'm sorry for his loss."

"Thank you, Tiny." *Time to start this.* Vic released a slow breath. "Computer, ship-wide broadcast. *Mula Pesada*, this is the captain speaking. Report to the docking bay. The shuttle leaves in ten."

The trip to the bay was in silence. No words were necessary. The plan was simple. The prisoners would pretend to be drugged captives. Once they were escorted into the facility, shit would hit the fan.

She loved the plan. Drafe hadn't wanted anyone to be harmed, hence why Nenn was along for the ride. As she slid down the ladder into the bay, she gaped at the shuttle which looked like a boxcar with strips of rusted metal. Pieces of painted letters formed no legible words but added to the dystopian feel.

"Caah, does this thing even fly?" She scanned it as they approached the lowered ramp. The closer she got, the worse it looked with gaps between the twisted or bent metal.

"I thought the same, but she's space-worthy." Caah leaned out of the shuttle, one hand gripping the door's edge. "I present the *Burro Lento*, or so the manifest claims."

Now *that* she'd believe. "Cute." She chuckled. "Just as long as this 'slow donkey' is safe." When she stepped into the shuttle, she smiled at those boarded with Dez in the front. "Weapons?"

They nodded, some held up daggers or blasters, and one had a rusted machete. It was the state of their hearts that mattered, not the condition of their arsenal.

"Vic," Grant panted as he stumbled into the shuttle. "I can't aid your cause, but if you could record it, you might capture incriminating information I can later claim I don't know the source of."

She laughed. "Sure."

"Stand still." He held a device over her eye. Blinded by the light and the image of a multi-colored hot air balloon, she waited. Something tickled the bottom eyelashes and pinched her eye. She jerked back. "Done." He pocketed the device and tapped his arm, swiping across a small screen to the right of the console. What she was seeing flickered into existence. "What you see, I'll record."

She blinked to clear her teary-eyed vision.

"Don't worry. By the time you land, you'll be fine." He winced. "It's just going to hurt in a few days when you pee out those bots."

She punched Grant on the arm.

He yelped and leaped away. "Sorry, should have led with that." Stumbling down the ramp, he waved and disappeared up a ladder.

"All aboard?" Caah claimed the pilot seat.

"Yes," Dez responded, his fingers twitching where he gripped a blaster.

"Initiating start up," Caah called as he typed on the console, his fingers blurring. "We are good for pre-flight. Final checks completed. Ready to launch."

"Okay, Caah, take us down." Vic faced the worried faces.

"Brace for detachment. Arm uncoupled." Caah chortled. "This is going to be fun."

The shuttle jerked, and with a high-pitched scream, its ass swung outward, filling the screen with the back end of the hauler and the retracting arm.

"Descending, reducing speed by a hundred knots. Temperatures are a balmy negative one-six-zero degrees Celsius. The atmosphere is a thin layer of oxygen. No marking to use as a point of entry, other than the red cruiser on a landing pad."

"Carne." Vic rubbed her hands together. "Hail *Vesalius*, this the *Burro Lento* requesting permission to land."

"*Burro Lento*, we've been expecting you. What's the delay?"

"Shuttle malfunction, *Vesalius*. Tends to happen with these rust buckets." Vic grimaced.

The man paused before he cleared his throat. Not a good sign. "Where's Nikko?"

"Had an emergency. Had to journey home." She grinned and whispered, "to hell." Raising her head, she said, "Left everything in my control."

"And Themba?" Doubt warbled the man's voice.

"Just found out his son died. Give me a break here. Leah has laryngitis, Dieter's busy with engine repair, which leaves me, the newbie, delivering the cargo. Man, it stinks too. Fargen lot of them need sol-baths stat."

Silence followed her outburst. She met Drafe's calm gaze. Knowing him, he would storm the place if sneaking in didn't work.

"No can do, *Burro Lento*. Permi—" The man paused. "Wait, my boss would like a word. Patching vidcon through."

The screen flickered to a face Vic hated more than her pa's.

"Ah, Victoria Harper, what a small galaxy. You'll be delighted to know your precious Ande lost his match. Of course, his death came as a surprise, and Devlin will be dealt with most severely. Alas, I digress. I thought Nikko disposed of you."

It took all her strength not to wince with the memories of her solo-flight still fresh. "Sebastian, I didn't know it was my birthday. I can't resist saying how happy I am to see you off-world."

She grinned, the need for revenge twitching her fingers. Slitting his throat came to mind and with Drafe's dagger in her boot, her plan would be realized.

The universe had blessed her. She would capture *Vesalius* and take her revenge at the same time.

CHAPTER TWENTY-SIX

Year: 2219

Moonside on Europa.

Carne snorted. "Permission to land denied."

"Fine by me, Carne. I'll just free your prisoners and issue an official statement to the Galactic News. They might be surprised to find I'm very much alive."

He laughed. "They won't believe you unless you travel to Earth." He tapped the console. "Then again, I would like another opportunity to kill you, and since you're being so obliging, by all means, land."

The screen flickered to black.

"Now we have the red carpet rolled out for us," Dez muttered. "Sonja will take over the shuttle when we disembark. She has piloting skills and will land out of firing range. The codeword to order the shuttle's return is 'humpback.'"

"Those with blasters will head out first." Drafe scanned the compartment before resting his gaze on Vic. "No heroics. You have survived so much. Dying now is stupid."

"I equipped the shuttle with gas canisters in case *Vesalius* is not friendly." Caah tossed a grin. "When we fire those, wait for them to collapse and the air to dissipate before we disembark."

Dez pursed his lips. "Could work."

"Good thinking, Caah." Vic squeezed Caah's shoulder.

"If all else fails, I added laser canons for sticky doors." He chuckled. "Was fun tweaking your human weapons."

Drafe tapped his chin before clasping Vic's hip. "I would suggest we land a distance away and go in on foot. Caah, Vic and I will take them by surprise. Once the area is clear, Sonja will fly the shuttle and land. Let's save our arsenal for emergencies."

Vic bounced on her toes, loving the idea of a little action.

Dez shook his head. "You don't have suits. It would be suicide. Europa may have oxygen in its atmosphere, that doesn't mean it's survivable and not at these temperatures."

She grinned and double-tapped her neck device. The shield rippled as it formed. "Has two hours of oxygen and traps our body heat. We'll be fine." With another double-tap, she deactivated it. "Everyone know the plan?"

They nodded.

"There are bound to be medical personnel. What we want are the chief surgeons, the director of the facility, someone in charge." She met each gaze. "If you have to fire, aim to wound or disarm."

"Agreed. For all we know, these people are as much prisoners as we once were." Dez checked his blaster then strapped it to his thigh.

"Landing the shuttle one klik from the facility." Caah spun its ass and lowered it with the slightest of bumps. As he slid off the pilot's seat, a brunette woman with a ponytail and a scarred cheek took his place.

"Remember 'humpback.'" Sonja ran a delicate touch over the console.

"I like the name *Vesalius*." Dez sidled closer to Vic. "It's a pity we'll have to change it."

Vic grinned. "Got any ideas?" With vengeance so close, she couldn't stem the flow of adrenaline. Her leg bounced as each second brought her closer to her target.

"Rebirth?" He twisted his mouth.

She shrugged. "The naming of it is up to you, Dez. Just don't die on me."

"Carne contesters are hard to kill."

She frowned, flashes of Ande's death gainsaying Dez's words. "But we *can* die."

He nodded and left her to lean against Drafe, who wrapped an arm around her to pull her closer. "Same applies to you, *gevatia*. There will be no dying today."

"The almighty Drafe Arrak has spoken," she teased before snatching a kiss.

"No, because Aehort has shared a vision. You live, my female." He chuckled. "But it pleases me that you think me all-powerful."

She wasn't about to mess with his ego by implying that wasn't what she meant. Besides, parts of him were mighty. "Bless Aehort. He should be here."

"He is inside me and you. Learn to listen for him." Drafe cupped her cheek, trailing his thumb down her neck. She shivered and nuzzled his palm. "Listen for me."

"I'll open the door a little. No need to freeze us all." Sonja tapped the console. The door groaned as it inched open.

Vic activated her shield and slipped through the crack. After waiting for the door to start closing, she hurried to catch up to Drafe and Caah, jogging toward the red ship but a blip on the horizon. She smiled. Yet another thing she wanted to thank Sebastian for—a free ship.

As fit as she was, by the time she climbed the ice shelf circling the base, she gasped for air. Men in suits patrolled around the red cruiser, military blasters in hand.

"A dozen. That means four apiece." She counted on her fingers. "They're a little blinded by their helmets. We can strike from behind."

"That is the coward's way," Drafe said. She would swear before the Q.C.C. that his scowl traveled through the neck device.

The urge to roll her eyes gripped her, but the infantile action was wasted on Qaldreth warriors. "Got any other ideas?" She arched a brow. "Divide and conquer. They're expecting us, so anything we do will be met with their full force."

Caah gestured to the ground. "Drop from the ledge. If we land well, we can disarm three."

Drafe peeked over the edge. "The rest will fire at us, but at least it will be face to face."

"As long as we can start this instead of debate it, I'm in." She peered at the soldiers closest to her. The drop was significant, two levels high. She would need to land on her cybernetic leg to absorb the impact. "Ready."

She waved at Drafe and threw herself off.

"Vic."

Laughing, she dropped on top of a guard, crushing his spine, then fired at the closest two, before rolling behind the landing pad of the cruiser. Confusion reigned with the rapid-fire of blasters. They aimed for the ledge, not realizing that Caah and Drafe had split, both planning to fall from separate positions. Sliding under the cruiser, she duck-walked across, prepared to add cover fire.

As Drafe and Caah plummeted, she fired, drawing the soldiers' attention. Seven more died.

"They're everywhere," a soldier screamed and banged on the door to be let inside. He died, smearing blood down the steel while his oxygen escaped in a hiss.

"Where's the twelfth man?" Vic asked, unable to see anyone's legs but Caah and Drafe's.

Behind you.

At Aehort's warning, she spun and fired without hesitation, catching the soldier by surprise.

"Got him," she chuckled. "See, what did I say? Easy."

"You will receive chastisement when we return to the *Aroagni*," Drafe growled as he hoisted her from under the cruiser.

"Oh, am I due for a good spanking?" At the idea, heat uncoiled in her core. She pinched her thighs together. Now wasn't the time.

"I am right here." Caah tossed her a glare. "*Burro Lento*, humpback."

Sonja responded, "Roger that, Caah. En route now."

"So, any ideas how to open the doors?" Vic smiled and pointed at the sec cams.

Caah scanned a panel with his wrist. It flickered green while he typed on the holographic images glowing in his skin. The panel flashed red. He pursed his lips and continued.

"You do know there'll be a fresh wave waiting for us." She pressed her shoulder to Drafe's.

"I expected as much." He tugged a ball out of somewhere. "One of Caah's gas canisters."

She studied his body, layered with his thick symbiotic armor. Where were the pockets? "I knew there's a reason I find you incredibly sexy."

He chuckled. "Only one reason?"

"I cannot wait for time away from you two." Caah raised his head to glance at them. "I am a little envious, to be honest."

"Find your own female." Drafe curled his arm around her waist.

Caah jerked back, and a slow smile formed. "Good idea. Perhaps I will return and help Dez repair this—" The doors glided open amid blaster fire between the growing gap.

Vic bolted forward and pinned herself to the door, firing on those foolish enough to be in her line of sight. Drafe did the same on the other side.

"Like fish in a barrel," she called.

By the time the doors had tucked into the walls, bodies littered the entryway. Alarms blared, and red lights flickered. The facility was on high alert. More boots thundered closer, as if Carne had endless security.

"Dying for Carne isn't worth it. Toss out Sebastian Carne, and we'll spare your lives." She smiled at Drafe who frowned at her. "Had to try," she whispered.

When he drew a symbol over his neck, his shield shimmered to black. He strolled into the facility and shot six times.

She gaped, mesmerized by the pale gray circles from where his shield had taken fire. "And you couldn't share that with me?"

Drafe's frown knitted his brow. "No, you would use it without thought. Once is all the shield can spare."

"Once?" She huffed. "We could have ended this a while ago."

"I would prefer you save yours for when it is necessary, *gevatia*." His eyes faded to pale yellow. "I will not lose you."

"So you don't believe I can do this?" She huffed. "I need all the information to make informed decisions, Drafe. Look at me, I have survived without your assistance."

"Fine, but no heroics, Vic." He captured her hand and drew on her palm a zero with a line slashed through it.

"I promise." She captured his hand and kissed it through the shield.

A blast of air whipped at the bodies in their suits. Snow eddies spiraled up. She followed them as they twirled until her gaze rested on the sleeping giant of Jupiter looming over them. The *Burro Lento* landed behind the cruiser. The prisoners disembarked, sprinting toward them. The dead soldiers across the doorway kept the doors open. As soon as the last person entered the foyer, Caah kicked aside the bodies and slipped inside before the doors sealed shut.

All gasped, able to breathe again. Snow coated their hair and eyelashes. Many shivered, rubbing their exposed arms.

"Ready?" Dez scanned his people.

Drafe led the way, single file along the passages. Employees in white coats screamed and threw themselves down. Dez made lightwork of capturing and placing them under guard in a large lab. So they went, capture personnel, kill soldiers. When they reached the end of the corridor and an elevator, Vic spun on her heel and grabbed the closest med tech.

"What is under us? How many levels?"

The man squeaked. She tightened her grip on his shoulder until he winced.

"There are six more levels."

"And what is on them? What should we expect?" Drafe shoved his face into the man's. The poor thing's eyes bulged.

"Level two has security and storerooms, living spaces, and entertainment areas." He swallowed so hard, his Adam's Apple almost popped out of his throat. "Levels three to six are labs and patients. You want level seven which is for top-secret projects only. That's where Carne will be."

Useful. Vic studied his beaded forehead then glanced at the lab Dez guarded. "Any chance we can convince your people to surrender? We're not after them."

The med tech nodded, sweat trickling down the side of his face. "Let me...speak to them on the comm system." He raised a trembling finger to point at a black box behind her.

She released him. He sagged then stumbled across the corridor to lean on the button. "Don't fight them. They want Carne. We can live, survive this, and return to our families."

"Thanks, McCarthy," she read his name off his keycard now in her hand. "Is there another way down?"

Caah strode along the passage, a bright grin on his dark face. His white hair and eyes glowed. "I deactivated the vids. They cannot trace our progress."

"The stairs." McCarthy pointed at a door but mere cracks in the paneling. "May I join my people?" At Vic's nod, he scurried to the door Dez hovered in and slipped past him.

The old man and a few of his people broke off and hurried to join her. "Are we going down?"

"Not in the elevator." She leaned on the button, summoning it. As soon as the doors opened, she aimed her blaster. It was empty. Dipping her head inside, she pressed all the buttons, going down six floors.

With a grin, she strolled to the hidden door, swiped the keycard she had stolen from McCarthy, and slipped inside.

CHAPTER TWENTY-SEVEN

Year: 2219

Moonside on Europa.

THE STAIRWELL AMPLIFIED SHOTS fired. Surprised screams and the moans of the dying meant one thing. Carne was killing his people, the key members Grant needed. She sprinted, taking the steps two at a time. Stopping at the next level was foolhardy, no matter how much she wanted to save these poor folks. The only way to end the carnage was to capture Carne.

"Vic," Drafe called, hot on her heels. "When we reach the bottom, let me go first."

"Why? He wants me, Drafe. You, he'll just kill."

"Female," he growled. "We are walking into a trap. I am most unhappy with this."

She shrugged. "What do you expect? Besides, Aehort had a vision, remember."

Drafe scowled. "That does not mean you can be reckless with my heart."

"What?" she squeaked and paused on a landing to catch her breath.

"You have my heart as I have yours. Dying will sever it from my body."

"Right. That makes no sense *and* should have been something you mentioned before a life-and-death mission."

"She has you there," Caah said as he ran past them.

Grunting, Drafe followed him.

She sucked in a deep breath and hurried to catch up. "Shorter legs here."

They ignored her, and she knew why. If they reached the bottom level first, she wouldn't be able to enter before them. *Smartasses.*

Farg it. She threw herself over the railing and plummeted the final two levels, landing on her cybernetic leg. Still, she fell into a crouch just to make sure she didn't harm herself.

"Vic," Drafe roared, but she ignored him, drew a zero with a line through it across her device, and opened the door.

The blaster shots hit her in the chest. She fired, taking down the five men surrounding Sebastian Carne seated at his wooden desk. The room was a replica of his office onboard the *Conqueror*, the training grounds for Carne combatants.

"You were always too skilled for your own good. And so damn righteous." He tapped his vapor pipe on a wooden ashtray.

Without hesitating, she shot him in the shoulder.

He cried out and cupped the wound. "I thought we could be civil," he gritted out.

"You don't know the meaning," she said and shot him in the other shoulder. While he writhed in his chair, she leaned across and pressed the button for the comm system. "I have Carne, cease killing your people or he dies." She nodded at Caah and Drafe. "Go, I've got this. Help Dez clear the levels."

"*Gevatia,*" Drafe hesitated. "Take care."

"I promise," she smiled and fired a shot into Carne's right thigh.

He whimpered, pushing his chair back. Across his knees lay a blaster.

"Reach for it and die sooner." She rested her ass on the end of his desk. "You can beg now, although, I will say, it won't make an ounce of difference."

"Ande wasn't my doing," Carne whimpered.

"Sure it wasn't. Not like I saw your message to Themba." She studied her fingernails then chewed on a torn thumbnail. "It's a pity Devlin didn't travel with you." She shrugged. "He was an eager puppet suffering from unrequited love. You always knew where to twist the dagger. I bet you convinced him that Ande was fucking me." She grinned and nudged the blaster off Carne's lap with the tip of her boot. "*Burro Lento*, patch me through to Grant on the *Mula Pesada*."

"Patched through, Vic."

"Grant, Carne's dead. We were unable to save him. His wounds bled too fast, too much. What a shame." She beamed at a pale Carne.

Silence fell for a minute before Grant asked, "And the facility?"

"Captured. Send in the I.L.E to sweep it clean and gather what intel you can." Carne spluttered, so she waved her blaster at him. Tilting her head, she studied the man she had hated for a decade of her life. Without hesitation, she shot him between the eyes.

A pause followed before Grant asked, "Was that a blaster shot?"

"Space rats. Best hurry. *Burro Lento*, end patch."

She withdrew her dagger and slit Carne's throat for good measure. There was no surviving that. "For Ande," she whispered.

Staring at Carne's slumped body, she felt no remorse. He'd taught her not to regret, not to fear death. Scanning his office, she smiled, allowing the weight of hatred, the memories of pain, loneliness, sadness, and grief to leak from her. Peace settled, and she laughed, letting her tears slip free.

There was freedom in vengeance.

As she climbed the stairs, she paused at each level and peeked through the door, finding strewn bodies, and nothing else. When she reached the first level, Drafe guarded the elevator, Caah was at the other end of the corridor at the entryway, and Nenn meandered through the prisoners, healing with his black box.

Dez had the employees in hand. He nodded at his people and approached Vic. "Is he—?"

"Yup, right between the eyes." She tapped her forehead. "*Vesalius* is yours. Chosen a name yet?"

"Libertas." He beamed.

"A good choice." She slapped him on the shoulder.

"Once we have inventoried everything, we'll destroy those pods, Drafe, and give those poor souls proper burials." Dez pressed his hand to his chest. "I promise."

"My thanks, honorable Dez." Drafe gripped the older man's forearm.

Dez's cheeks flushed at the compliment. "Now what?"

"The I.L.E. should be visiting you soon." She gestured to the facility's employees. "Sorry you have to clean this up."

Dez shrugged. "It's our home now, and housekeeping is an eagerly awaited chore."

"Fair enough. We'll take the *Burro Lento* to the *Mula Pesada*." When Nenn glanced up, she gestured that they were leaving. "Dez, need anyone to come with?"

"No." Dez scanned the floor, contentment in his lingering smile. "Those who wanted to remain on board did so. Sonja will pilot the shuttle for you."

Made sense. Vic nodded. "Thanks, Dez."

"No, thank you, Vic, Drafe, Nenn, and Caah." He waved at Caah. "You have given us back our lives."

Vic strolled along the corridor, activated her shield, and walked through the gaping doors. They closed behind Nenn, the last one to leave.

She smiled at Sonja as she stepped into the shuttle's compartment. "To the *Mula Pesada*. I wish to bid Themba goodbye."

"He will be asleep for many days, Vic." Drafe unflipped a wall-mounted chair and lowered himself onto it. He captured her hips and tugged her onto his lap, wrapping his arms around her waist as he buried his nose in her hair.

"True." She smiled through her tears. Since leaving Earth, she had cried more than the last twenty-seven years combined. She snorted. It had better be a passing phase.

"I wish to remain on the *Mula Pesada*," Caah said when Sonja launched off the moon. "Without having to ask the Q.C.C. for permission. You know how long they take to debate."

She could imagine with seven commanders or udaps on the Q.C.C., no doubt with volatile and dominant personalities. Focusing on the whispers inside her, she zoned in. How had she known about the udaps, what that word even meant? Or that there were seven of them, one for each tribe: mountains, sky, jungle, canyons, volcano, water, and Drafe's desert, hence the colors of their hair and eyes. How simple yet so radiantly beautiful.

Drafe tilted her to stare into her eyes, his warmed to amber. "I shall inform them it was my decision." He didn't glance at Caah. "Your skills are needed here, and you will serve as a bridge between humans and Qaldreth. If the Q.C.C. wish to send an ambassador, they may do so at their leisure."

Caah beamed and gripped Drafe's forearm, snapping his gaze from hers. "My thanks, *darasaho*." He joined Nenn in leaning against the interior bulkhead.

"Drop us on top of the *Mula Pesada*, Sonja." Drafe pointed over her shoulder to the ice hauler.

"What?" she squeaked. "Okay, if you say so." Her brows knitted, but she angled the shuttle anyway.

"Get the *Aroagni* to send a shuttle for pick up," Nenn said to Drafe. "I do not want my female walking across a ship, not until I have repaired her vision."

Drafe chuckled. "Protecting her is your right, Nenn." He rose to his feet, bringing Vic to hers.

"Thanks, Caah, and good luck." she smiled. Without him, they wouldn't have made it inside the facility. Double-tapping her neck device, she laced her fingers through Drafe's and leaped out as soon as the door opened. They landed on the *Mula Pesada's* exterior and, together, thumped toward the *Aroagni*.

When they stepped inside, she laughed and wrapped her arms around Drafe. "We did it."

"Yes, we did." He grinned. "Now the trip to Ivoy, time with the Q.C.C., then home, *mhi'vatia*."

"You did as well as I expected." Aehort greeted them, his hands clasped in front of him and the widest smile splitting his cheeks.

"Thanks for your help." She squeezed his wrist as they strolled past them.

"What happened?" Vaen asked, wearing his customary scowl—further information the symbiotes shared. Also, Drafe was fond of him. "Aehort has been secretive about your disappearance. Where's Caah and Nenn?"

"Foq, Nenn." Drafe burst into a run, abandoning Vic.

"Nenn's on the *Mula Pesada* and will be joining us shortly. Caah chose to remain while we travel to Ivoy."

"What?" Vaen spun on Aehort. "See what becomes of a half-baked idea? Disrespect, flouting our laws and protocol. No, this makes no sense." He tapped his throat and strode off, barking orders with his brown hair rising and falling.

Vic shrugged and winced, tired to the core. "Dez said he will destroy the pods and no more will be sent."

"I know." Aehort gave a slow nod.

She huffed. "I'll head for Drafe's quarters."

"Go, rest, you have earned it." Without waiting, he glided off.

Each placement of her foot trembled her knees, but she made it to Drafe's quarters, was able to peel her clothes off, stand under the spray and dryer before sprawling across his bed. Her eyes closed as soon as her head hit the pillow.

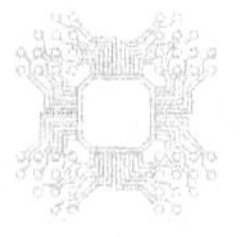

THE RETURN JOURNEY WAS spent mostly in bed, on her back, knees, or ass. When Drafe wasn't proving how much he adored her body, she visited with Aehort. He taught her how to listen to the symbiotes, their whisperings. The images...no, memories, played like old movies, showing the past lives of the Meorri eking out a living in a desolate land.

At night, before they drifted off to sleep, Drafe would tell stories of his childhood, of his time with his parents, of what he loved most about his homeworld. Not that the symbiotes hadn't revealed those already, but it was more personal when he shared his memories in his husky baritone.

She was eager to meet her sister, Larya and her mate, Kael. Vic knew her as if they'd been family since birth. Such was the efficacy of the symbiotes.

We draw near to Ivoy, Aehort informed her.

Thank you, friend. I am ready.

He had prepared her for the Ivoyan curiosity and the Qaldreth weariness. Tiny and Nenn would stay onboard the *Aroagni*. Aehort had decided it was best to shock the Q.C.C. only once a day.

Drafe rose and tossed her a pair of breeches and an armor vest. The black was bold against her pale skin. She left her hair down since he preferred it loose and snapped on her boots. When she stood, he caught her wrist and tugged her into his arms. Love for her crossed their bond. Like the warmth of a UV light on her skin after a cold shower, it touched every part of her soul and leaked into her body.

"I want you again." She flicked her tongue around his earlobe.

"And I you," he growled, his eyes molten amber. She loved how expressive they were, not that she was in doubt as to how he felt, about anything. Dominating their connection was a sliver of fear, of the unknown, of what the Q.C.C. could decide.

"Why are you nervous? Aehort will ensure we are not separated for long."

Drafe grunted. "Let us pray they are in a benevolent mood."

He clasped her hand and led her off the ship and down the ramp. Pausing, she gaped at the lilac skies, tall, majestic spires that were their buildings, and the flying crafts. She peered over the edge of the platform at the endless waterfalls and rivers beneath them, some enshrouded in gray-lilac mists.

"It's breathtaking." She smiled, admiring the vistas again. "Water is not scarce here at all. Like you said, Drafe. Despite the symbiotes sharing your memories and those of the Qaldreth who came before you, I refused to believe it."

"As did I." He kissed her knuckles. "Come, they do not tolerate tardiness."

They sound like they have sticks up their asses.

Drafe jerked back, his mouth twisted in horror. *Is that possible?*

She means, they hate for anyone to enjoy themselves. Aehort glided behind them, his hands clasped before him.

She giggled. *It is a saying, gevatia, and not meant to be taken literally.*

He chuckled. *Good to know.*

Willing her armor to remain hidden, she let Drafe escort her in silence along a narrow bridge beautifully patterned and carved with what she now knew were hudu, vasquva, and massive flying birds she did not yet know the name of. Excitement burst in her belly and butterflies fluttered, catching her breath. Soon, she would see her first sandworm.

Chapter Twenty-Eight

Year: 2220
The Qaldreth Command Council
Planet of Ivoy

As they strode into the hall, many Qaldreth, in a kaleidoscope of hair and eye colors, quietened and watched them head to the center. Despite being used to thousands observing her, this small gathering of warriors twitched her fingers and scattered her heartbeat.

Drafe squeezed her hand. *Breathe, mhi' vatia, you will not be harmed. I am forever your guardian.*

She met his gaze and winked. *As I am yours.*

They paused in front of a dais where seven Qaldreth warriors sat. One had the same coloring as Drafe's—Meorri aac Kish Udap.

His scowl was monstrous to behold. "We receive no recent word of your mission, no status updates, then you arrive with a live specimen. I am not impressed, Meorri aac Drafe Arrak."

Red hot fury exploded across their bond, but when she snuck a peek at Drafe, only his jaw clenched.

"Our mission was successful, revered members of the Q.C.C." Aehort stared down each man. "The source of the pods were discovered and vengeance taken for the Ots killed."

"Good." Kish Udap studied her. "You are without Awayar aac Caah Taed, the finest in his field. How did his death serve the Qaldreth?"

Drafe scanned the council. "I tasked him to remain with the humans, to help rebuild, and to serve as a bridge between our species, Kish Udap."

A white-eyed udap nodded, his hair flowing down his back unruffled. "An excellent choice, Drafe Arrak. We of the Awayar make outstanding ambassadors."

"He is not trained in such a capacity, Rath," Kish Udap growled at the white-haired commander at his side. "But the deed is done, the Ivoy avenged, and your bond with Aehort has strengthened, Drafe Arrak." He tapped the desk. "Yet before me, I find a stranger."

"She is as I foresaw." Aehort chose to sit on a stone bench, his face a mask of boredom.

"Oh?" Another commander, Zuphayr aac Srim, arched a blue brow. "And what did your visions reveal?"

"An ally."

Oh, Aehort, thank you. She smiled at him then looped her arm through Drafe's. *You have helped me heal, my love. The loss of Ande still haunts me, but with you and Aehort, I am whole again.*

Warm adoration from Drafe crossed their bond.

It has been a pleasure, Vic of Earth, Aehort sent.

She laughed at him. *It's Meorri aac Victoria now.*

He dipped his orange head. *So it is.*

"Now I see." Kish Udap leaned back in his chair. "And how did it come to be that she has your symbiotes, Drafe Arrak? The Jakar has performed no symbiotic transfer, nor would we have condoned such an action."

"Calm yourself, Kish." Eran Udap stared at Vic, his brown eyes almost human.

She appreciated that the symbiotes shared their names and ranks, but still, to be studied as a specimen irritated her. Drafe squeezed her hand. She drew in a calming breath and willed her leg to stop twitching.

"This was unexpected." Eran Udap rose and climbed off the dais, pausing in front of her. He captured a lock of her hair to test between two fingers. "Yet her bond with Aehort Uz and Drafe Arrak is strong. Her species must be remarkably acceptable to the symbiotes." He flicked a wrist. "Summon the Jakar. We must test her."

Her blood ran cold. Aehort had expected as much and warned her accordingly. She could do this.

Drafe tensed. *I cannot lose you, Vic. I have tasked Vaen to await you on the shuttle. Run if you need to.*

She shook her head. *I can endure, besides, I won't abandon you, Drafe. Do not ask me to.*

"We have run tests on the return voyage and have made the findings available to the Maed Board," Drafe said, scanning the udaps.

"I will determine which tests are necessary, young Drafe," the black-eyed, pale-skinned Jakar glided toward them amid a cloud of incense. "Come," he gestured to Vic.

She fell into step behind him. *Argh. How old is he? I mean no disrespect, but a robo-dog can walk faster than this.*

Drafe smothered a chuckle. *Patience, Vic. Ceremony and protocol matter here.*

She forced herself to stare ahead even as laughter barreled up her throat. *Imagine the expression on his face if I swept him off his feet and carried him to the temple.*

Aehort snorted. *If we must flee, then I insist you carry him, Vic, and let the symbiotes record it for posterity.*

Do not encourage her. Drafe widened his eyes at Aehort. It was the last image she saw as she left the chamber.

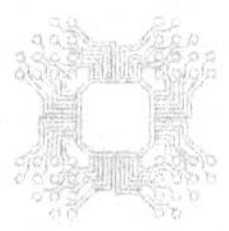

"The newest ots were expecting you, Aehort Uz. Since the mission was a success, they have taken an interest in policies regarding the categorizations of newborns. They await your input." At Eran Udap's news, Aehort rose and glided out of the hall, leaving Drafe to face the Q.C.C. alone.

"We are all Qaldreth warriors, and there are no outsiders. What say you, Drafe Arrak?" Srim Udap threw out his hands, encompassing the gathered males.

Drafe shared each step of their investigation, as Vaen had communicated to the Q.C.C. They knew all this until Vic had found her way onto the *Aroagni*, and with the retaking of the *Mula Pesada*, communication had become sporadic. So he shared the footage from Vic's eye implant. His chest swelled with pride at her actions, that of a warrior. The hall was privy to where her gaze lingered on parts of his anatomy when she leaned in to hug or kiss him. They witnessed her killing Carne without hesitation. He ended it before they suffered through two days of mating until she had, at last, purged the implant. Shuffling from foot to foot, he scanned the council, trying to read their thoughts while enduring a surge of lust. She did that to him, had from the moment their gazes first met.

"You mated a non-Qaldreth?" Kish Udap pointed at the door she had disappeared through.

Drafe gritted his teeth. "She is my *vatia sahaar*."

Gasps rippled through the hall.

He scanned the council without fear. "As you know, when it happens, it is unexpected and cannot be denied."

"And you did not reveal this to me, why?" Kish Udap growled. "Such an event is to be cherished, Drafe Arrak, not used in this callous manner."

"I am not ashamed of the warrior female who is mine for eternity. I needed you to see her for yourself. She is beyond worthy of my affection, to birth my sons. But...there is more. The human she killed hurt her and, in doing so, inserted into her their version of symbiotes known as nanites. I now carry these." He withdrew his sword and sliced his palm. The cut healed before it could bleed, but the idea of pain lingered.

Kish Udap leaped over the desk and grabbed the sword. He sliced Drafe's palm again with the same result. "She carries these in her?" At Drafe's nod, he faced the hall. "Summon the Jakar. Bring the female."

"This is remarkable. How did this occur? Do the humans have the same symbiotic transfer ceremony?" Eran Udap took Drafe's sword to test the blade. "The sword has not been tampered with."

"Could we harvest these *nanites*, insert them into our warriors?" Kish Udap slapped Drafe on the shoulder with a hearty chuckle. "You have done well."

A growl pierced the excited murmurs. "You congratulate him?" Ulvus called from the rear of the hall. "He abandoned Caah, mated another species, and this mating sickness has spread to Nenn Maed with a blind human female. Do not be so easily deceived, my udaps."

"I have read your reports, Ulvus Sava. They reek of bitterness. Your hatred for Drafe Arrak is well-documented by symbiotes and personal accounts. Anything you say will be measured against this." Srim Udap captured Drafe's palm to stroke his thumb across it. "Incredible. We had healing before but never to this degree. It is as if there was no wound."

"Ulvus Sava is correct." Drafe smiled at the shock contorting Ulvus's face. "Nenn wished to heal a blind female and formed an attachment to her. She is onboard the *Aroagni*, having agreed to travel with us. She is a Maed for the humans and her knowledge on her species might be of help to the Ivoy and Qaldreth."

Eran Udap laughed. "You excel in unexpected ways, Drafe Arrak."

"I am nothing without my crew, my udaps. Their performance was beyond all that I could have asked for."

"They will be rewarded accordingly." Udap Kish flicked his fingers.

I'm here, Vic whispered. *Why did I need to return?*

Drafe relaxed, relief sliding down his body. *Are you well?*

He hasn't done anything yet. I have so much pent-up energy, I need a good, long fuck after this.

Drafe groaned, closing his eyes against the expected wave of hot need she aroused. *Vic, I cannot sport a hard koq before my udaps.*

She halted beside him and slipped her hand into his. *What did I miss?*

As one, the council gathered around her, stroking her hair, her skin, or splaying her five fingers, so delicate against theirs.

"If you cut her hand, does it heal as fast?" Srim Udap asked, running a thumb along her palm.

Huh? She glanced at Drafe, her brow furrowed in concern. *What healing are they talking about? You cut your hand?*

"She does not know, my udaps. Vic, your nanites heal me. Watch." He asked for his sword, then sliced his palm and held it up for her to see.

"What the farg?" She grabbed his hand. "Nanites encourage healing, but I didn't know they were this good in you. Try me." She offered her palm and didn't wince when the sharp metal pierced her skin. Before blood could pool, the skin knitted together. "Huh."

"Her blood is red," rippled through those gathered.

"I have had enough of this garak shit." Ulvus withdrew his sword and leaped over the heads of males.

"Drafe." Vic vaulted to meet Ulvus, her skin shimmering under the venai lights.

Drafe wasn't quick enough to stop her and was helpless to aid her despite the instinct to do so. She collided with Ulvus, but as they plummeted to the floor, it was Ulvus at the bottom, her knee at his chest, and her hand on his throat. Ulvus tried throwing her off, but she spread her thighs and gripped his torso. He tried stabbing her with his sword, but she was too close to him. When they landed, his sword clattered to the side amid his deep groan. They glided to a halt at the base of the council's desk.

Drafe bolted forward. "Don't kill him, Vic."

The udaps gaped, but he couldn't take the time to explain.

She did not glance his way. "He's an asshole."

Drafe held out his hands, showing her he was unharmed. *He has sinned in front of the* Q.C.C. *Let them handle it.*

She snorted, tossing a derisive glance at the udaps. *Like your elder did when he stole your water pouch?*

Drafe crouched beside her, sensing her crumbling resolve. "Vic, *gevatia*, please, hide your armor and leave him be."

Ulvus's cheeks paled as she met Drafe's gaze. "Fine." She leaped off Ulvus, kneeing him in the ribs as she did so. "But only because I love you, Drafe. That's twice now. The third time, I'll kill him."

"There will not be a third time." Kish Udap gestured to the guards, and they descended upon Ulvus, escorting him out of the hall. "You have the Q.C.C.'s gratitude, Meorri aac Vic. I would like to extend a formal welcome to the Qaldreth and my Meorri tribe. Please, dine with me this night."

EPILOGUE

ENDURING THE MANY TESTS, the honoring ceremony, and the formal dinners had taken a few weeks. Vic had drawn the strength from Drafe and Aehort. At last, they approached the Qaldreth planet. It had the look of Earth—blue, white, green, and brown.

"If Meorri is without water, but Awayar has it in abundance, why not trade?"

Drafe grinned. "Why do you ask questions you know the answers to?"

She chuckled. "We need another resource we can barter with besides salt."

The Ivoyan shuttle touched down. She scanned the empty compartment where Aehort should have been. The male had stayed behind on Ivoy, his life having changed after he was honored for his service. Depending on his choice, he was to be trained as a zi—a traveler, or a lo—a teacher. In addition, Ivoy agreed to improve their testing process. All Ivoyan children categorized as uz could earn a higher rank.

Still, she missed him.

The door slid open to sweltering air, bathing her. She sighed. The scent of hot sand greeted her, just like on her sol-farm. Drafe captured her hand and pressed a kiss to her knuckles. As one, they strolled down the ramp, the wind whipping her hair.

Whispers began in the recesses of her mind and built until the cacophony slammed into her. Emotions surged, zigzagging as she endured thousands of memories, of joys and sorrows, victories and deaths. Every nerve sparked and tingled. She froze, allowing the sensations to flood her. Tears slipped free, the welcome too overwhelming for her to bear. Then there was peace, the gentle blanket that was Drafe, protecting her.

"Thank you," she gasped.

"It is good to see you, Drafe Arrak." An elderly Qaldreth stood before them, leaning on his walking stick. "You bring a gift to Meorri." He reached out with a shaking hand to touch Vic's arm. "Welcome, daughter. The sands whispered of your arrival."

"Elder Bavu, may the sands be at your back and the suns on your face." She bowed.

Bavu beamed. "You have chosen well, Drafe."

Thank the symbiotes. I didn't expect a welcoming committee.

Neither did I. Drafe grinned.

She raised her gaze to the people gathered to greet her. Some did not have the hair and eyes of the Meorri. *I thought tribes did not intermingle.*

Drafe scanned the crowd and jerked back. "This is an unexpected welcoming, Elder Bavu."

He snorted and gestured with his walking stick. "They have come to meet your *vatia sahaar.*"

"What?" she squeaked. "How did they know—?"

"Any returning Qaldreth shares his experiences from off-world." Drafe crushed her against him. *And if you do not close your mouth, I will take it as an invitation.*

She wiggled her eyebrows. *For what?*

To kiss you.

She laughed. *You don't need an invitation ever. Help yourself.*

He grinned and kissed her, plundering the depths of her mouth until breathing didn't matter anymore.

"Enough. Mate later." Bavu whacked Drafe's thigh with his stick. "I have had these people on our doorstep for days. Oh, for a little peace." He waddled past Larya and her mate, Kael.

Shyness struck Vic. She frowned. Never had she been nervous or self-conscious about meeting people, but Larya wasn't just anyone. Her fingers twitched where they gripped Kael's forearm.

Vic drew in a deep breath and stepped out of Drafe's embrace. "Hello, sister."

Larya's smile was beautiful, bright, and her eyes shimmered with unshed tears. She sniffed, not letting them fall—to do so was wasteful. "Greetings, sister." She lunged, engulfing Vic in a hug. Drafe laughed and hugged them both. Kael followed, embracing them all.

"Our family has grown, brother." Larya smiled when the hug unraveled. She rubbed her belly in a sign as old as time.

Drafe gasped, then roared, whipping his sister into his arms.

"Careful now." Kael threw out his hands, his brow knitting.

As soon as Drafe set Larya's feet on the sand, Kael snatched her into his arms, his gaze vigilant should Drafe feel the need to hoist his pregnant mate into the air again.

Vic laughed, reading Kael's expressions and listening to the symbiotes when they whispered of past celebrations.

"We have prepared your home..." Larya giggled. "This night will be yours alone. After the suns rise in the morning, expect many visitors."

Impatient, the crowds grew rowdy, calling out Vic and Drafe's names.

I don't see why the excitement. Vic pasted on a smile and grabbed Drafe's hand.

You are not Qaldreth nor Ivoy. He stole a kiss. *You are mine.*

Fine. One more thing I need to endure. Releasing Drafe's hand, she strode forward and paused a meter away from the crowd. "Greetings, Qaldreth."

Silence fell as they waited for her to continue.

She sighed. "I am a human of Earth. My name was Victoria Barnes Harper." They blinked at her. "But you may call me Meorri aac Victoria."

They cheered and stamped their feet, casting up clouds of fine sand.

The suns baked down on her, and she raised her gaze to the two glowing orbs traversing the blue sky so like Earth's. "Thank you for your kind welcome." Farg, she hoped that was the end of it.

Voices bombarded questions at her. Her head snapped from one side to the other as she tried to find the sources.

"Are all humans as pale as you?"

"How many tribes are on Earth?"

"Why don't your eyes match your hair? Are you a half-breed?"

"It is forbidden," leaped across those gathered.

Vic waved her hands, shushing them. "We have many colors, and sometimes the hair matches the eyes. No, we don't have tribes, and on Earth, you may mate with whomever you choose. It is not forbidden."

"Truly?" someone called out.

"Yes. Giniiri aac Nenn Maed has mated a woman named Tiny. She has purple hair." Vic smothered a wince. She didn't know what Tiny's eye color was other than the white she once had.

Gasps followed, along with whispers about lightning.

A child broke from the crowd, carrying a wrapped bundle. Vic kneeled and smiled at the boy. "Hello."

He skidded to a halt. "Hello?"

"It means greetings."

"Oh. My mama says to give you this." He shoved the bundle at her and prepared to dart away.

Vic caught him. "Wait, I don't know your name. And wow, your muscles are amazing. Are you training to become a fine warrior?" She squeezed his upper arm as if it was the largest set of muscles she'd ever encountered.

He grinned, wide enough to twitch his ears poking through his head of blue hair. "I am."

"I'm sure you will bring honor to the Zuphayr tribe." She gestured to the bundle. "Want to help me open this?"

He nodded, and within seconds, the aroma of salted meat teased her nose." *What are they?* she asked Drafe.

Dried kurrula.

So not helpful, she said, wishing she could roll her eyes.

Drafe chuckled. *The flesh of birds.*

Like chicken? She could get behind that. "Mm, this smells so good." Closing her eyes, she inhaled deeply. "Please, choose one for me and you."

"Me?" His eyes widened and burned a bright blue.

"Of course. It's rude to eat alone, isn't it?"

He nodded, his hungry gaze on the dark strips of meat. With eager fingers, he chose the biggest piece for her. Right then, her heart melted. She accepted it, took a massive bite, and hummed her appreciation. Once he had chosen his, she clamped her lips on the strip, wiped her hands on her pants, and ruffled his hair. "Tell your mom these are the best kurrula I have ever tasted."

The boy weaved through the crowd hollering his mother's name.

You did not have to do that, but it is appreciated. Drafe rubbed her lower back as he joined her. *Yet another reason why I love you.*

She offered him a strip while chewing on her own. *Children are precious. Every word said to them has impact.*

One by one, folks stepped forward, blessing her with gifts from their tribes. At one point, Kael rushed off to fetch his wagon. He and Drafe loaded the rugs, woven blankets, homemade garments, weapons, foods, and as wonderful as their generosity was, none of it mattered as much as the simple leather necklace with an amber pendant.

As she stared at it draped over her palm, tears pressed behind her eyes. A young man stood before her, his spine straight, his chin high, his orange hair blowing in the hot breeze.

She sniffed, and he dipped his chin, his shoulders drooping. "I apologize. I meant no offense."

"No." She squeezed her eyes shut and willed the tears to abate. "I apologize. This is incredible. It's the exact shade of my *vatia sahaar's* eyes. I will cherish this always." She looped it over her head and stroked the pendant where it rested below her collarbone.

The crowd cheered and slapped the young man on his back as he returned to their midst.

Drafe raised his hands. "Thank you for your warm welcome. Please, take care as you return home and send Osnir's blessings to your tribes."

In an orderly fashion, the crowd dispersed.

Vic gaped. *Why couldn't you have started with that?*

They would not have left until they met you and judged for themselves the validity of the rumors.

She huffed. Under their vigilant gazes, she dared not wipe the sweat from her brow or sweep aside the tendrils sticking to her neck. Drafe escorted her into the caverns, the temperature cooling the deeper they strolled. Kael pulled the cart with Larya nestled in the middle of it, protected.

Curious faces peeked out of their caves, nodded, waved, or came out to watch them pass. By the time they reached the farthest doorway, exhaustion pounded at Vic. She entered Drafe's home and sighed, spreading her arms wide to better relish the shade.

Kael and Drafe carried the gifts inside as she sat on a fur-covered ledge. By the width, she would hazard a guess it was their bed. The variegated walls were ridged and curved as if millions of years ago, water had carved it. The ambers, umbers, and beiges were pretty. Small venai stones glowed like flickering candles. She rose and captured one, marveling at the smooth, cool-to-the-touch stones.

"Thirsty?"

She smiled at Drafe, then placed the stone on the mantle above the firepit. "Yes."

"We shall leave you for the night," Kael said, dragging a hesitant Larya from the cave.

Come, gevatia.

Vic whipped her gaze to Drafe and approached him as he poured water into a stone cup. He offered it to her, then kneeled to unsnap her boots, peeling each one off and stacking them to the side. Her pants followed. She laughed between sips and watched as he folded her pants then tucked them into a stone alcove. Offering him the empty cup, she peeled off her shirt, bra, and panties, then folded them, stacking them on top of her pants.

Still kneeling, he tapped the rug-covered rock floor. She crossed the room and paused in front of him. With a cool, damp cloth, he stroked her body, from her face to her toes, lingering under her breasts and at her sex. She moaned, arching her back as his touch intensified. Gripping his hair, she rocked across his fingers, whimpering when the intensity built. Tossing the cloth aside, he clasped her hips and tugged her to the floor. She draped her arms around his neck, straddled his lap, and kissed him. He was hot to the touch but matched the heat inside her.

"Drafe," she panted, writhing in his arms as he trailed kisses down her neck to suck a nipple into his mouth. She rode his hard thigh, crying out at the sparks of pre-orgasmic joy along her sex.

He switched to her other nipple, flicking his tongue before nipping it.

Farg, she needed him now. Reaching between them, she stroked his thigh until his armor faded, exposing his erect cock. She rubbed her palm across the head.

He released her nipple to groan, and with his eyes closed, arched his back. Without hesitation, she lowered herself on his length, inch by inch. He gazed into her eyes, his mouth parted as he panted. Grinning, she rocked her hips, sliding along him while tilting her pelvis until he gasped. The growing throbbing within her had her heartbeat roaring in her ears. She needed more, faster, harder.

He leaned forward, pinned her back to the floor, and pounded into her. Crying out, she wrapped her legs around his hips then pressed her open mouth to his throat to smother her pleas and moans. Everything within her tightened. Her senses heightened. She clung to him, riding the anticipation and the skittered tingles along her nerve endings. Her breath caught, her thoughts froze, and for a moment, the symbiotes quietened...until her world exploded. He didn't stop plunging into her and triggered another explosion. He stilled, his fingers digging into her hips. Releasing her, he threw out a hand to catch himself as he collapsed across her, his eyes an intense amber.

Peace descended. She smiled.

Laughing, he brushed her hair off her face, stroked her jaw, and stole a sweet kiss. "Welcome home, Vic."

She hugged him, forcing him to rest his full weight on her. Sighing, she nuzzled his neck and held on. She awoke once when he pulled out and carried her to their bed. After that, she knew no more.

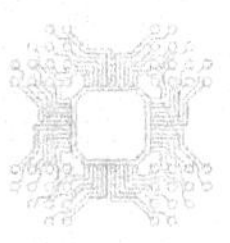

DRAFE AWOKE WITH VIC curled against him. He lay there, rubbing his hand up and down her back while pressing kisses to her temple, watching her sleep. Tiny spots marked her cheeks, so he tried to kiss each one. She had some idea how he felt about her, but she couldn't truly understand how she had changed him, blessed him.

He glanced at the door, measuring the suns' light as it traveled. It would be dawn soon, and he would prefer to start across the plains before then. He grinned, and before the well-wishers descended. Best for them to find their home empty.

Cupping a breast, he stroked his thumb across her nipple until she gasped and rolled onto her back. He captured her mouth with his, his breathing faltering as his nostrils flared. It was as if he couldn't get enough of her, couldn't draw the essence of her into him.

"Vic, it is time."

She moaned and pressed a sleepy kiss to his chest. "Ten more minutes."

He chuckled. "The suns are rising."

"Let them rise," she mumbled.

He slapped her backside.

Squealing, she shot up then fell off the bed.

"Good, you are awake."

She huffed the hair out of her eyes and glared at him.

He pointed to the alcove. "Larya set aside garments for you. If you hurry, we can reach the cucooya tree before the suns bake the sand."

"A real tree." She scrambled to her feet then hopped from one leg to the other as she yanked on the breeches without strips of cloth to cover her sex. He groaned his approval.

With her tunic on, she stamped her boots in place while tying up her hair with a strip of garak leather. He watched her as he dressed, loving the sway of her hips while she whistled a jaunty tune. Reaching for the water pouches, he paused, his hand hovering over one not his own. Branded in the leather was a fresh burn, a vasquva, and alongside that was his father's symbol. His chest swelled when he ran his thumb over it. The leather was soft, meaning someone had recently killed a hudu to make this. He would thank Kael later.

With pouch in hand, he offered it to Vic. "This is yours. The star is my family's symbol, passed down from father to son. The vasquva is...mine." He clipped the full bladder onto her hudu belt, also new. "And now yours."

She sheathed his dagger into her boot then studied the etched symbols. "Is this because you killed one?"

He shrugged. "I have much to speak to Kael about. Ready?"

When she nodded, he marched from their home, along the climbing steps, then out, waving at Umda and Tijl on duty.

"Greetings, Drafe, Victoria. Osnir has blessed us with a great day." Umda bowed his head, then raised his face to the sky.

Vic did the same and smiled, her expression one of contentment.

"We should return by nightfall. I wish to show my *vatia sahaar* our world, Umda."

He thumped the butt of his spear on the rock floor. "May the sands bless your journey."

Hours passed as they hiked across the plains, the salt crunching beneath their boots, the hot winds tugging at their hair and garments. Many times they paused in the shade of a rock outcropping to enjoy the cooler air and savor five droplets of water. Not once did she plead for more or complain about the heat. Only sighs and smiles filled their bond.

I love your Qaldreth. It is so peaceful. And I have missed the feel of the sunlight on my skin.

He grinned. *It pleases me that you see the beauty in* our *home.* He pointed ahead at the bulbous tree from where Ulvus had stolen his water pouch.

She gasped and sprinted across to it, leaping onto the rocky platform to stand in the tree's shade. "*Gevatia*, is this a cucooya?" She leaned against the tree and plucked the closest white-petaled blossom, cupping it in her hand.

Yes, and as pretty as it is, it is not your equal.

ABOUT THE AUTHOR

Sevannah Storm is a fiction writer who immerses herself in fantastical worlds both magical and science fiction. She has a flair for the creative having studied art and interior architecture and spends her time drawing, oil painting, and writing. An avid reader from an early age, Sevannah finds her inspiration from various sources: games, novels, music, and the land of make-believe. The unique versus the practical has brought on numerous debates.

In her spare time, she does Krav Maga, CrossFit, and rereads novels that snatch her breath away. Having embraced the social media world, you can find her on most platforms.

Her home is a land south of Wakanda, where animals roam free. Born in Zimbabwe, she grew up in South Africa. The crisp blue skies with cotton-candy sunsets expand her heart and soul, encapsulating a sense of freedom.

Words she lives by: "Know your pothole and dodge it. Don't work in a pencil factory if you're a vampire."

Sevannah loves to hear from her readers. You can find and connect with her at the links below.

Website/Newsletter:

https://www.sevannahstorm.com/

Facebook:

https://www.facebook.com/sevannah.storm

Instagram:

https://www.instagram.com/sevannah.storm/

Twitter:

https://twitter.com/sevannah_storm

Thank you for taking the time to read Sol Survivor. If you enjoyed the story, please tell your friends and leave a review. Reviews support authors and ensure they continue to bring readers books to love and enjoy.

https://sevannahstorm.com

SOUL FORGED

THE GIFTING SERIES #1

Know-it-all Oriana agreed to travel with aliens who need women. But she didn't agree to abduction, life/death battles, and escaping with a bossy, arrogant man. She was sabotaged, attacked, and kidnapped, but she is far from beaten. Forced to participate in an alien battle arena with no promise of freedom, she has to forget the loss of her family and focus on surviving.

Enyl has given up hope. His people are dying due to a genetic modification gone awry. Darkness is consuming his warriors, and his world, as he knows it, will end. His father, the king, has rolled out a plan to save them all. But Enyl doubts a solution will be found in time.

And when a compatible female is found...and lost, he must rescue her, a human female capable of surviving despite all odds. However, freeing Oriana serves to anger the aliens holding her captive. Ensuring she is cared for—as per Etterian protocol—he is stunned by the strong connection between the two of them. Such a bond was only experienced between Etterian mates.

Is she his salvation or is that wishful thinking on his part?

Read it here:

https://books2read.com/u/mlAWr9

THE SHIKARI

www.ingramcontent.com/pod-product-compliance
Lightning Source LLC
Chambersburg PA
CBHW061013120726
47910CB00006B/1907